FIC
KEL

MAR 0 7 2002

P9-DJV-317

BRADLEY PUBLIC LIBRARY
296 N. FULTON AVE.
BRADLEY, IL 60915

Also by

JACK KELLY

LINE OF SIGHT
MAD DOG
PROTECTION
APALACHIN

MOBTOWN

BRADLEY PUBLIC LIBRARY

MOBTOWN

JACK KELLY

BRADLEY PUBLIC LIBRARY

HYPERION

NEW YORK

Copyright © 2002 Jack Kelly

All rights reserved. No part of this book may be used or reproduced in any
manner whatsoever without the written permission of the Publisher. Printed in the
United States of America. For information address: Hyperion, 77 W. 66th Street,
New York, New York 10023-6298.

Library of Congress Cataloging-in-Publication Data

Kelly, Jack.
 Mobtown / by Jack Kelly.—1st ed.
  p. cm.
 ISBN 0-7868-6615-2
  1. Private investigators—New York (State)—Rochester—Fiction. 2. Rochester
(N.Y.)—Fiction. 3. Organized crime—Fiction. I. Title.

PS3561.E394 M63 2002
813'.54—dc21   2001024361

FIRST EDITION

10 9 8 7 6 5 4 3 2 1

Everything is a racket today.
—WILLIE MORETTI, gangster

BRADLEY PUBLIC LIBRARY

BRADLEY PUBLIC LIBRARY

MOBTOWN

WEDNESDAY

1

YOU DON'T JUDGE IN this business. You judge, you climb aboard the emotional roller coaster. It takes you up and down and around and around and leaves you off right where you started.

You don't judge, you don't get distracted. Your attention wanders for two seconds, your man slips, you spend the next five hours staring at an empty rabbit hole.

Trouble was, I did judge. I was following a guy, a matrimonial job, Eddie Gill, thirty-seven, four kids, squiring a sixteen-year-old to an after-hours joint and then to a five-dollar motel on the truck route.

Now, if he'da been thirty-two and she was eighteen and it was only two kids and he took her someplace nice, I might have said what the hell. I was thirty-two myself and divorced. Who was I to talk?

But I had a daughter who was going to be ten, and I didn't want to think of her growing up in a world of Eddie Gills. Plus, I had listened to the wife's side of it, and just the suspicion was giving a good woman a lot of pain.

So, okay, I judged the guy.

God, it was hot. That summer, '59, was a scorcher. The county had opened Durand Beach for night swimming. Driving past, I could see the glow of the big floodlights groping the black enamel of Lake Ontario, whole families of ghosts wading in the tepid water.

All the hot dog stands and frozen custard joints along the shore were mobbed. Beach resorts were crowded from Hamlin all the way out to Sodus. About midnight, Earl Clear and I, using a leapfrog tail, had followed our subject's car to a stand he owned that said EDDIE GILL'S TEXAS HOTS and GROUND ROUND in big letters. He wasn't hard to stick to. He drove a new apple-green Edsel, with that grille that looked like an Olds sucking a lemon, the square rear end, and the chrome in all the wrong places.

I parked across the street and watched the carhops running around in their short flounced skirts. Gill was a heavy, wheezy man who couldn't keep his shirttails tucked in. His elaborate comb job failed to cover his bald dome. He spent some time crabbing at the counterman and chewing out the cook. Then he sat down to count the night's receipts.

He doused the lights on the sign and the staff went home, all except one of the waitresses. She slipped into the ladies' and came out wearing a party dress tight enough to show the world she had more body than she knew what to do with. She was coltish, long in the thigh, unsteady on her high heels, a kid auditioning for adulthood. While he locked up, she laid one hand on her belly and pirouetted, anticipating a dance. Gill caught her from behind and ground his hips against her slim backside.

She held on to his arm as they walked to his car. I propped the telephoto lens on my dash and got them passing under the streetlight.

Earl and I followed them to a Polynesian restaurant on Clover, one of those places with tiki lamps and bead curtains. Gill gave no sign he suspected a tail.

They were inside just long enough to polish off a couple of mai tais and a plate of sweet and sour. Next stop was the Tic Tac Club on Winton Road. I was surprised—the Tic Tac seemed a little classy for a guy like Gill. It was a place that catered to high rollers, moneyed playboys, and politicians on the make. It was done up like a Roman circus, with plaster statues of satyrs peeing into goldfish ponds and a twelve-foot-high Bacchus covered in pigeon droppings.

I steered into the parking area of the shopping strip opposite.

"His mind's on her," I told Earl when he pulled alongside. "You might as well turn in." Earl's older than me and he needs his rest.

"Why not bust his ass? That kid's jail bait."

"If I still had a badge, maybe."

"What badge? Need a badge to kick a guy's teeth in?"

He was right and we both knew it, but I said, "Client's paying me cash. I watch, I report. I look, I don't judge."

"You're the boss," he said. He palmed his suicide knob and disappeared.

My eyes fell into a sentry rhythm. You can't stare, you can't look away. I checked a woman waiting for her clothes to spin in a late-night launderette in the strip, her legs crossed, I looked back to the club. I watched a green-and-blue parrot gnawing its perch in the window of a pet store, I looked at the stars piercing the hot haze. Near the entrance opposite, Michelangelo's *David* was glancing at the sky himself and looking like he'd give a week's pay for a fig leaf.

I checked the dashboard clock. I saw two women emerge from the Tic Tac, laughing as they lit cigarettes, the guy with them a dead ringer for John Cameron Swayze. I noticed the woman in the laundry holding up a black brassiere, I switched back to the club. A box of Tide, a nervous hamster, a gum wrapper in the gutter.

The gaudy Edsel was parked right across from me. I guess Gill was the type of guy they'd intended it for, a loser who wanted to show off on the cheap.

When my party came out, she was having trouble walking and he was doing things you don't do to a girl in public. I snapped some more photos. This was a private eye's meat and potatoes.

I know in the books the detective sneers at matrimonial work. In real life, it's your meal ticket. Mix up sex, love, hate, jealousy, and suspicion, throw in some fear—it's a stew that brings them in the door eager to pay hard cash for a scrap of certainty.

He tumbled her into his car, thumbed his shirt under his waist-band, and drove to a long brick building with MOTEL in lipstick-red neon. He already had a key to room number 6. I waited in the parking lot of a used car dealer across the road.

I hadn't been sleeping well. Was there a time when I did sleep well? Those hot summer nights I spent a lot of hours lying alone on damp sheets and wondering what it all added up to. As soon as I turned off my engine, a wave of fatigue washed over me.

I poured a last swallow of iced coffee into the plastic cup of my Thermos and shook out two tiny pills from a brown glass vial. I put them on my tongue and washed them down.

I'd picked up the Benzedrine habit in the army. Bennies were your friend when you needed to stay awake, or needed to goose your morale, or needed to keep the darkness at bay. They put a knife edge on your mind, at least for a little while. Later was a different story, but behind a couple of bennies, later was beside the point.

The metallic taste filled my mouth. I gritted my teeth as time turned into a polished rail and my thoughts began to accelerate, steel on steel.

I found myself thinking about Korea, nights in Asia, guys I had known over there who were missing every one of these moments that would have been their lives. And for what?

One of those high-pitched voices that whispers in your ear said, You know for what, Ike. For a trip to the end of night. For a vision of something wild. See the world, they said. Well, you saw the world.

For some reason, I remembered reading about the first white man to reach western New York, a Frenchman named Étienne Brûlé. Got this far and heard the drums and went native. The story was he'd had a falling out with the Hurons. They killed him. I don't know if they cooked him, but they ate him.

I steered my thoughts to Gloria, to her dimples, her birthday coming up in a couple of days. Ten already. She had told me she would be a teenager because it was two digits. Jesus.

I thought about a girl I had known during school, before Eileen, and wondered what had happened to her. I even thought about Ei-

leen for a little while, imagined ways I could have kept my marriage
from going down the drain.

You think a lot of things, waiting. I turned on the radio low. I
was glad to hear the DJ on WHAM playing Billie Holiday. That
station, it was usually Perry Como, the human tranquilizer.

Billie sang "Travelin' Light" and, right after, "What a Little
Moonlight Can Do." Oo, oo, oo. It was a voice with the surface
stripped away, all heart. The voice of somebody who's way out in
front of the parade.

Then the announcer said the music was a tribute. Billie Holiday
had passed away. Dead at forty-four. It didn't seem possible.

I thought about a lot of things that night. And for a time, I didn't
think, just listened to the crickets as they crinkled the air, just
watched a lazy orange slice of moon float down behind the saw-
toothed roof of a factory building.

Somebody once said it's not the places you go, it's the odd hours
you keep—a church up the street in the early morning fog can be as
magical as Notre Dame in Paris. That was another thought that wandered through my mind as I watched the air go pearly over the motel
and then watched the sign begin to leach pink into the eastern sky.

When they came out, the girl was gripping her elbows and walking with her head down. Gill held his hand on her neck and steered
her toward his car. I should have taken him apart. He'd just stolen
her innocence, which was probably all she had that was worth half a
damn.

I followed them across town to a rundown section off West Main.
He let her out on Cicero Street and drove away.

I was the only one who watched her mount the sagging porch
steps of a disheveled two-family house. She walked slowly, as if she
were climbing into a bleak future.

2

I DROVE TO MY apartment on Oxford Street and took the shower that would have to stand in for a night's sleep. I turned the water to cold and stayed under the needles until I felt relaxed and my breathing slowed to normal. I put on a clean light-blue shirt, a smoke-colored summer-weight suit, and a narrow-brimmed fedora.

Down at the stainless-steel Empire I ordered two poached on buttered rye toast, a small T-bone, home fries, and a broiled grape-fruit. I put away three cups of coffee and two Luckies, enjoying that feeling you get, when you've been awake all night, that you're a step ahead of the suckers who are just getting up.

The traffic in Rochester had been getting bad the last few years. Everybody had a car. The city was busy dumping federal money into six-lane bypasses that would solve the problem. For now, we were stuck with congestion that ground to a standstill nearly every rush hour.

Newsboys hawked papers to drivers locked in the jam. I bought one and glanced at it as we inched along. I read about how Eisenhower wasn't going to let the steelworkers push him around. I was no Republican, but I had a soft spot for the president because we shared a name and because he looked a little like my father used to.

I turned to the sports pages and read about the rhubarb that the Red Wings had gotten into in Havana. Everybody was wondering where this thing with Castro would end.

I finally made it downtown and strolled over to my office building on Mortimer Street. The sun was shining and I felt like a human being. It was one of those mornings, clean and luminous, the heart of summer, full of juice and joy. I was glad to breathe the air.

In the lobby I ducked into the barbershop for a shave and a trim.

"Believe what happened, Mr. Van Savage?" the elevator boy said. "What a crazy game."

"Those Latins can be pretty wild when they get on the rum, Mike."

"Wings better take hand grenades next time."

"Or some dependable pitching," I said.

He honked through his nose, pulled back the accordion gate to let me out. The pebble glass on my door said DWIGHT VAN SAVAGE, INVESTIGATIONS. Inside, Penny told me, "You just missed her. Too bad."

"Who's that?"

"The mystery client. Very urgent. Hush-hush. Couldn't leave a number."

"Sound like money?"

"If desperate means dollars. She was nervous. Said she'd call back later."

"Something to look forward to."

"Hear about Billie?" she asked me.

"On the radio."

"Damn, huh? I knew she'd been sick. Now they'll all say how great she was. Wait and see. When she was alive, they lifted her cabaret license."

Penny Nichols liked jazz. She liked to hang out in coffeehouses and listen to earnest young men recite poetry. But she wasn't a dope and she wasn't a phony. Her eyes went moist for a second, then she tucked back the corners of her mouth and shook her head and moved past it.

I handed her two rolls of film. "I got some good stuff on the Gill case. Put the lab on this and have the wife come in tomorrow. What else is cooking this morning?"

"That guy Doyle is supposed to come by, let's see, ten minutes ago."

"He's an Irishman, maybe he can't tell time. Let's start on Gill while it's fresh."

She followed me into my office, sat down, crossed her long legs, and waited. I noticed her rolling her head, so I stood behind her and gave her a shoulder rub while I talked. She could take dictation at a phenomenal rate and polished my prose when she typed it out so that I sounded half literate.

"Began surveillance, ten forty-five P.M. Proceeded to subject's place of business, Gill's Texas Hots on Lake Shore Boulevard. Observed subject leave in the company of a female employee at twelve twenty-seven A.M."

I kept it clinical for the wife's sake. She could read between the lines. She could look at the pictures, too. One night and we had a case that she could leverage into a nice chunk of alimony. Not bad at all. Tell your friends—Ike Van Savage, the scorned housewife's best friend.

The buzzer on the outer door rang as Gill was going up the girl's blouse.

"Just when it was getting good," Penny said. She went out to usher in the client.

"Paddy Doyle." He was a wide man with dark hair and one of those broad red faces that remind you of a football field after a hard scrimmage. He cracked my knuckles, smiled a gap-tooth smile at nothing, and spoke with a polluted Kerry brogue.

"They're burning me out, the Italians. I got this house and that house, soot and smoke, water damage. I'm losing the shirt off my back here."

"Okay, sit down and start from the beginning."

"These places up the northeast, the old seventh, nice income properties. Guy says, You wanna sell? No, says I. You better, says he. I says, Get your ass outta here before I kick it through your mouth. Then four of my places burn, two in one night. You just point me toward 'em, I'll . . ." He mimed crushing a stone with his bare hands.

He finally took a seat. He put his hands on his knees, like a peasant at church. He wore incongruous patent leather pumps on his rather small feet.

"Who's the guy?"

"Whaddaya think I'm hiring you for?"

"You didn't get his name?"

He shook his head. "A stout lad. Something Realty. I got a slew of houses out there. I'm not sellin'. That's my retirement."

"You think it's arson?"

He laughed a machine-gun laugh. "Italians is what it is. I know that. This city."

"The man who approached you was Italian?"

"Not him. He's just the front, see. That's how they work it."

"What about the police?"

He ratcheted off another laugh. Oh, I was a real comedian.

He told me the locations of the fires and where his other buildings were. It was out in the no-man's land on the edge of the city, an area that changed hands every few years, from Irish to Italian to Bohunk. I wouldn't have been surprised if Doyle was one of those landlords who had busted blocks out there, moving a family of blacks into one house and picking up places in the panic sale that followed.

"It's these racket boys," he concluded. "This Petrone."

He might have been right. Rochester was a mob town in 1959. You think of Kodak and maple-shaded streets and white-shoe suburbs, you might not imagine that hoods ran the place. Sure, the city fathers jaw-boned about civic responsibility and chamber-of-commerce virtues, but the mob had the inside track on vice and knew how to push the doorbells of gimme. Every city has its dark side, and the Arm was a power to be reckoned with in all those upstate burgs.

Different guys handled different ends of it, but everybody said a boom-kis named Joe Petrone was the one who pulled the most strings. They'd scooped up his brother Manny at the Apalachin party two years earlier and then Manny got bumped. Word was, Joe raked something off the top of every game in town and all the politicians knew his name and knew Christmas was coming.

"That can make it a little delicate," I said to Doyle.

"Delicate? I'll fuckin' delicate them. You point me, Van Savage, I'll walk into the back room of the Tic Tac, make'm wish their mamas knew how to use a coat hanger."

I told him I would look into it. I was glad for the business. I had just set up that spring and the overhead was eating up my profits.

"What's it gonna cost?" he asked.

I told him how much I charged and explained about expenses. He gave me the fish eye. Like a lot of shanty Irishmen, he thought the world was out to pick his pocket. He forked over the fifty-dollar retainer and told me he wanted results fast or else.

I had just started back on the Gill report with Penny when Earl Clear showed. He leaned against my desk and rolled a cigarette, which is a pretty good trick for a man with one arm. His left got blown to pieces during the Anzio landing. "Ticket home" was the way Earl summed up the experience.

I had met him when I was still on the force and hot for the bit. Somebody had knocked over a card game on North Goodman. It wouldn't have surfaced, except one of the players had dropped from a heart attack in the middle of it. His pals told us what happened, two guys, one of them, his arm lopped above the elbow. I guess one arm is enough if it ends in a sawed-off twelve-gauge.

I'll show you how smart I was: I figured, a couple of pros, this has to be a pattern. I checked with the VA, local vets on disability for an arm. There were fifteen of them. The ones who were married and the two from the first war I ruled out. I focused on a guy who lived in a little flat on Vine Street downtown, unemployed, a couple of arrests going back to the thirties.

Friday was a popular night for card games, payday. I staked out his place Fridays. The third week, I followed him to a split-level on a leafy street in Gates. He and his friend went in. I called for backup and went in after them. Earl put down his weapon and turned to me with his dreamy that's-life smile.

The smile was justified. The captain patted me on the back, but Earl and his buddy were out on bail in twenty minutes and beat the rap easily when none of the poker players showed to press charges. They had him on a weapons violation, but what judge wants to toss a one-armed vet inside? Eleven months' probation and he walked. He bought me a beer when the trial was over.

We would meet for a drink now and then afterward. He was no stoolie, but he filled me in on the strings that connected various parts of the city, connections I was still in the dark about. When I went private I was looking for a helper and he was interested.

"Paddy Doyle?" I asked. "Know him?"

"I've heard the name. Used to be a hod carrier. Did some slugging during that strike at the overall factory in '47."

"You know Orlo Zanek, don't you?"

"Sure."

"See if you can run him down. And Penny's got a couple of skip-trace jobs you can get started on."

He went out with her to get the files. I swung my feet onto my desk and flicked on the futile fan. The mounting heat increased the force of gravity. My eyelids were giving up the struggle when the phone rang.

"It's her," Penny told me.

"Can you meet me?" the woman's voice said. It was a voice that knew things, almost harsh, a smoky Lauren Bacall voice.

"What's it about?"

"I can't say. I was given your name. They claimed you were reliable. It's very serious."

"Come to my office."

"That's not possible."

"What do you suggest?"

She laid out a plan for me to meet her on neutral ground at five that evening.

"How will I know you?" I said.

"I'll know you. Please be there, Mr. Van Savage."

I told her I would. The old cloak and dagger. I didn't mind. Everybody likes to turn their problems into melodramas. If citizens weren't paranoid the detective business would dry up.

3

I PUT ON MY hat and went out for some early lunch. The sparkling day made up for my lack of sleep. Cold consommé was the special at Gray's Mainstreeter, a crowded eatery downtown. I nodded to a table of dicks from the property crimes unit I used to work with, found a place at the counter, and ordered a BLT to soak up the boullion.

Some want their lives predictable. You go to work, come home, no surprises. You put in your years, retire, collect your pension. Perpetual care at Holy Sepulchre and you're all set.

I wasn't like that. I needed possibilities or I don't know what I would have done. It was in my blood. I needed creeps pawing teenagers and gangsters torching houses and mystery women cooing danger over the phone. That was the tune I danced to.

After lunch I walked back to my office through the diesel heat of Main Street. Earl had left an address for me. I got my car, drove out Scio, and stopped near the railroad tracks. I stepped out onto a street of broken glass.

I climbed two flights and banged my knuckles on the door. It opened on a security chain. A face peered at me through horn-rimmed glasses held together by friction tape. He exhaled smoke over a loose lip. "Hey ya, Officer Van Savage. Long time."

"Didn't you get my Christmas card, Orlo? And it's plain mister, I'm not on the force anymore."

"I forget. Where'd you send it?"

"Auburn. Or was it Dannemora? Want to let me in?"

He closed the door, then swung it open. The two-room flat reeked of nicotine and dirty socks.

"This is a real honor. Sorry about the place, it's trash city around here. I been trying to get my mother to come down, clean it up."

"All this paper lying around, makes for a real firetrap."

"That's a good one, Officer, I mean Mister." His chest heaved a poor imitation of a laugh and he followed it with a spasm of coughing. "Hey, you seen *Ben Hur* yet?"

"Yeah, I saw it. It was long."

"Great, though, right? That chariot race, jeez. 'Your eyes are full of hate, Forty-One. That's good. Hate keeps a man alive. It gives him strength.' "

I told him he was a decent actor, he should get on TV. He liked that.

"You're not playing with matches anymore, are you, Orlo?"

"Me? Hell, no. Strictly straight and narrow, nine-to-five city. Soon as I get a job. I was just looking in the want ads when you knocked. Something outdoors, I'd like. In the zoo, maybe. You know anybody there?" He ground his cigarette in an ashtray that overflowed with butts. A few were filter tips stained crimson. I formed a quick image of the type of woman who would go for a guy like Orlo. I fought an urge to empty the goddamn thing into the trash can that stood against the far wall.

I said, "I'm looking for some information. I've got four fires in the old seventh ward."

"I told you, I'm done with that, Mr. Officer. I'm on parole, I can't take no chances. I'm reformed. I go to church now." He tapped a Chesterfield out of a crumpled pack.

"I'm glad to hear that. But you still know people. These were professional jobs, no obvious accelerant. Not as clean as yours, but clean."

"I knew how to light a place, not that I'm proud of it." He palmed a chrome Zippo and snapped a flame to light the butt.

"And you know who's available if somebody should want to collect some insurance."

"This an insurance job?"

I shrugged. On the far wall he'd hung a calendar with a picture of Santa drinking a Coke. The pause that refreshes. He hadn't ripped a month off since February.

He exhaled smoke through clenched teeth and said, "Whaddaya want, anyway?"

"If you wanted to light a fire and you weren't around, who would you turn to?"

"If I wasn't around? Jeez. I wouldn't want to accuse somebody. Plus which, I can't be sure exactly who might be able to pull off something like that."

"You know you owe me."

"I sure do. And—let me think about it, I'll ask some people, get back to you."

I gave him the long stare. He nodded, smiled, looked away.

"What is it about fire?" I said.

"Fire?"

"You're not a burglar, you're not a car thief."

He thought about it, if what went on inside his head could be called thought.

"Fire," he said, "it's final city, man. Know what I mean? You get sick, you get well. You get wet, you get dry. Married, divorced. Eat, you're hungry again. Fire, it's all over. The whole world's on fire, Officer. 'At's the way I see it. Something satisfying about it. 'Cause it's final. It's forever."

"It wasn't you, was it, Orlo?" I had half a notion it was him, but he didn't let anything slip.

He acted indignant, flattening his palm against his chest. "I told you, church. Our father which aren't in heaven, hollow be thy name."

"Think it over." I handed him one of my cards.

"I'll do that. I'll put some brainpower into this one, Officer." He sucked on his cigarette and bared his brown teeth.

I was glad to get outside and breathe the sweet air.

4

I WENT BACK TO the office and put in a couple of hours of phone calls and paperwork. I tried to fight the big hump of a yawn that was building on my palate by doing a bunch of push-ups. I stared out the window at the shadows lengthening in the street.

Penny came in and reminded me about the mystery client.

"I almost forgot. Did I tell you where she wants to meet?"

I told her and she laughed.

I drove to a new shopping center they'd built on Empire Boulevard. All the big department stores were putting up branches in the suburbs. I circled behind the Sibley's there and parked near the loading docks. Then I walked around to the front entrance. Young mothers, career girls in a hurry, and blue-haired ladies with mammoth pocketbooks moved in and out of the store. Which one would go with that dusky voice? I wondered.

I needed a couple of highballs bad. But I didn't drink during the day—at least I told myself I didn't—and the sun seemed stuck just above the western horizon. It blazed loudly off the chrome of the cars that filled the lot.

A perky blonde behind a glass counter asked me if I wanted to sample a whiff of "My Sin." I shot her a quick grin. Did they actually pay people money to think up names like that? I moved on, past umbrellas and jewelry, wallets and belts, women's and men's shoes.

I figured she had chosen the lingerie department because not many men would spend time browsing there. I tried to appear casual examining the nose-cone brassieres, front-panel girdles, and a complicated lace and elastic contraption that the sign said was a merry-widow. I was just beginning to contemplate the mystery of the strapless bra when I heard that voice.

"Mr. Van Savage?"

I hadn't really formed any expectations—it doesn't pay in this business. Still, I was surprised. Under the compact hat, her hair glowed with the luster of white gold. Not many women wore veils anymore, but she had a web dotted with black stars arrayed stiffly across her face. Her sharp jawline, elegant cheeks, and radiant fore-head had a perfection that you rarely see outside a darkened movie theater. She was expensively dressed and wore dark glasses. The way she kept glancing over her shoulder you might have thought she was making off with the H-bomb secrets.

When I acknowledged my identity, she said, "Can I trust you?"

"Sure," I said. "I'm licensed by the state of New York and fully bonded."

"I don't mean that."

She removed the sunglasses. After all the rigamarole, I wouldn't have been surprised if her face had been decorated with a shiner. Instead, she looked at me with a pair of ultramarine eyes.

"You can trust me," I said. "What did you want to talk about?"

"Not here," she hissed. Her gaze jumped around before she slipped the glasses back on.

"I know a place," I said, getting into the game. "We'll go in my car and I'll bring you back."

I had already noticed the rings, a wedding band and a sparkler that was only half as big as the Ritz.

On the way out, we passed through sporting goods. It reminded me that I still had to pick Gloria up a baseball glove for her birthday.

She was a superior second baseman. I'd had to make quite a stink, but finally they were letting her play on the regular Little League team with the boys.

We descended a short flight of concrete steps to the rear parking area. The sun had disappeared and the sky was taking on a milky turquoise veneer. In the car, her perfume hit me. She was reluctant to talk.

I was excited. It wasn't lust—not directly, anyway. It was the excitement you might feel if you were meeting a movie star. I had never met one, but I could imagine how worked up I would get if I were riding in a car with Kim Novak. How daily life would pale.

"This heat's bad," I said.

She looked at me as if she had never noticed it, as if she lived in a climate of her own. "I guess."

"Where did you hear about me?" I needed to keep talking.

"A friend."

"Anybody I know?"

"I doubt it."

"You got lucky."

"I hope so."

We rode another mile in silence.

"Could I ask what it is you want to hire me to do?"

"I haven't decided whether I do want to hire you. It's a very delicate matter. I must have someone I trust implicitly. Someone discreet."

"I wouldn't be in business ten minutes if I blabbed about my cases at the beauty parlor."

"No, I don't suppose you would."

Before I could probe any further, we arrived at the Anaconda.

5

THE GENESEE RIVER USED to flow into a wide bay east of town, but during the last ice age they switched it to run through the gorge that now cuts Rochester in half. The old outlet, Irondequoit Bay, was the site of a big Seneca Indian camp. They ruled the local hunting and gathering racket around here for about four centuries. LaSalle came across them when he and his boys paddled down the lake in canoes. The bay is now rimmed with marshland and fed only by a small creek.

They'd been dumping in a landfill at one end for years. Burning garbage permanently tinted the air down here. A few businesses had opened along the road that crossed the fill.

I stopped at the low-slung bar and grill that sat at the bottom of the steep slope. A billboard right above it urged passersby to TIP A TOPPER—HAVE A HAPPY BEER. A neon bottle poured neon brew into a neon glass right above the Anaconda's chimney.

Inside, you had to stand for a moment to let your eyes adjust to the dark. The only light came from a few of those flickering bulbs that are supposed to look like candle flames and from the blue-white illumination under the bottles.

We slid into a booth in the far corner. She removed her hat and used her fingertips to fluff and smooth hair that was a luminous shade of blond you usually see only on children. Her tongue darted to wet her ripe-cherry lips. I asked her what she wanted to drink.

"You decide."

The bartender was a former middleweight I used to watch fight now and then at the Armory AC.

"A couple of Canadian Clubs with ginger, Jerry."

He mixed the drinks and slapped down my change. For a minute I thought he was shooting a curious look toward the booth, but I let it pass. She was the type who inspired curious looks.

The drink tasted good, cold and sweet and nicely scented with rye.

"Okay, you've had a serious falling out with your husband," I said. "He's the type of guy who runs amok pretty easily. Maybe you want to call it splitsville, but he's the one with the bank account, so you have to finesse it."

Her face wavered and she turned her attention to her swizzle stick. Her skin caught rays of dim light, caressed them, and sent them on their enchanted way.

"How do I know all this?" I continued. "You don't want me at the house, so it's gotta be domestic. You didn't want to show at my office, it means your breadwinner's both jealous and rich enough to have you watched. Anybody far enough along for a detective is usually thinking about who gets the dough—that's only natural. How am I doing?"

"You guessed right, it's about my husband. But it's much worse than what you say." Her voice was saturated with a bedroom intimacy.

"What's the problem?"

She drew a cigarette from a pack she kept in a damask-covered holder. I snapped my lighter for her. She took a long drag and nervously tapped the butt against a glass ashtray printed with an ad for Carling's Red Cap Ale.

Finally she said, "He's planning to kill me." It struck me as a line from a movie.

"What makes you think that?"

"He's going to do it. Our marriage has become a war."

"Welcome to the club. Murder's another matter."

"Have you ever heard of Bluebeard?"

"The fairy tale?"

"It's a story. Bluebeard left his wife with the keys to his house and went out of town. He told her not to go into a certain room, but she got curious and opened the door. She found the bodies of all his other wives. Blood got on the key, and she couldn't wipe it off. When he got back, he knew she knew." She stared earnestly into my eyes.

"You got a room like that in your house?"

"No."

"But your husband killed his other wives?"

"Yes."

I looked at her closely. She was a beauty, no doubt about it. Yet I couldn't get over the feeling that her looks were an exquisite facade, that her eyes were looking out from behind a mask. They reminded me of the eyes of a lizard, sharp, stunning, but completely impersonal.

We had both downed our cocktails. I returned to the bar for refills.

"You like to live dangerous," Jerry said when he'd set me up with another round.

"Do I?"

He glanced toward the booth and nodded. "You know her?" I asked.

"I saw them together once."

"The husband?"

"Yeah, the husband. Sure, the husband."

"Just having a drink with the lady, Jerry. Totally innocent."

"Tell Joe Petrone."

The whole equation shifted. I was trying to work out some calculations in my head as I carried the drinks back to the booth, but I never liked algebra, all those unknowns.

She quickly poured out the story about her predecessors. The first, a convenient accident. Then her husband had married a society girl. She hadn't lasted six months. Another mishap. A woman friend had clued her in to the dark suspicions. The police had been paid off, nobody had dared to question the official story.

"And you believe all this?" I said.

"Yes."

"Because you're married to Joe Petrone and he has a reputation as a torpedo? Don't look so surprised, it's my business to know things."

"Then you see why this is so delicate." It was the second time she'd used the word. I remembered using it myself once that day.

"Who was the friend who wised you up to the secret room?"

"Angela Grecco. She has a kind of reputation herself—she runs that amusement park—but she seems to know about that world, Joe's world."

"And you don't?"

"When I married him I was looking for security. I didn't take any interest in his business. I was naive. Joe can be charming when he wants to. No, more than that. He has a gift for making you feel that the world—that it's a magical place. Now I see that he's evil, truly evil."

Evil? Magical? Charming? This was the way a person talks when they live in a fairy tale. You'd be surprised how many do. They see a bogeyman lurking behind every bush, a knight in shining armor riding every cloud.

"So why do you think he wants to kill you?"

"He knows I've come to loathe him. You have to understand, Joe desperately wants a son. He talked a lot about it before we were married. It's a very big deal to him. I haven't been able to have children. And now, knowing what he is, I can't bear to—to go to bed with him."

I tried to imagine what it would be like to be married to this woman and have her hold out on you. Would it drive you to murder? Maybe. Especially if the drive was a short one to begin with.

"So leave him."

She brushed at a stray strand of hair. "Defy him? Humiliate him? I'm not a fool."

"Go away then."

"Where? On what? I have no money. And he would track me down as sure as I'm sitting here. He has friends. You don't know."

She finished her drink—we were burning them up. A couple of guys came in while I was at the bar buying a third round. Now, anybody who comes into a joint will look around. But I found myself watching these guys and trying to gauge just how curious they were, just where they were looking.

Back at the table, I took a big swallow. The weariness had dropped away now. My mind was running in high gear.

I asked her, "Have you considered the police?"

"Police? I'm no longer naive." She meant that Petrone had plenty of friends in the department, which I knew was true.

"Just what do you want me to do for you?"

"I'm desperate. I need something that I can use against him. If I had some hard evidence about his previous wives, it might make him think twice. It might give me some leverage."

"You're talking about blackmail."

"Yes, if you want to call it that. Blackmail with the truth. If Angela is right, this might be the one area where he's vulnerable. But I can't do it on my own, I need help, Mr. Van Savage."

"Make it Ike. I don't think I got your first name."

"Vicky." She put a lot of lip into it. Then she whispered, "You carry a gun, don't you?"

"Sometimes." I did strap one on now and then to amuse the client, part of the show. Uncomfortable, though, especially in summer.

I wished I had my Colt with me that night to show her. I could tell she would have been impressed.

"I need someone who's on my side, someone I can call on in case Joe—in case my husband doesn't listen to reason."

Reason. I would have laid money that the whole thing was hooey, the product of an overactive imagination. I imagined I could dig around for a couple of weeks, hold her hand if she needed it held, and collect a nice fat fee.

But I knew it wasn't as simple as that. Here I was, big as life, having a drink and whispering secrets with Joe Petrone's missus for all the world to see. Suddenly I wanted to get out of there. I emptied my drink and stood. She slipped on her dark glasses. I took her arm as we left.

"I'll find out what I can," I said in the car.

She thanked me. I asked her for more details. She told me she had met Petrone soon after the death of her first husband. Joe had courted her like a gentleman and suddenly she was able to stop wondering whether to buy soup or stockings.

Back at the shopping center I rolled to a stop near a new Chrysler.

"You don't know how much this means to me," she said. She smiled briefly for the first time, all peaches and cream. "And thanks, Ike. Thanks for not being afraid."

Afraid? No, I wasn't afraid.

I always checked my mirror when I drove. That night I kept seeing the gleam of headlights, the flash of chrome, and blackness.

THURSDAY

1

"I FIGURED A SKIRT in it. *The Seven Year Itch,* did you see that picture? Underwear in the refrigerator?"

Earl Clear had come in the next morning to report on a skip-trace he'd run to ground outside Batavia. The man had been a bookkeeper for a furniture wholesaler, and after seven years he'd walked. The audit found eleven thousand missing, the bonding company hired me to find him. Earl was good with that kind of thing.

"Sure," I said, "Marilyn's skirt getting blown."

"I was wrong. It was his mother. Liver cancer. No hope. Guy wants to impress her before she goes over. Guilt? I don't know. Buys a new Merc, tells her how well he's doing. Plans to take her to Bermuda. Had the tickets and everything. Told me all about it. Shame."

Earl was a great listener. Maybe because of his injury or his basset-hound eyes, he inspired trust. He knew how to pick up on the clues everybody drops about what they're not saying. He would gently steer them toward just the things they had no intention of going into.

"Company going to press?" he asked.

"They'll see what's left of the money and decide. We did our bit."

"It don't leave me feeling good."

"That's the business. Maybe you'll like the next one better. I need some background on a guy, grapevine stuff. Strictly on the Q.T."

He lit the cigarette he'd been making and said, "Name of?"

"Joe Petrone."

He laughed smoke out his nose. Then he stopped laughing.

"What's the joke?" he said.

"I know his reputation. I want personal dope. Family life, hobbies, that end of it."

He laughed again. "Hobbies? Joe Petrone?"

"Discreet inquiries, Earl."

"On account of what?"

"He's married to a looker who thinks he's plotting to bump her off."

"That's always the way. The guy wants a woman who can wear the clothes, the woman wants the guy who can buy them. They both end up with the short end, looking over their shoulder."

"You're a regular philosopher," I said.

"Sure I am. You know what you're poking into?"

"Just doing a job."

"Listen, back when I was . . ." He tilted his head to sum up his criminal career. "Certain games, no go. Why? Petrone's pals. Games I did hit, twenty cents on the dollar I gave to a guy. I never shorted him. How come? He knew Petrone. Get me?"

"Yeah, Petrone's King Tut in this town."

"Not just, either."

"This county, this end of the state."

"Ask Ernie Canale, had that jukebox operation out in Charlotte. Or Jojo Dunlap. He used to run a horse room in the back of a cigar store on Commercial Street. Ask Pattycake Pulaski, operated them chair-rent bingo parlors. Only you can't ask any of them, unless you want to go out to the graveyard with a table knocker. Canale, only his dentist recognized him. Little Maxie Norris used to peddle Mary Jane down in the third ward but he didn't clear it. Somebody's dog dug him up in Genesee Valley Park."

"You're blaming Petrone?"

"Except you'll never prove nothing."

"Fine. I'm not pissing in his beer, I'm just looking for some information. A nervous wife, a check in the bank. You don't want it?"

"I'll ask around. Why not."

He headed for the door, and I could hear his chuckle fade down the corridor.

I sent Penny to the lab to pick up the Gill photos. I got on the phone to Tom Cahoon, a detective in the persons unit downtown, and invited him to lunch.

Penny came back and was explaining the plot of a *Peter Gunn* episode to me. Her long fingers made hieroglyphics to summarize the action. The outer bell jangled just as she was describing the solution to the case.

"And they lived happily ever after," she said, and went to answer it.

2

MRS. GILL WAS A heavyset woman who spent a lot of time in a beauty parlor. Her nylons whispered as she crossed my office.

On her first visit she had poured out her life story, no stopping her. She and her family had joined the flood of refugees during the war. She named places in a distant and dark corner of the world: Petroseni, Budapest, Bratislava. They had seen their clothes go to rags, felt the cold, eaten moldy potatoes. The experience had shaken her faith in life itself. Hope had become a dream.

They were Szekelers, a tribe from Transylvania that was supposed to have descended from Attila and the Huns. They had powers—spells and evil-eye stuff. I imagined Dracula. A person's sixth sense, she assured me, means little in war, means little when reality turns to nightmare.

Her shred of hope had taken the form of Eddie Gill. He was a buck private on occupation duty in Germany. His round, well-fed form represented to her the bounty of the New World. He was her ticket to America.

The arrangement, she assured me, was a practical one. She owed him children and a home. He owed her fidelity and a paycheck.

"Love?" she had said. "This is something you talk about in America. Love died for us."

Now she thought she was getting the short end and I was there to tell her she was correct. It was my duty, but I hated to do it. Through the filter of her accent, she struck me as an intelligent woman. She deserved better.

Matrimonial cases, you generally work through a lawyer, sometimes you don't even meet the client. A few come in directly–Mrs. Gill was one of those.

Square jaw, hard eyes, but a lot of vulnerability in the corners of her wide mouth. She perched on the chair opposite me. Penny closed the door and the sound of her typing warded off the silence.

I felt like a doctor who has to tell somebody that, yes, the tumor is malignant. I was glad I had the pictures. I handed her the stack of eight-by-tens and waited.

When she looked down, a double chin formed at the top of her throat. She went through the photographs slowly, studying each one. She looked up at me with egg-white eyes.

"Did not take you long," she said.

"I'm afraid your suspicions were correct, Mrs. Gill. Here's my report."

"Tell me what says."

"I saw him with that girl. She works at his restaurant. They went out to a nightclub. They went to a motel. They stayed there three hours and twenty minutes."

"Three hours and twenty minutes? He says he is playing cards."

I shrugged.

"Who is she?"

"It'll be easy to get her name."

"She is young."

"Yes."

She turned back to the black-and-white glossies. I was the man who brought salt to the wounded.

"Mrs. Gill, if you're thinking divorce . . ."

She looked at me as if I had said a dirty word. "Divorce?"

"The threat of a statutory rape charge can be a very potent bar-gaining chip in any negotiations."

"Chip?"

"A threat."

"But I want my husband!" She was overflowing with cold fury now. "You don't understand? Divorce? I need Eddie. These young girls, they lure a man. There is no way a man can resist. Isn't that right?"

"I didn't observe any resistance."

"She is slut. Look at her." She held up one of the indistinct pictures. "She do this. My Eddie, he is a boy. Always was a boy."

You never know how they're going to react. They hate the spouse, they hate the lover, they hate themselves, they hate the world. You never know.

"I hope it works out for you," I said.

"You think I am big fool?"

"No, I think you're a loyal and generous woman."

"He loves her?"

I shook my head without committing myself.

I watched her face age in front of me. She didn't cry or even grimace. It happened very simply, the way a shadow passes over a landscape. This was her reward for four pregnancies, four rounds of diaper changes, thirteen years of sleeping beside a farting, snoring clod.

I admired her. I imagined her taking the dope I was giving her and hitting him in the balls with it. She wasn't going to run away from her marriage, she was going to fight.

It made me think.

I had lost a lot of sentimentality in Korea and come out of the army restless. I needed to be on the edge. A job with the police gave me that at first. But you know how it is, you're always looking for a little more. I drank too much. Drinking, I ran into women. I didn't resist, either.

Eileen had not hired a private detective. When she had suspected I was tomcatting, she had gone out and done the same. By the time the thing came into the open we were both so bitter that separation seemed the only way out.

Things didn't improve, so we figured let's call it splits for good. It made sense at the time, but now Gloria was paying the price for two people's selfishness.

Mrs. Gill moved her lips silently as she counted out a stack of wrinkled bills, five and tens.

3

I DROVE OUT TO the old seventh ward to have a look at some of Paddy Doyle's buildings.

It was a squalid area. The place had been used up long before Negroes started moving up from the South after the war. The houses were built close together, some of them wedged in along alleys. Their fake-brick siding was crumbling, tar paper showing, windows broken, stairs sagging, weeds taking over where little patches of grass had been trampled to dirt. Two-by-fours and strings of Christmas lights held up a front porch. A hubcap served as a planter for pansies.

These places were moneymakers for the landlords. They could divide an old house into four or five apartments, spend the bare minimum on maintenance, and line their pockets.

One of Doyle's houses had burned to the ground. The place next door had caught, but they'd managed to save that; only two windows were covered with plywood.

Over on the next street was another of Doyle's. Gutted. As I drew even with it, a dog stuck his head out the gaping door and barked. Another propped his paws on the front windowsill and looked at me with cocked ears. Maybe they had lived there before the fire or maybe they had moved in after. They gave the impression of being regular householders, worried about taxes, water rates, and the make of cars their neighbors were driving.

A building on the next block that belonged to my client was a palsied old crone leaning on the pillar of a porch. The roof sagged, the corner had given way, and the whole thing seemed about to topple. Black eyebrows sprouted over each vacant window. The char smell was still strong.

A child's bike lay in the front yard, the tires gone, paint blistered, the wheels and frame covered with fresh rust. Some kids were playing around the precarious porch. Each wore an eyepatch and carried a wooden sword, little pirates.

An old woman, her dark face puckered with a million wrinkles, shuffled past pulling a bag of groceries in a battered American Flyer. She gave me a look, glanced at the ruin, shook her head.

"What happened?" I asked, innocently curious.

"The Lord said it. No more floods. No good learning to swim. Build all the boats you want. Where there's fire, there's smoke, mister."

"How did it start?"

"Electric, they say. Rats gnaw at the wires, burn theirselves up. Burn the whole place. Sure, electric."

"You think different?"

She nodded, came close, and squinted up at me. "Fires around here all the time. Burnin' and burnin'."

"What's causing them?"

"Miracle." She gave me a four-toothed grin.

"Act of God, you mean?"

She shook her head slowly. "Not God, money. Mammon. Miracle mile. You hear? That's what. I know things."

"Somebody's making money?"

"Somebody. Somebody else. Not me, I don't want to make money that way, burning. No sir. Not for no miracle mile." She walked on, hunched over to grip the handle of the child's wagon.

In among the blackened rubble they'd thrown into the yard, I noticed bright yellow dandelions blooming. I walked around for a while, not knowing what I was looking for. The seat of my car was hot from the sun as I climbed back in and drove ten blocks.

On Mohawk Street I knocked on the door of a man named Tyrone Power. A rotund black woman told me her husband was out.

We had picked up Power on a numbers rap a few years earlier. I'd recognized him for a decent citizen and had thrown a lot of juice into getting the charges reduced.

"You can probably find him down at Willis's," she said. "He spends about all his life in the barbershop. Kind of funny for a bald man, ain't it?"

She didn't laugh but scowled at me as if I might challenge the statement. I thanked her and walked the two blocks.

Some people were sitting on their porches this warm morning, plenty of them out of work. Kids were whooping up and down the sidewalks, deep into summer vacation.

A slowly revolving barber pole marked Willis's corner. Two benches and four or five bentwood chairs on the sidewalk were all occupied. Four old men sat around a rickety card table playing dominos. The rest were just jawboning.

"Tyrone!" one of the men shouted without getting up. "Man want you."

"Don't ask me about my name!" said the portly man who emerged. I knew he remembered me, but he went on with his act. "My grandpap was Tyrone Power and I'm Tyrone Power. No third, no junior, no nothing. And no lame-ass matinee idolater is gonna tell me who I can be named after."

"Way he handled that blade when he was Zorro," a poker-faced older man said, "he was *almost* slick as you, Ty."

This was some kind of standing joke and they all laughed.

"I don't need no blade to whup you ass, Leroy."

"Our Tyrone was in the movies, too," the man said to me. "I seen him there last night. Third row."

"Give a man a chair, Mr. Bones. You still young enough to stand on your feet."

He commandeered two chairs and moved them around the corner into the shaded alleyway where the morning glories clinging to the side of the building were blooming a virginal blue.

"How you doing, Ike?"

"I'm interested in some fires."

"From what end?"

"I'm working for Paddy Doyle."

"That son of a bitch?" He rubbed his palm along his shiny pate. "What are you on his side for?"

"He may be a shark but he's not burning his own buildings."

"No, they're burning them down for him because he swimming against the stream."

"Which way is it running?"

"Man want to buy, you sell—that's which way. He's not the only one who's had fires. Anybody else, not so pigheaded to turn their back on money, even if what they're offering is chicken feed. Word is out."

"Whose word?"

"Man upstairs, man with the dough, man who knows. Why ask?"

"You been approached yourself?"

"Sure. I've sold half a dozen buildings. Why? Look around you. They're poor people's houses. So if the man discover oil under them, want to drill a well, what's the point of standing in his way?"

"Drill the well yourself."

"What do I know about oil? Or gold? Or who knows what? They say gravel's worth money. Stones. Dirt. If you've got the market. I learned a long time ago, when it comes to money, you gotta finesse it. Doyle, he don't see it that way."

"Who's buying?"

"Search me. The check clears, why ask questions?"

"They're picking them up through an agent?"

"Some little office out on St. Paul, Caliban Realty. Some front."

"What do they do with the buildings?"

"They rent them out to colored folks, same as me. Or they leave 'em sit, some of 'em. I'd be careful, I was you."

"Why's that?"

"Certain people in this town, you don't ask questions. Ain't worth your hide. Besides, you hear about Superman?"

"What about him?" I asked.

"Dead."

"Kryptonite?"

"Nope. I'm talking about that actor, what's his name? He played Superman. Was gonna get married next week. His fiancée and some friends are sitting in the living room, big house in Hollywood. They hear *pow pow* upstairs. Guy shot himself. Goes to show. More powerful than a locomotive. You keep that in mind, start thinking you can fly."

"I already know I can't. I've tried."

"They're waiting, is what I think. Waiting for the oil to come in. Did I say Caliban? I think it's Cavalier."

4

AT NOON THE BAVARIAN House on South Fitzhugh roared
with the midday crush. It was a place where men still sat at the bar
and lunched on pickled eggs and beer.

Tom Cahoon was a big man and a big eater. He used wax to
keep his crewcut just so and stared at the world through squinty
cowboy eyes. He took time out from leveling a mountain of mashed
potatoes to devour four fat Forlini bratwursts and a man-sized helping of sauerkraut. I sweated as I worked on a plate of fresh ham and
applesauce. We both had quart steins of lager in front of us.

As I said before, when I'd come back from Korea, I'd needed
something with more edge to it than selling Chevies. I had taken the
civil service test and joined the Rochester Police Bureau. Eileen had
sulked about it for two weeks—late hours, bad pay, and the way it
kept me keyed up. I told her you'd better get used to it, and she
did—she tried, anyway. I was keyed up anyway and I had this taste
in my mouth.

Back then I was gung-ho, a real crime fighter. I hadn't endured
Heartbreak Ridge to have lawbreakers turn up their noses at truth,
justice, and the American way. I worked overtime. I set up a Saturday

basketball league for kids from the neighborhoods. I put my own time in on cold cases.

The bosses liked that. After I made detective a couple of years later, I kept it up. I couldn't let off on the gas. The rugged pace was shredding my marriage, but I was on a mission.

Working vice in '58, I got wind of a prostitution ring, organized stuff, call girls, not street level. I should have asked around the department, but to me it was a cause, a moral thing. That was a mistake. I talked to people, started to make some headway. A guy named Lucky MacAdoo was the front man. I managed to get something on him and was pushing to find out who pulled his strings.

Finally my big break came. A stoolie offered to spoon-feed me the inside dope, MacAdoo and a lot more. He had a burglary case coming up in state court and he needed a pal, he said. I arranged to meet him in an alley off of Clinton Avenue.

He handed me a package that he said contained business records. When I looked inside, I saw money instead, nice green bills. That sight punched me in the gut. Four cops and a couple of newspaper reporters came around the corner at the same instant. My picture showed up on the front page of the *Democrat and Chronicle*. VICE COP IN BRIBE RAP. They offered to drop the charges if I resigned.

Was that the straw that broke the back of me and Eileen? I don't even know. It all happened about the same time, and it's all lost in a blur of booze and resentment.

I supposed I was swimming against the tide and they would have got me sooner or later. Some guys fit in—I saw it in the service. It's a square hole? Fine, I'm a square peg. That never worked for me.

After the bust-up, I mooned around for a few months, drank even more. Then decided to go into business for myself. I figured one thing I've got, it's instinct. I know when to trust my hunches. I knew that being a detective was 90 percent legwork, but I figured it was the gut reaction that gave you the advantage.

By that summer, '59, I had managed to pick up some routine cases from lawyers I knew and was keeping my head above water as a private dick.

My buddies from the job had mixed feelings. I was Judas or I was the last upstanding man in Gomorrah. I was a simpleton, a conniver, a holier-than-thou gobshite. Some even thought I had communist leanings.

Tom Cahoon was one of the ones who stuck by me. I asked about his wife, who was going blind from diabetes, and his son, who would be starting at left tackle this fall for Aquinas. He asked about Gloria. We talked for a while about the heat and about this one and that one in the department.

"Petrone?" he said when we got down to it. "They all claim he's the nicest guy you'd ever want to meet. Sponsors that March of Dimes gala every spring. I hear he never swears, farts out loud, or blows his nose on his sleeve."

"You hear, I hear. But who the hell is he?"

"What's the key to the world, Ike? Who you know. Join the force, you could be a captain in a year or never. All depends on who you know. Petrone, he knows people. That's all. Who the hell put you onto this one, anyway?"

"The wife."

"I don't envy you."

"She's scared of him."

"Hasn't she heard about better or worse?"

"It's the death-do-us-part angle that's got her worried."

"She's dreaming."

"She'd be number three."

He rolled his eyes, thinking back. "The last one I remember. Went down the gorge off Maplewood last year. A mess." He lit a panatela and blew a ring of smoke.

"Let me guess—not many questions were asked."

"Why should they be? It was an accident or it was suicide. She had a psych history. Her family wanted to keep it quiet. Society people."

"What about the first?"

"I don't recall that one."

"Any chance of looking over the files on them?"

"Sensitive stuff."

"I'll owe you."

"You already owe me."

"I think it's best to be careful on this, Tom."

"Careful is right. I'll see what I can do."

"That's white of you."

He tapped an ash into the remains of his kraut and belched.

"Keep your eyes open," he said, patting the back of his head. He moved his hard bulk across the restaurant and out the door.

I walked to City Hall and spent a couple of hours looking over deed registrations. Legwork and research. So much information is lying around in the open if you know where to look. In this case, it was written in big leather-bound ledgers and recorded on documents filed in a room that smelled of mucilage and old ink. It was so hot in there that I sweated through my shirt even with my coat off.

Cavalier Realty had purchased a slew of buildings out in the old seventh ward. I knew it wasn't unusual for a real estate company to acquire property for later resale. But this firm must have had an awful lot invested in these places, and they seemed to be buying at an accelerated rate.

I came across at least five other companies that all listed the same St. Paul Boulevard address. Sure enough, Caliban Properties was one of them. Also PT Realty, EG Management, Castle Homes. All were busy acquirers of property in a wide swath that traced the city line out to the northeast.

I copied down a list of addresses and title transfers and left.

As the lady said, Where there's fire, there's smoke.

5

WE HAD BOUGHT THE little house, two blocks from Highland Park, in the spring of '48. The Russians had blockaded Berlin around that time and there was talk in the air of another war. We wanted to have a place of our own.

The night we moved in, with hardly a stick of furniture and orange crates for bookshelves, the light breeze came through the screens and we caught the lush bouquet of the lilacs. There was a lot of happiness in that smell.

It was before Korea, when I was working for Peterson Chevrolet and trying to fit. Trying to hack a mortgage and stay home nights.

We used to go up to the Bowl and lie on the grass and listen to opera under the stars. We didn't know the first thing about it, but that music just streamed into the summer night and took us with it.

Lots of memories.

Eileen, my ex, wasn't expecting me today. She told me so.

"That's the idea," I said. I was trying to keep a smile in my voice. "I like to surprise her once in a while."

"She doesn't need any surprises." She did a thing with her mouth that I once thought was sexy. Now it bugged me.

"I do so," a voice behind her said. "I need a surprise. I gotta have a surprise."

She had a paper bag over her head, two eyeholes ringed in crayon.

"Now who is that? Is it the monster that devoured Cleveland?"

"No-o! You're cold."

"Agent S-11, Kelly?"

"Warmer."

"I give up."

"It's Fury!" she yelled.

"The vicious daughter of Ivan Shark? No, it can't be!"

"Ha-ha!" She pulled the bag off and brushed light-brown bangs out of her eyes. "You are in my evil power clutches, Captain Midnight!"

"But this is just a disguise," I said. "I'm really Ivan Shark himself."

"I knew you were."

I leaned over and she gave me a smacker on the cheek.

"Want to go to Gleeland, kid?" I said, preempting Eileen.

"Yes! Can I, Mom?"

"You said Nancy was expecting you."

"No, Gleeland. Please please please."

Her mother couldn't think of any objections, so the deal was done. "Get her back by supper," she told me.

"Of course."

Gloria filled me in on the latest as we drove toward the lake. "They said on *Mr. Wizard* that honey is made of bees' spit and Robin and me found an old bees' nest in a tree but I think there was only eggs in it so I'm going to hatch them, only Mom says it's wasps."

She was overflowing with the fervor of nine years old. She was interested in everyone and everything. It delighted and pained me to listen to her, to know only a sketch of her life, to catch only the glimpses from weekend visits, holidays, the odd surprise.

My consolation was that we shared a delicious sense of conspiracy that we might have lacked if I had been the daily disciplinarian. We kept up a running gag about *Captain Midnight*. I remembered the show from radio. She had watched it on television when she was little and had dutifully sent for her Ovaltine decoder ring. In our version either of us could be any of the characters, and she sometimes made up new ones.

"I learned a new song, wanna hear? 'Good-bye old Paint, I'm . . .' No, wait. 'I'm a-ridin' old Paint, I'm a-leadin' old Dan . . .' Daddy, what's a hoolihan?"

"It's a kind of rope or a slingshot."

"Like a lasso?" She gave a yip and went on with the song. The windows were open and the air was sweet.

She got sidetracked onto a different tune: " 'I'll tell you the truth, not lyin' or jokin', I'd rather be in jail than to be heartbroken.' "

For some reason she thought that was a sidesplitter. Her laugh was more musical than her singing.

A minute later she was asking me, "Do they burn cows?"

"When they cook them?"

She shot me her suffering-fools look. "No. Because Kathy told me they burn them and that's how they get the brand on the calves, like Rocking A?"

I had to admit it was true. "Cows are tough, though," I said.

"But calves are children."

She made her mouth pouty and was quiet for a while. The breeze caught a strand of her hair and lifted it.

The cloud passed and she wanted me to guess her favorites.

"Candy," she said.

"All-day sucker."

"No, M&M's, yellow ones. TV show."

"*Roy Rogers?*"

"*Have Gun Will Travel.*"

"Mom lets you stay up for that?"

"Sure. Paladin. He dresses in black and he has this card, with a horse's head. Baseball player."

"Luke Easter." He was a home-run–hitting first baseman the Wings had picked up that year. Gloria was stuck on him.

"Right. Um, car."

"Olds?"

She shook her head. "T-bird. No, Corvette."

We came in sight of the highest curve of the Jackrabbit.

"Oh, boy!" she squealed.

It was one of the oldest amusement parks in the country, built by the streetcar company a hundred years ago to get citizens to ride the line on weekends. It was a little shabby now, but a kid wouldn't notice.

We paid our admission and headed right for the Jackrabbit, Gloria's favorite ride. She was willing to wait in order to get the front car. Once we had our spot, we stayed on for three tours, the last strictly no-hands. Part of the thrill was a fast section with a lot of humps that was all enclosed in a tunnel so you hurtled through pitch darkness. A real screamer.

Next we headed for Gloria's even more favorite ride, the bumper cars. I liked this one myself. We careened around the slick steel floor in our tubs, the contact sparking above us, rear ending, T-boning, and maneuvering for spine-jarring head-ons. Gloria gave me a jolt from behind that threw my head back and set her howling with sadistic joy. By the time I had her in my sights for payback, the power died. I handed over more tickets and the chase was on again.

We bought a couple of Belgian waffles and some orange pop and sat at a picnic table in the shade. Marsha, one of her school friends, came by with her mother. Gloria challenged her to Ski-Ball. I gave the girls five dollars and told Gloria I would meet her at the arcade in a little while.

I walked around to a building behind the carousel and mounted a flight of stairs to a door that said OFFICE. It wasn't latched properly and swung open when I knocked.

Yellowed shades made the light dim. A curled strip of flypaper hanging from a ceiling fixture was the first thing that caught my attention. The gaping mouth of a pistol barrel was the second. My hands floated as if attached to two helium balloons.

"You're that close to death and still smiling," the woman who held the gun said. "My, my."

"I'm trying to look friendly. I didn't come here to rob you." The table in front of her was covered with money, a hay mound at my end, neat stacks at hers.

"That's lucky, Jeremiah. Whyn't you go to confession, maybe I'll forgive you your trespasses."

"Angela Grecco?"

"Who's asking?"

I told her who I was and mentioned Vicky Petrone.

Her hard face had dark circles under the eyes and incongruous cupid lips. Her eyebrows nearly met over her prominent nose. It was a handsome rather than pretty face, a face you might have seen in the Roman Forum, the face of someone plunging a knife into Caesar.

She wore little rubber nipples on her fingers for counting the money.

"Don't worry about the gun," she said. "It's not loaded."

"They say those are the most dangerous."

"It didn't make you tinkle on my floor, that's a good sign." She laughed. "Let me buy you a snort."

I've learned never to turn down what's offered. She took one of those bottles with the basket and poured two tumblers of dago red.

Yes, a hard face and a peasant face, good looking and homely by turns, wild.

She motioned for me to sit on a ratty green couch. She wasn't fat, but she certainly filled her plaid Bermuda shorts and sleeveless blouse. She sank into an easy chair and propped a pair of surprisingly slim legs on the coffee table.

"How much of what you said can you back up?" I asked her. The wine tasted sharp and dusty.

"You get right down to it, don't you?"

"Did you want to dance a cha-cha first?"

She laughed a Santa Claus laugh. "I love to dance."

"You think Vicky's really in danger?"

"I'll tell you something about Joe Petrone—he never grew up. He's a two-year-old with a gun in his hand. Mess with his little red wagon, take your chances."

"You know him?"

"You been to Gleeland before?"

"I bring my little girl," I said. "One of her favorite places."

"My family's had it, three generations. Three generations. So what am I doing handing Joe Petrone cash every month?"

"You tell me."

She began bending her fingers back one at a time. They were unusually flexible and cracked with each word: "Unions. Linens. Beer license. Ice deliveries. Even the goddamn permit to put on our fireworks show. Grease. Baksheesh. It stinks to high heaven." She held out her hand and brought the inside of the opposite elbow hard against it.

"How does all that make you privy to his family life?"

"I know Joe. I know him from around and we're friends in a manner of speaking, used to be. He can charm the pants off you. He wanted a showpiece just like he wanted a ticket to the society ball. He gets what he wants, but he doesn't necessarily want what he gets."

"That give you a reason to sour the sauce?"

"If I was the type. But he sours his own sauce. She came to me. We had met each other here and there—Rochester's a small town. She knew I knew Joe and wanted my take. Girl stuff. I told her what I told her for her own good."

"How did you come across the info?"

"I know how to talk to a man. They whisper little things in my ear."

"Like what?"

She pushed away the delinquent curls that tumbled around her eyes. "Just hints. My uncle's sister was Joe's first wife. Uncle Leo knows."

"Who is he?"

"Leo Forlini? He's the sausage king. He knows what happened. Louisa was talking divorce, couldn't take it anymore. Believe me, she had grounds. Joe brought chippies right into the house. She'd open the paper, there's his picture, some young gadget on his arm. But divorce wasn't in the cards, lawyers digging into his business, the humiliation of it. He had other ideas."

"Such as?"

"Electrocuted. She was listening to the radio taking a bath. The set fell in. It was nasty, like the punch line of a bad joke. He said she drank, she was careless. That's probably true. Then he cried so much at the funeral, two guys had to hold him up."

She splashed more wine into our glasses. She reached with her lips for the cigarette I offered. I lit a match and she guided my hand, all the time keeping her eyes on mine.

"What about the second wife?"

"The Kerr girl? She was frail. Joe, you don't want to be frail. It wouldn't surprise me, she was a virgin before she married him. Too bad."

"Why do you think these accidents were murder?"

"Because things happen for a reason, Ike. You know that. There are no coincidences. In Petrone's world, you're inconvenient, you're gone."

"So you have no evidence."

She tapped her temple. "I have a brain."

She smiled and for a second she let me look a long way into her dark eyes. In the quiet I heard the distant rush of the Jackrabbit, the screams of the happy riders.

Then her look went opaque again and she said, "I'm surprised she hired you, but I'm glad. It shows some pluck. You, I hope you realize what you don't know."

"What's that?"

"Wheels within wheels." She made spinning motions with her fingers and jutted her tongue out as she laughed.

When I was young, I read the comics every day. My favorite was *Li'l Abner.* All the girls in Dogpatch were stacked to the ceiling, but the one who really did it for me was Moonbeam McSwine. A grimy girl, dressed in tatters and sucking a pipe, she lounged in the pen with the hogs and gave off an aroma that discouraged suitors. I don't know why I found her such an aphrodisiac, but I did.

Now, this woman showed no grime, patches, or corncob, but there was something of the barnyard about her, something fertile. The warm day and the raw wine had me sweating.

"I'd like to talk to Forlini."

"Sure. Come around tomorrow, say five-thirty, I'll take you over there, you can have it from the horse's mouth. Just keep my name out of it. I'm not interested in committing suicide, not yet."

I assured her I was discreet. I thanked her for the drink and stood to go.

"I hope you can help her," she said. "I hope you live long enough to help her."

"I'm a big boy."

"I see. Wait a minute." She reached into the drawer where she had left the gun and pulled out a five-foot string of ride tickets.

"For your kid," she said. "Have fun."

6

GLORIA HAD A KNACK for Ski-Ball. By the time I returned, her girlfriend was gone and she had won two Kewpie dolls, a green-and-white stuffed donkey, a couple of pinwheels, and a set of ceramic see-no-evil monkeys.

"Watch, Daddy, a ten." She squinted one eye and rolled the ball down the lane. It flew up the slope, plopped directly into the center hole. She jumped into the air and clapped her hands in front of her mouth, shocked by her own skill.

"The little lady wins another prize from the second shelf," the man said.

"One of those." She pointed. He handed her a blue glass dish.

We collected her loot and headed for the car. We drove down to Durand Beach to look at the water.

I loved the lake. Ever since I had been a kid and had biked eight miles from the shadows of Kodak Park to get to the water, I had been drawn to the shore. The sight of that endless stretch of emptiness always eased my mind. I loved the fishy smell, the way the wind would raise angry tusks of whitecaps and tint the water with ominous blues.

It was comforting to know that in this one direction at least, the fussy, cluttered world came to an end. Here all the fever and fret stopped and turned to the cool void of a clean horizon. On a calm night like this you could barely tell where the water left off and the sky began.

During the war, my teenage years, I had worked as a lifeguard here. I had sat on a wooden throne wearing a pith hat and a whistle, lording it over dimpled children, ladies with pudgy knees, sunken-chested 4-Fs, and exciting, flashing-eyed girls my own age and a little older, whose watery squeals ran hot and cold up my spine.

Later I would come here nights myself, swim out into the cold inky water, keep on going until the landed lights glimmered only in the far distance, until I could see along the shore beyond Charlotte lighthouse and catch the feverish glow of Rochester to the south.

Even farther. I imagined swimming all the way to Canada. Johnny Weismuller had done it, but at a narrower part, not here where it was a good sixty miles. It was a feat beyond even Tarzan.

In my dreams I would swim on and on, until all was dark, just me and the stars. I would drag myself up onto that northern shore, into another world, another life.

Later still, the lake had been the scene of some of our most honeyed family moments. Eileen would put water wings on Gloria's arms and take her in. I would sit up on the beach and feel the hot sand under me and imagine that life was as good as it could get.

That night, the sun was scrawling an orange smear as it descended. Gloria had left her saddle shoes in the car. She drew designs with her big toe down where the lazy ripples tickled the beach. We fought to a draw in a stone-skipping contest. She found a rock with a vein of fool's gold and put it in her pocket to take home.

We sat down on a smooth driftwood log and she borrowed my matches to light up a porous stick of what she called smokewood. She puffed on it, pretending it was a cigarette.

Then she threw it away and, suddenly serious, said, "Will you tell Mom something for me?"

"Sure."

"We have to have a shelter." She picked at the remnants of polish on her fingernail.

"What do you mean?"

"For fallout. Everybody's supposed to have one, only Mom says we can just go down in the cellar and eat canned peaches. But you have to have a steel door and water and stuff so you can stay a week. And games. They said at school."

She had brought this up before. The papers were full of Khrushchev and kilotons.

"I think your mom knows best about that."

"She doesn't. What if there's World War III?"

"It probably won't ever happen."

"But what if it does? Wendy's family has a shelter. They have Sorry and Monopoly and flashlights and Kool-Aid."

"I'll talk to Mom about it."

"Make her do it, okay?"

"We'll see."

The price of liberty, they say, is eternal vigilance. It was pitiful, though, that we adults couldn't work it out to save a child from worries about atom bombs.

As we started for home, she announced that she was starving. She couldn't wait for supper, she would perish from hunger in five minutes. Only a hot dog could save her, a white hot.

Rochester was a mecca of hot dogs. The stands competed for the plumpest and juiciest. Different parts of town, you could smell the distinctive spicy aroma of roasting hots.

We were passing Eddie Gill's, which she declared was her favorite hot stand. I turned in. We ordered a porker and a red hot at the window, fries, onion rings, and milk shakes.

"The girl will bring them," a pimply guy said. I took a quick look around for Gill himself.

We found seats at a picnic table and waited. Gloria quizzed me about why we couldn't all go away on vacation that year. I told her I had to work and that she and her mother would have fun in the

Adirondacks and could watch real bears at the dump. I was talking too much and even she knew it.

I hadn't stopped here purely for Gloria's sake. The case was over but as I said, I judged. I didn't have a plan, just that uncomfortable feeling you get when you know something's not right with the world.

The sinking sun was casting copper light into the canopies of the locust trees on either side of the restaurant. We sat there trying to guess how many June bugs were flitting around up there and what they might be talking about.

"I betcha they're saying 'Why do we live in the ground, any-ways?' " she guessed. "And the smart ones are saying, 'Cause it's safe is why. Do you want to end up in the stomach of a redwing black-bird?' Right, Dad?"

"I think they're saying 'Vzzzzz!' " I buzzed the back of her neck and she squealed.

The girl I had been watching two nights before brought us our food. She was fair and had the high cheekbones and narrow eyes that make a girl look pretty when she's young, gaunt later. Her smile was all cookies and milk, not a trace of Pall Malls and gin slings. She wore her youthful body as if it were a dress and she was unsure of the fit. Narrow wrists, skinny legs, breasts pushing assertively against her blouse.

"Who's got the porker?"

Gloria raised her hand, then demanded, "Where's the mustard?"

"Please," I prompted.

"Mustard, please."

"Mustard coming up." She kept her lips tight to hide her slightly bucked teeth, and when she let them go, a smile blossomed that made my heart catch its breath. "And you've got shakes coming. That was one vanilla, one ketchup?"

"No! Chocolate."

"I thought you ordered a ketchup shake."

Gloria closed her eyes and tittered. "No, pickle."

They both laughed. The girl returned with the mustard and the two milk shakes.

"Those monkeys are funny," she told Gloria.

"I won them. Ski-Ball."

"I love that game. I used to play it." They talked Ski-Ball tactics and traded names in the casual way girls have. She was Sandy.

"You're lucky to have a dad who takes you to Gleeland." The waitress smiled at me.

"He's Icky."

"He is?"

"Ichabod Mudd. And I'm Captain Midnight. And sometimes"— she put her hand to her mouth—"he's Captain Midnight."

"Like on TV," the girl said. "High on a mountaintop, overlooking a great metropolis . . ."

"Right, and I'm Fury. I'm evil. Only really he's a policeman. Or, what is it, Dad?"

"Private detective."

"Now he's a pirate detective." She couldn't wait any longer. She filled her mouth with hot dog and bun until her smile drooled mustard.

The girl tucked a wisp of hair behind her ear and bit on her lower lip. I wanted to tell her to get out, quit her job, keep as far away as she could from Eddie Gill and anyone who looked like him. I might as well have told her not to grow up.

She watched Gloria eat for a few seconds, then slid her eyes to me and caught me looking. She smiled again. "You do things for people? I mean, they hire you?"

"That's the way it works."

"He let me ride in his police car," Gloria said. "Remember, Daddy?"

"How much would it cost?" Sandy said, and quickly turned her glance to the sky. She was just finding out about the world, that money can buy and sell just about anything, including people.

"That depends. What would you want me to do?"

"Just, if a person was in trouble."

I told her and she winced. "Oh."

"But I'll talk to somebody for nothing. Sometimes I can steer them in the right direction."

Her eyes were as clear as water. I thought of Eddie Gill's hands moving over her young shape. I said, "Here's my card. Call me anytime." Ike Van Savage, knight in tarnished armor.

She looked at the business card as if she'd never seen one.

Gloria said, "I can do a trick with a card. Wanna see?"

Sandy thanked me and tucked the card inside her shirt, next to her heart, before hurrying back to pick up more orders.

"I want to be a waitress."

"You do?"

"Yes, because then you could make your own milk shakes and have them all the time. It'd be fun."

"You'd get tired of them."

"Nnn nnn." She made a loud sucking noise with her straw to let me know she had already finished hers.

We drove back in warm darkness, splashing through the pools of glow cast by streetlights. Gathering up her prizes from the seat, Gloria handed me the glass dish. It was an ashtray, I saw now.

"I won you this," she said, "to put your cigarettes in."

"Thanks, sweetheart."

Her face was a votive candle in the dim light. "Let's go to Gleeland tomorrow. I'll win more."

"We can't go every day."

"Why?"

"I'll pick you up soon. I'll surprise you."

"Do you know what's Saturday?"

"Somebody's birthday?"

"Mine. The party. Don't forget."

"I'll be there. Promise."

"Are you going to talk to Mom?"

"About what?"

She rolled her eyes in frustration. "The shelter. And don't you two argue."

I nodded. I watched her disappear through the door of a house I didn't live in, back to a life I had no part of.

7

BASEBALL WAS INVENTED IN Rochester—most people don't know that. I don't mean the game itself, which had been around for a while. But it was first played in an organized league right here in the 1830s.

That night, the Wings had just gotten back from their road trip and were taking on Columbus in a twi-nighter. The management had hired me that spring to keep an eye on a wandering prospect, a boy from the country who had found that there were women in the big city who would reach right down into his pants pockets to relieve him of any wad of greenbacks he might be keeping there.

So they knew me and I was able to get into the clubhouse between games. I found Luke Easter relaxing with a bottle of Orange Crush and playing Spanish checkers with Gene Green, the right fielder. I asked Easter to sign the fielder's glove I had picked up earlier.

"She's president of the Luke Easter fan club," I told him. "She's writing a song for you. Next February she's going to get all the fifth-grade girls to send you Valentines."

"I'll look forward to that," he said in a deep drawl.

I hadn't met him before and was impressed by the size of him when he stood. His face had the relaxed folds of a well-worn mitt itself. His eyes, behind thick glasses, were as mild as milk.

For Gloria, he wrote, *your pal, Luke Easter.*

I explained about her playing Little League.

"Now she'll be able to look into her glove and get a little encouragement whenever she needs it," I said. "She loves you. She actually cried the other night when you went oh-for-four."

"Tell her not to," he said with a grin. "We all gonna go oh-for-four sooner or later."

He was a gentleman. A close look told me he was a hell of a lot older than most of his teammates. Later it would come out that he was forty-eight years old that season. Everybody was surprised and said he could have burned up the majors in his prime if colored players been allowed through the door then.

I asked him about the dust-up in Havana.

"Hell of a game. Cot got chucked in the eleventh after he argued the ump made a bum call."

"Was it?"

"If you had the stands full of Latinos with burp guns," Green put in, "don't you think you'd come down on the hometown side?"

"You'd already heard shooting?"

"Hell, yeah," Easter continued. "So Verdi took over. Then in the twelfth Verdi got hit in the head with a bullet. They was shooting in the air, but what goes up, you know. Knocked him cold."

"This's a tough league you're playing in."

Luke laughed. "If Cot'd been out there, he don't wear a helmet when he's coaching the way Verdi does. He said getting the thumb prob'ly saved his life."

"I heard you guys got off the field pretty quick."

"I was the first one down that dugout, man. No, I think Green here beat me, all the way from right field."

This set off a couple of hoots. The players all had something to say about it. The shadow of the excitement remained and they were a little in awe at the way history had intruded into their game.

"Mr. Castro came right down in the dugout," Luke explained. "Big as life and smoking a cigar this long. Apologized for the shootin'. He knows ball, asked Joe McClain how he throws that nickel curve."

"La cucaracha, la cucaracha." McClain, in uniform pants and undershirt, danced past us.

Nobody knew for sure if Castro was a red, but that morning in the paper I had been reading how he'd said they didn't take over the government down there to play games. He was talking about a classless society, and I wasn't the only one wondering what would happen if that idea ever caught on.

I had planned to take off right afterward. Instead, I sat down in an empty box seat as the second game began, thinking I'd watch a couple of pitches. I got involved in the action and stayed.

There was nothing like minor league baseball. Sure, you got a few flubs, mental errors, but you also got desire in its purest form. These were guys who could smell the turkey in the oven and their mouths were watering. They all knew what was at stake, that many were called, few chosen. They couldn't coast. They played their hearts out.

That gave Triple A ball a special excitement. We sometimes lost our best guys to the majors at a crucial point in the season, but we couldn't complain. We were with them, our hopes went up with them. We loved the young kids whose world was opening with their talent. We loved the guys who'd been around the block, maybe up to the bigs and back a few times, who knew they would finish their careers in the bush but who gave it everything anyway, just for the sake of the game.

We were all minor leaguers, when it came down to it. Few of us ever got the call. We spent our lives on the assembly line, walking a beat, running down matrimonial cases. But we held on to our dreams, no matter how tattered they became, and we played our hearts out, no matter how slim the hope of glory.

I ran into Larry Warnke, who used to cover the police beat for the *Democrat and Chronicle*. Now they had him on features. He sat down and told me about a story he was writing about Rochester's last Civil War veteran, because of the upcoming centennial.

"He was just a drummer boy," he said, "but he saw action at the Wilderness. I mean, he actually remembers what it was like. First time he heard the bullets whisper he shit his pants."

"Some things don't change."

"Maybe I'll do a story on you, Ike. Real-life private eye."

"It's not like on television, Larry. Nothing but lies and half-truths."

"That's why it's real life."

I stayed until the sixth. The Wings had squeezed three runs out of a couple of walks, an infield hit, and a looper over second. They managed to hold Columbus scoreless. I decided to call it a night and went home.

It wasn't unusual to see a car parked across the street from my apartment. It wasn't even so strange to see a man sitting in the front seat. Mild nights, you found a guy sitting out listening to his radio or reading the paper, maybe escaping a house full of kids or his wife's voice, maybe waiting for somebody to come home.

Spotting the Mercury, though, I drove a few driveways down from where I usually park, made a U-turn, and pulled in on the same side, half a dozen car lengths back. I grabbed a flashlight from the glove box and walked along the street side of the parked cars.

Leaves were clustered around the streetlights, casting a lacy pattern on the macadam. A cricket started and stopped a few times, too lazy to chirp. Approaching from behind was something they'd taught us in our police training. It's hard for a driver to twist around and get a clear angle on you, assuming he wants to shoot you.

In my years on the police, I never once drew my revolver. I rarely carried a gun now. Being unarmed, I figured, kept me on my toes.

I was just coming even with his rear bumper when a chrome spotlight swiveled and ignited, dazzling me. I put a forearm up to shield my face and heard a voice say, "Think I was laying for you?"

The light died and Tom Cahoon climbed out.

"New car?" I said.

"Sure, I get a new one every year. This is nice, with the Dynaflow, push-button."

"Come on up."

I lived on the second floor of what had once been a single-family home. The tenant downstairs was a professor of psychology at the U of R. He told me you could learn a lot about humans by making albino rats run through mazes. I said I wouldn't be surprised. His wife had left him, so he thought we had something in common. Maybe we did. Anyway, he was quiet.

Tom and I went up the stairs. I grabbed a couple of cold Toppers out of the icebox.

"Sharon's got a girl comes in to read to her," he said. "You know how she always liked to read. They're halfway through *Peyton Place*. Damned if I didn't get hooked on it myself."

"I hear it's pretty racy."

"You can say that again. You should get over to the house now and then. She talks about you."

"Tell her I was asking, will you?"

"Sure. I brought up Petrone at the station house. Casual, like. Picked up what's common knowledge. He's been consolidating things—gambling, unions. Some say narcotics. The old-line racket boys back him. They like order. He's got connections out of town. Joe gets respect and not just from his side of the fence. He's reasonable."

"Walt Duffy was trying to organize the sheet metal workers, he might not have thought it was too reasonable," I said. "Petrone capped him behind the ear and threw his body out there, Bushnell's Basin."

"Duffy was a red."

"Now he's a corpse and the case's been open eighteen months. Tell me something that's not common knowledge."

"Try this," Tom said. "They were laughing about it. Seems a patrolman stopped an Eighty-eight out on Portland Avenue last week, a darky driving and a marshmallow in the seat beside him. He thinks it's a little off, asks them both for ID. The blonde hands him a license, Victoria Weller. The name sticks in his mind, he looks it up. Victoria Weller is none other than Mrs. Joe. That was her maiden name."

"And who was he?"

"Melvin Slade. Or he goes by Night Train, decent middleweight, lost to Basilio years ago."

"Nice."

"Somehow I don't think anybody's going to volunteer to take the information to Joe himself. But if it's the true blue, Mrs. P. is playing with some fire there."

"You speak the truth, kimosabe," I said.

"Anything good on television?"

"You can try it."

"I'll do that. There's some stuff in the paper you might be interested in."

He handed me the newspaper he'd been holding under his arm. I took it into the kitchen and opened it. Two manila folders were tucked inside.

I opened the first and went right to the pictures. The one on top showed a naked woman submerged in a bathtub. Her long dark hair floated, obscuring her face. A plastic radio set rested on her legs, the cord snaking over the edge of the tub.

Then the water had been let out and the radio removed, and she lay wedged in the bottom of the white enamel trough, eyes staring at a fly on the ceiling, looking cold and uncomfortable. Her skin was white, the patch of pubic hair and two broad nipples dark.

A wide shot showed a lavish bathroom with framed mirrors, vases of flowers, marble tile, fancy plumbing fixtures.

Then she was lying on a stretcher. She was a woman with wide hips and muscular shoulders. Her relaxed face looked younger than thirty-nine, which was the age listed among her vital statistics. It was a handsome face with a lot of character. Eyes glassy. Mouth in a position of speech, as if she'd been interrupted while saying something. Forehead blank as marble. Even in death, she showed a vitality that made you think she was about to spring up, throw on a robe, and cook some spaghetti sauce.

I turned to the report. Whoever had written it up hadn't wasted a lot of time on legwork. Interviews with the maid who had found the body, a couple named Sebring whom Mrs. Petrone had gone out to eat with, dinner at the Kemper House. Mrs. Petrone ate lamb chops. She drank, no more than usual. Despondent or nervous? No.

The maid had cleaned the whole house before coming to the bathroom. Assumed Mrs. Petrone had gone out early. She had vacuumed, waxed the kitchen floor, done the laundry—all the time the lady was lying up there in a tub of water. She didn't like to think about it, she said.

Interview with Mr. Petrone. In Cleveland on business. Knew his wife sometimes listened to the radio while she bathed. He couldn't remember whether he'd warned her of the danger or not. Should have.

One of the neighbors, a Mr. Lucas, thought he remembered seeing a man leaving the house the night before. Limping, he said. Sometime after eleven. Lucas was hurrying home to catch *Jack Paar*. The man wasn't acting suspicious, just walking down the Petrones' front sidewalk.

No follow-up on that noted. Maybe, with Joe out of town, she'd had a late-night visitor. If so, it was something nobody wanted to know much about.

The medical examiner gave the cause as cardiac arrest induced by electrocution. Blood alcohol rendered her "moderately intoxicated." The water found in the lungs was assumed to have entered after death. One finger had been fractured sometime in the past and, unattended, had healed improperly. An appendectomy scar. Early stages of liver cirrhosis. A slightly enlarged heart. The verdict: death by misadventure.

Clipped to a page of the report was a snapshot of Mrs. Petrone in life. Bathing suit, Lake Ontario in the background. She was smiling, but her eyes were curious, as if she were trying to peer into the future.

And what if she could have? What would she have seen? What would any of us see? Our own deaths? Time ended by an H-bomb? Misadventure.

"Well, Mr. Dillon, I guess I kin use a shotgun as good as the next fella, if I have to." Chester's twang drifted in from the living room.

I turned to the file on the second Mrs. Petrone. Born Avis Kerr. Twenty-nine. Married eight months before her car had gone off Maplewood Drive and plunged into the Genesee Gorge.

The car was a two-tone Lincoln that had been battered by a giant fist. The flash-lit photo showed it hanging from the back of a wrecker. The roof was smashed right down into the passenger compartment. One wheel had been torn off. The front end was seriously deformed.

A broken neck is a nasty-looking injury. In the photo of the body laid out on a tarpaulin, the head didn't line up with the torso. One leg was broken and jutted off toward China. The face was a mess.

The accident had happened the summer before. Driving too fast for conditions, missed a curve, and plunged down the ravine. The report noted that this Mrs. Petrone was an inexperienced driver, having learned only a few months before.

The dead woman's husband was out of town at the time of the accident. He had to be called back by ship-to-shore from his fishing trip off the Florida Keys. Mrs. Petrone's twin brother identified the body. I didn't envy him.

No alcohol or barbiturates in her blood. Under the care of a psychiatrist, a Dr. Bigalow, who had prescribed Miltown. She had tried suicide once while attending the College of St. Rose. The victim's friend, a Miss Biltmore, had seen her a short while before the tragedy. She said Avis had not been despondent, though she had seemed "nervous" in the days before the accident.

The one witness, Mrs. Rita Stancil, had not actually seen the crash but had been walking near the scene on Maplewood Drive. She heard a screech, a loud noise, and when she turned around she thought she saw the taillights of another car disappearing around the corner. She wasn't sure.

For some reason, the file contained a wedding photo of Joe and

Avis. His face bore the expression you used to see on crooners in the forties, all hair oil and self-confidence, the tense smile ready to shape a song, the unfocused eyes taking in the audience without making contact. He looked no more like a gangster than I did.

She was pretty but tentative, a cute face drawn on a toy balloon. You could imagine a strong breeze obliterating the little pug nose, thin lips, and delicate ears, leaving behind a mild oval blank. You could hear the tentative voice, see the easy blush. She might have been quite pretty if she had smiled, but she stared at the camera as if it were an accusing eye.

Hollow laughter drifted in from the living room. I went to the kitchen, opened two more beers, and took one in to Tom. He had switched over to *What's My Line?*

"This guy's a casket designer," he said. "Satin pillows and polished mahogany. They'll never guess it."

"What's going on with the Arm these days?"

He reached over to flick off the set. "You gonna ask me questions, Ike? They go too far, we step in."

"What's too far?"

"Too far is what the public says is too far. Whores, gambling—people want to get laid, they want to cover a bet. If they didn't, gangsters wouldn't exist."

"You're really doing a public service."

"Don't get on your high horse. I did you a favor."

"I'm asking you to talk straight."

"Okay, what's too far also depends on how many politicians you got in your pocket. How many judges. It's the ground we walk on. Anybody wants to do a job as a cop, he lives with that. You wanted to be independent, more power to you."

"Funny thing, Tom. We're always drawing lines in the sand. Then the waves come in and we have to draw them all over again."

"Makes for a complicated world."

"Anyway, how many judges do you have to know to get away with murder?"

"Who's dead?"

"I'm taking the lady at face value." I dropped the newspaper, the files back inside, onto the arm of his chair. "These things smell of last week's fish."

"Give me a shred of evidence on either one. Your client's spooked. My advice, tell her playing house with a Negro palooka ain't any good for her health, and that's got nothing to do with any syndicate."

"Her stepping out is certainly something to think about—if it's true."

"People start talking, sometimes it doesn't matter if it's true or not. You've covered the waterfront on this. Tell her what you found out, charge her enough to make her feel good, and say bye-bye."

"I might, Tom. Or I might walk downtown, kick Joe Petrone in the nuts, see what happens. Something I can do, being independent."

"Sure you can. See you around—I hope."

FRIDAY

1

GEORGE EASTMAN LIVED HIS whole life a bachelor. His mother's maiden name was Kilbourn. Maybe that's why he thought the letter "k" had a nice sound. Kodak.

When his fifty-room mansion was finished, he stocked it with old masters and threw a gala. The eighth course of the feast was pumpkin pie and cheese, the ninth was chestnut and candied-fruit pudding. He installed a concert organ and kept an organist on hand to fill the lonely house with cantatas. He wandered the halls, figuring ways to dole out his millions. When he'd completed that chore, he blew his brains out.

They turned the house into a museum. It was the biggest joint on East Avenue, but the rest of the places weren't shabby. The bishop had a nice spread there. Porticos still stood ready so that the residents could climb into carriages without getting their feet wet. Only now it was cars, stables full of Cadillacs. Elegant copper beeches graced the front yards. Any one of the houses could have doubled as a tony funeral parlor.

Of course, with the Eisenhower recession and a stiff income tax even millionaires were cutting corners. Weeds sprouted in lawns here and there and the fire escapes hanging off a few of the manor houses told me they'd been turned into apartments.

The section where the Gerard Kerrs lived was still pure swank. Their brown sandstone chateau had been designed with peasant revolts in mind—all parapets, bastions, and towers to pour boiling oil from.

They were one of the families that had tamed the wilderness in Rochester. The old man was a prominent architect and builder, recently retired. His wife was an organizer of charity cotillions and of societies to plant tulips in parks and to teach pregnant teenagers the art of bootie knitting. It was said that the family had once owned the largest motor yacht on Lake Ontario.

Legwork is what the detective business is about. I could have telephoned the Kerrs and been sloughed off a dozen times. Instead, I was out camping on their doorstep bright and early. Once they opened the door, I was able to get a foot inside in the form of a suggestion that I knew things. Detectives have a lot in common with salesmen.

Inside, the stale air smelled of dust and rubbing alcohol. Plush had gone out of fashion for home decorating—we were in the Danish modern era—but here the drapes were thick maroon velvet. They cut both light and sound. A three-tailed pasha's dream was woven into the oriental carpets.

A cadaverous lackey let me in, looked me over, and told me he would see if madam was available. I gave him the impression I was with the police and said I wanted to talk with her about her late daughter.

Mrs. Kerr pointed her bladelike patrician nose at me and firmed her sharp jaw. Her mouth was drawn in, as if she had a habit of sucking her teeth. Her eyes sparkled with life, like two jewels set in the face of a mummy. She was not old. When she was eighty they would say she was well preserved. Now she was a dry woman of sixty, used to living in a world populated by inferiors.

"Appointments are usually made over the telephone," she informed me. "We've gone over this thoroughly with your superiors. I don't see why—"

"Your man was confused, Mrs. Kerr. I'm not with the police. I'm an investigator. I've been paid to look into your daughter's death."

"And you think you have found a way to make it even more unendurable, is that it?"

"I can imagine that it's very painful."

"No, you cannot imagine. Painful does not describe what I feel. Do you think painful describes it?"

"I'm sure it doesn't."

Feelings did not pass over her face, they were stamped there. Yet I could see that my interest interested her.

"You want to investigate?" She waved her hand at me as if shooing a fly. "Avis was a wonderful girl, intelligent and strong-minded. Every day, every minute, every second, I live with the thought that Avis was robbed of her life by some foolish chance. No, not every second. Minutes go by—yes, hours—when I *don't* think of her, when I suddenly realize that I've forgotten her. For that brief time, she isn't even a memory. And that hurts even worse."

Her bony hand reached toward a portrait. It rested on a credenza between two silver monstrosities that begged to be melted down. It showed a boy and a girl, their smiles as innocent as ice cream.

"But you were never completely satisfied that it was an accident," I said.

"Do you imagine you can get us to hire you to find out?"

"Maybe." People like the Kerrs suspect you unless they can see how you're working the money angle. "But I already have a client, a person who's given me information and is interested in getting to the bottom of the matter."

"What information?"

"Threats," I said, improvising. "Other incidents."

Her lower lip quivered for an instant. What she said surprised me: "She came to me—it was a few months after the wedding. What do I have to put up with? she asked me. The same thing any woman puts up with, I told her. Being ignored. Being demeaned. Being brutalized even. Oh, I know she was looking for a different answer, but you can't hold a child's hand after they've left the nest."

"Nest?" The voice came from behind me, a baritone played at the wrong speed.

"Yes, dear," she said.

The old man in the wheelchair had a translucent complexion and stripped blue eyes. He looked at me and blinked twice as the nurse pushed him silently forward.

"This is my husband, Gerard Kerr."

"You riding your hobby horse?" he asked me.

"No, I came in a car."

"You're a long way from home."

"I am?"

"We all are. Like no tomorrow."

I nodded. A blue vein zigzagged down his temple.

"Mr. Van Savage is an investigator, Gerard."

He blinked at me again. For an instant his eyes grew icy. Then his wife made a sign and the nurse wheeled him on toward the entrance of a sun-drenched conservatory.

"My husband had a stroke soon after Avis's death."

I made a sympathetic noise.

"You don't know what that man was like," she said.

"Do you think Joe Petrone killed your daughter?" I meant the question to hit her straight on and it did. Our eyes connected for an instant.

She was about to answer when a voice from the entryway called, "Hello, Mother. I didn't know you had a visitor."

Two young people entered and Mrs. Kerr made the introductions. He was the son, Duncan. His dark hair had been parted with precision, leaving a white line along his scalp as sharp as the creases in his powder-blue suit. I told him I recognized him from the youthful photo.

The woman in the yellow sundress was his fiancée, Cecilia Biltmore. She tensed, as if the sound of her name made her want to laugh. Her short blond hair went well with her petite figure, pointed chin, and flawless cheekbones. Her smile dazzled, but she quickly bit it off when it had served its purpose. She had a feathery presence, pretty but indistinct.

"Avis and I were twins," the young man said. "I was older. Ten minutes, wasn't it, Mother?" His words had the hollow ring of a worn-out witticism.

"Mr. Van Savage thinks Avis was murdered," Mrs. Kerr stated flatly.

"Murdered?" He pronounced the word as if he had never heard it before. He looked at the others and said, "I'm afraid I don't understand. Who in the world . . . ?"

"Joe," his mother said.

"You have evidence?" he asked me.

"Serious questions have been raised. I was hoping that you could help me find out more."

He wiped his hand across his forehead and licked his lips. "I don't know. Avis, her death is still—it's hard to think about. It's torture."

"How did she come to be married to a gangster in the first place?"

People like to talk. You ask a question, they feel compelled to answer—unless they have something to hide. He gave me a queer look, but he immediately said, "They met while she was working on a charity dinner, wasn't it, Ceecee? Avis and Ceecee were friends."

"Best friends. Avis was on the organizing committee. The March of Dimes puts on a ball every spring. Mr. Petrone was a contributor. He took an interest. He was very charming, very Old World. Avis found men our age juvenile. Mr. Petrone was very attentive, very mature, very proper. She liked that."

"She had never been in love," Duncan said. "She didn't think of it as a passing fancy. She was, as they say, head over heels."

"Did she know about Petrone?"

"Know?"

"How he made his money."

"Joe was a businessman," Ceecee answered. "He sent her flowers every day. Sometimes a single rose, always something. He was very thoughtful. He gave her a necklace set with her birthstone. It really was romantic, what girls dream of."

"Dream?" Duncan sneered. "Nightmare, more like it."

"She was not a good driver," Ceecee offered.

"Did Avis ever talk about the first Mrs. Petrone?"

"Not to me," Ceecee said.

Duncan shook his head, then paced back and forth across the large room. A couple of times he puffed his cheeks and let his lips flutter as he struggled for composure.

In the silence his mother said, "I really cannot bear any more of this, Mr. Van Savage. Duncan, could you?"

"Of course, Mother. I'll handle it."

"Whatever my son decides, Mr. Van Savage. I'm sure you understand how difficult this is, how little it matters, in the end, if . . ."

"I appreciate your assistance."

"Let me help you, Mother Kerr," Ceecee said. She and the older lady nodded their farewells and left the room. Duncan motioned me to follow him into a stuffy den lined with bookcases. A walnut desk was piled with papers and old books.

"I'm sorry to see Mother so distraught." His words were a mild scolding. "Avis's death ruined my father."

He sat in the chair behind the desk and I settled into a leather easy chair.

"Before his stroke," he told me, gesturing at the papers, "Father was researching our family tree. It seems my great-great-grandfather came here in the 1830s from Lowell, Massachusetts, and went into the seed business. The year he arrived, they killed the last wolf in the county. Stuffed it."

"Fascinating."

He emitted a brittle laugh. "I know. There's nothing more tedious than another person's family history. I brought it up because Father didn't stop there. He tracked down records that indicated our people had originally hailed from Sunderland, in the north of England. Had some part in the Jacobite rebellion, whatever the hell that was. He decided that our ancestral lands were located just beyond Hadrian's Wall, which cut across England up in that area. We were the Brits the Romans were afraid to conquer. See?"

"You're going back a ways now."

"I mean, you see my point—Joe Petrone did conquer us. That was the way my father saw it."

"He didn't like Italians?"

"The idea of his daughter sleeping with a dago, as he put it—he was livid."

"How did you feel?"

"I recognize that people are different. We've learned to restrain our impulses. They choose not to. It's really very simple. On an every-day level, it means we waltz at the country club and they do the hokey pokey in their church basements. Fine. But on another level, that lack of restraint turns septic. They are capable of real savagery."

"They?"

"A certain element. You think I'm exaggerating. Joe Petrone is an animal, Mr. Van Savage. I know. He lives in darkness. I'm not sure if you have any idea how corrupt this city is, this country. Re-member Kefauver?"

"Sure. He turned up gangsters under every rock."

"The law of animals is the only law a man like Petrone under-stands. Take whatever you can lay your grubby hands on. Feed on those who are not as strong as you are or not as lucky. Humiliate those around you with your brutish behavior. He brought women into his house."

His face had turned red and a vein jumped out at his temple. I thought he was about to have a stroke himself.

"Women?"

He pounded his fist on the desk.

"Into the house he shared with my sister," he growled. "He sug-gested to her . . ." He scraped the inside of his mouth with his tongue, as if tasting something noxious. "Not suggested, forced her to participate, to engage in acts. Do I need to elaborate?"

Apparently he did. He went into quite vivid detail, an account that reminded me of barracks stories I had listened to endlessly in the army.

"Avis was not worldly," he concluded. "She was childlike in many ways. She had a child's trust, a child's susceptibility to attention. She was easily dazzled by someone who appeared urbane and knowing. But make no mistake about it, he turned her life into a living hell."

"That's the way she felt?"

"Avis was stubborn. The more I tried to convince her to get out of his clutches, the more she dug in her heels. A coolness developed between Avis and me that I very much regret."

"How much credence do you give to the idea that Petrone was responsible for your sister's death?"

He stared at me intently. "Anything's possible. I simply don't know. But if he were involved, I certainly would want to know. I would want him brought to justice."

"To be frank," I said, "I can't hold out much hope of that. He would have gone at it indirectly. As you know, he has friends and influence. He can pull strings and he can intimidate. Pinning a cold case on him is a big order."

"But you intend to try?"

"I have a client who is interested in the matter. I plan to do what I can."

"My family obviously has an interest. I would like to engage you to provide us with whatever evidence you uncover. It's something I've thought about ever since Avis died. I'm glad you came by. I assume a retainer would be appropriate?"

The banknotes he was extracting from his billfold looked very fresh and crisp.

"You understand I already have a client in this matter," I said.

"Of course. All I ask is that you keep us informed, report anything you find out about Avis's death. I know that it may not be enough for the authorities to act, but if it were sufficient to give us some insight into what happened, it would be a boon. You can't know what a burden it is to live with the kind of doubts that we've had to endure."

"I know it must be hard."

"I trust you, Mr. Van Savage. I sincerely hope, for my mother's sake, that you can help us."

"I'll do my best."

A telephone rang in another part of the house. A woman wearing a black dress and a fancy white collar entered the room and said, "Mr. Kerr, I'm sorry."

"I'll be right there, Nan." He turned to me. "I sincerely appreciate your coming by."

Ceecee was waiting in the hallway.

"I'll see him out, darling," she told Kerr.

He shook my hand.

She walked me into the entryway. Sunlight was streaming through the ornate glass over the door. When I turned to say goodbye she put a hand on my chest and went up on her tiptoes as if to kiss me.

"I have something to tell you," she said. "Can you come see me this afternoon?"

I nodded. She whispered the address and held her face close to mine for a second, staring intently. Then, glancing over her shoulder, she stepped back. I moved out into the summer air and the door shut on her worried face.

2

"WHAT'D YOU THINK OF the Patterson fight, Lewie?" I asked.

Lewie Bimberg had wrapped himself around the metal folding chair like a vine, one foot hooking the back leg, the other around the front, his upper body twisted sideways.

"I think Floyd peeked when he should have booed."

Once, when one of his fighters had scored a TKO that moved him into the top ten, they said Lewie had actually broken into a grin. Personally, I had never seen him smile. His lipless mouth was an indictment of the modern world. But his eyes, sharp as flint, sparkled with wit.

"Still, they say Johansson has a hell of a right."

"They say you can build a cathedral out of Popsicle sticks, too. A guy like that as champ, it shows you something's screwy with this country."

He turned his head and made a little spitting sound through his teeth. The Swede heavyweight kept his girlfriend in camp with him—as far as Bimberg was concerned he might as well have gone on a training diet of Necco Wafers and lemon chiffon pie. You didn't waste your juices in the weeks before a big one, and that Birgit was most definitely a juice waster.

"Put him against a real heavyweight. One punch doesn't make you a fighter. Who the hell is Patterson? Moore was forty-two when Floyd beat him. An old man."

"Johansson's supposedly bucking the system, Frankie Carbo and them."

"More power to'm. You asked me can he fight. Against a guy like Louis, that Swede'd been one dead turnip."

Above us, two welterweights were going at it with twenty-ounce gloves. Lewie divided his time between watching them spar and packing burly into his pipe.

I said, "There's a middleweight around town, Night Train Slade."

"Him? Sure. He's fighting the main at the Armory tonight, against a comer name of Kid Blik. Hey!" He waved for the two boxers to cease hostilities. "Terry, when he does that thing with the shoulder, you gotta go underneath. You fall for it twenty times, what the hell? Throw to the body. You're staying upstairs too damn much."

"Slade a prospect?"

"Was. Tough kid. Came up here, he was a farmhand, used to pick fruit in the orchards out along the lake. Somebody saw him spar in a migrant camp, hooked him up with a colored trainer. He had a punch, it didn't just hurt a guy, took a piece out of his soul. Didn't get the right training, though. Shame. Could have been something."

"He go for the ladies?"

"That was part of his problem, so they say."

"White meat?"

Lewie probed his cheek with his tongue. "Search me."

"I hear things."

He yelled into the ring, "Don't punch at his belly! Punch through him. Make him feel it." To me he said, "Hear?"

"Him and Joe Petrone's goods."

"I don't know nothing about nothing. Believe me, Ike, it's the only way to stay alive in this crazy world. Hear no evil, do no evil."

"A lot of people seem to be saying that these days."

"Slade, from what I understand—I've met him a couple of times—he don't care. That, I love to see that in a fighter. It makes a guy dangerous. He'll do anything. It also makes him hard to handle."

"Slade still picking cherries?"

He shook his head. "He drives truck, a place called Neville Transport. I also understand he does odd jobs for guys like Leo Forlini."

"What kinds of jobs?"

"Looks after some lotteries, crap games out in the colored wards. Goes around to deadbeats and puts on a mean face."

"Any idea where I might find him?"

He shrugged. "His handler's a colored guy, Willie Christmas, runs a dive down to Joseph Avenue. You might drop around to the Armory tonight during the prelims. I can't get you a seat. It's a popular card and Marciano's gonna be there."

"No kidding. The champ's in town?"

"To pick up some Boy's Club award."

"There was a fighter for you," I said. "You ever see him in the ring?"

He shook his head.

"I went all the way to New York to watch the second Charles fight," I said. "Remember? Charles's elbow caught Rocky in the nose and split the damn thing right in half. He was going to lose the championship that round unless he could knock out Charles. He went out and destroyed a good fighter the way you chop down a tree."

"Sure, I remember. Now he's retired. If he's smart, he'll stay that way."

"This Slade have a chance?"

"I wouldn't bet my paycheck on him. Blik's got backing."

"What kind of backing?"

"What kind is there? Money. I like to think the fights in this town are honest, pretty honest. But money's the sickness of this sport. The sickness of America, maybe."

"Tank job?"

He shrugged. "What do I know? Blik's a good fighter, too. Should be interesting. Go down there, if you can get in. See how honest the world is."

5

PENNY WAS STANDING ON her head when I arrived at the office. Yoga, she had told me, was a scientific technique developed in ancient India for achieving peace and serenity. When I'd suggested that a dry martini might accomplish the same thing with less fuss, she'd laughed as if I were joking.

"I didn't know you wore blue panties," I said.

She scissored her legs back and forth gleefully—they were tan enough that she didn't need stockings.

"Earl was here," she told me, still topsy-turvy. "He'll be back."

"I'm glad you're not overworked."

"It's my break. Instead of coffee. You had a client." She dropped her legs, smoothed her skirt, and stood. "A Miss Mink. Said she knew you or had met you."

"Mink? What did she want?"

"Dunno. I tried to draw her out—she was a scared little thing. She said she'd met you, had to talk to you. She had money, quite a wad, surprising for a kid like that. She said she knew you'd want money. Sandy Mink."

"Okay, now I connect it. Leave a number?"

"She'll stop back later, she said. I told her to call first, make sure you were here. Who is she?"

"The third party in the Gill case. I met her out at the restaurant last night."

"Her? She's a child."

"That's the world we live in."

"Jeez, that burns me, a greasy old man pawing a girl like that."

"We're in the business of turning over rocks, sweetheart. Bound to run into a few worms and beetles."

"If I'da known, I would have told her a well-timed kick in the family jewels can work wonders."

"Talking from experience?"

"You betcha."

"Call up Moss Dunlop."

"The ward heeler?"

"Yeah. See if you can get me tickets to the fights at the Armory tonight. He's supposed to have an in. Then check with your girlfriend who writes the society page. I'm interested in if she's got anything on a Cecilia Biltmore. Ceecee."

The heat was revving up again. I pulled my office blinds to keep the sun out, but confinement made it feel even hotter. I flicked a switch. The fan began to spin its blades frantically, tinting the air with machine oil.

Earl arrived and sank down onto my red leather davenport.

"Euchre," he said.

I waited.

"You wanted hobbies, I'm reporting."

"Petrone?"

"Heavy-duty euchre, ten bucks a point, games go on for hours. Joe's a master of the lone hand."

"That's helpful, Earl."

"It was hard to get that much. Nobody wants to talk about the man."

"What else?"

"Every hand book in town, he gets his cut. And that's a lot of birdseed."

One thing you could say about Rochester, the people loved to gamble. Maybe it was true everywhere.

"What else?"

"The old guard is behind him. Leo Forlini, Danny Paretta. The Ruggieros up in Buffalo. His official dodge is labor negotiator. He works sweetheart deals on the one hand, diddles the pension fund on the other."

"That's it?"

"Kidding? Jukeboxes, cigarettes, soft drinks—he's got a Nehi franchise he runs out on Dewey. Produce, meat, ice, anything that spoils he's got his finger in the pie. All he's got to do, hold up delivery, they come around to his way of thinking fast. He carries weight with the Teamsters, it gives him the edge."

"He's the king of kings."

"Around here, yeah. Lots of stories floating, maybe he starts them himself. He cut off a guy's head, he boiled some alkie cooker in his own vat. It's convenient if people believe it. Makes them think." .

"What about his wives?"

"He's living the dream. Starts out, talka like this. But he's the type of guy, changes his name and takes speech lessons at night school. His first wife cooks lasagna real good. But whaddaya know? She dies. He makes the jump into society. That one drives off a cliff. Next, he goes for glamour. Third time lucky, maybe. Anyway, when he takes the stage at the City Club now, he knows his woman's going to outshine them all."

"You know anything about the Kerrs?"

"Old money. The daughter marries a gorilla like Petrone, you explain it."

"Maybe it was love."

We both laughed. I told him to keep his ear to the ground and he left. A few minutes later, Penny poked her head in and said, "Mr. Doyle." She scowled and showed me her canine teeth to let me know the client was in a fighting mood.

"Mr. Doyle, warm enough for you?"

"Fucking shit." He wore a dark suit with a ketchup stain on the lapel. He was sweating into his yellowed collar.

"Hey." I nodded at Penny, who had shown him in. She made an "o" with her mouth and stuck her fingers in her ears.

"Sorry, miss." When she closed the door, he spit out some more ungentle terms.

"Another fire?" I asked.

"A garage I got over on Reliance. Six stalls, a moneymaker. Lit it up, burned it down. Ruined the guy's Olds, he says he's suing me. My insurance man is having fucking kittens."

"You're going to burst a blood vessel yourself if you don't calm down."

"What have you got for me, that I'm paying you so much for?"

"The police—" I started.

"Cops don't give a tinker's damn."

"Only one of the fires was definitely arson in their book. They don't see any pattern."

"They wouldn't see a pattern on the wallpaper there, would they? Somebody's after me."

"The fires were suspicious, yes. Just the number of them." I held up a hand to keep him from interrupting. "But you've got a lot of violations in those buildings, electrical, whatever. I've talked to some of the residents—"

"Bah! They wreck the places themselves." Doyle dismissed an entire race with a wave of his meaty paw. "You know what I told you, who's doing this. Have you looked into that yet?"

"Those boys work behind the scenes."

"What the hell is your job? You go behind the scenes, find out."

"A lot of property has turned over in that area you're in, but there's always a lot of turnover in the slums."

"Fucking residential properties, what you calling a slum?"

"What we want to work on is who's buying into that neighborhood. I've looked at the deed registers. They've got shell companies."

"Shells?"

"Fronts. It makes it almost impossible to trace the real owners. If you could point me toward the guy who offered to buy you out, it would help."

"That fat fuck comes around again, I'll grind him into powder."

"Let's talk turkey here. You think these guys have something against you, but it's just business to them. They set a few fires. Unless you've got a comeback, you cave or you're ruined."

"Cave? I'll never cave. I'll be lying under six feet of sod before I cave. I'll burn those buildings down myself. I swear, I'll light 'em up before I'll ever sell to those dagos."

I told him I was still waiting to hear from my underworld contacts. He wanted to know how much I'd run up in the way of expenses in the two days I'd been on his case. We went over the accounts until he was satisfied. He told me again to point him in the right direction and walked out the door.

"Dunlop is sending over a couple of tickets," Penny told me. "He says they're worth their weight. Everybody wants to see Marciano. I called Janet but she's out covering a flower show at Seneca Park."

"Okay. Hold the fort till I get back."

4

I FOUND MYSELF HURRYING to my car in spite of the heat. I smiled at that. I knew myself too well. Miss Ceecee Biltmore had pushed my buttons in just the right way, a touch of mystery, a promise of a lead on a tough case, and that little something extra that shoots right into the bloodstream. Oh, I was eager, all right. I was chomping at the bit.

You have to do your job, Ike, was the way I explained my enthusiasm. The silly, serious voice in my head was saying: You have to follow every lead. This could be important.

But my rational mind wasn't biting. It was too familiar with my hairy ape, a creature with his own dirty ideas. That personage was afflicted by mixed feelings when it came to the rich, a repulsion and a fascination. Does money add to a woman's allure? It always has.

Sure, money. A guy like Duncan Kerr, somebody who had had it easy all his life, he couldn't appreciate what money did for a woman. He was soft at the core. And she knew it. And I knew she knew it. And . . .

Maybe the heat was driving me a little nutty. By midday the

thermometer was tickling ninety. It was a gritty heat, the type that sandpapers you.

I drove out Browncroft Boulevard, down through Ellison Park, and into the wide-open spaces of Penfield. Off of Creek Road a neatly spaced lane of elms led to a big Georgian mansion. It was a gentleman's idea of a farm. White fences and green grass. Horse stables with elaborate weather vanes. Intricate flower gardens.

She knew I was coming but she didn't greet me at the door. Instead, a colored butler in a hot wool suit smiled me inside. He said Miss Cecilia was riding and had left instructions. He offered me a cold drink and led me to the verandah.

Verandah, that's what he called it—a long porch with painted wrought-iron furniture. Off to the side a nymph was spilling water into a goldfish pond from what looked like a martini glass.

There was a swimming pool, of course, very blue and surrounded by a wide expanse of flagstones. I imagined her going for an early morning dip in her birthday suit, blond between the legs, the servants partially averting their eyes.

I told the butler an iced tea would do me fine. He returned with sweating pitcher, several glasses, one goblet of lemon wedges, one of mint sprigs.

I carried my glass over to the fence and peered across the rolling meadow to where Ceecee was riding a big brown-gold palomino.

I have always found that a woman on a horse makes an interesting sight—I don't know why. I could have watched her bobbing across the green for an hour without being bored.

Halfway up a knoll, she noticed me. She gave a quick salute, urged the horse to a canter, and took the rises and dips smoothly. She rode Western, not English, gripping with her thighs.

Then she was at the fence and I was feeding the steed some of the sugar cubes that had come with my tea. The animal liked that and so did she.

"Oh, Tarawa, he's spoiling you awfully. Thank you for coming, Mr. Van Savage."

I demurred at the formality and we got down to a first-name

basis. Another Negro, a man of about my age, took charge of the horse. Ceecee swung down and patted the sweaty beast on his haunch and told him to be good. She gave some unnecessary instructions to the groom.

She opened the gate and joined me. She wore tight blue jeans, tooled cowboy boots, an elaborately embroidered shirt, and a ten-gallon hat of white straw. She licked the sweat that beaded her upper lip and smiled at me when I caught her doing it. Her face was moist and glowing.

We sat in the shade. On cue, the hired man brought out a plate of tuna salad sandwiches with the crust cut off, a bowl of tiny sweet gherkins, and more tea.

She didn't want to talk about Avis at first. She wanted to talk about Duncan.

She loved him, of course. But Duncan was cold. Duncan was distant. Did I think he might still be getting over the loss of his sister? I said that was possible. She thought that twins did have a special bond. Or was it his family? His mother was a domineering woman. His father, before the stroke, had been a regular Caligula.

"I think that Duncan is having a hard time establishing his manhood," she said.

"He's young yet."

"Not that young. He'll be thirty in two years. So will I. God, I never thought I would be this old."

"Ol' man river."

"What?"

"Just keeps rollin'."

She tittered. "Of course. I think it was one of the things that pushed Avis to marry. She was afraid of ending an old maid. She thought she could be happy with Joe and she was happy, at first."

"So you said. What changed?"

"God, I want to be happy myself. But I'm so inexperienced. My folks died when I was twelve. Do you remember that plane crash out at the airport, the Chicago flight?"

I shook my head.

"They were on it. My aunt moved in here afterward. She thought she had to be very strict. I guess she did. But it didn't leave me with much of a view of the world. What do you think of Duncan?"

"I just met him."

"But you're a detective. You should know."

"He seemed sincere. Reserved. A little immature, maybe."

"You're so right. He is immature." She showed me her imitation of the Bardot pout. "Once I agreed to marry him, he started taking me for granted. He never takes any initiative. Always busy, running around making deals. Sometimes I think he was only interested in my money."

"Doesn't he have money?"

"Of course. But I have a lot more." There was something of the six-year-old in her voice.

She talked on about her life. She had grown to loathe her aunt, but now that the poor dear was gone, she missed her awfully. This existence was a golden cage. She could dream, but she couldn't find the key to unlock the bars.

"I really don't know anything about men," she said. "I've been so sheltered."

On and on, none of it very original. Whenever I probed about Avis, she managed to steer the conversation back to her favorite topic, Ceecee. That didn't surprise me. I played along.

We ended up talking about horses. She knew a lot about Arabian stock, and what the difference was between a pastern and a fetlock. All the time, she was making gestures that seemed more calculated than nervous: playing with her blond hair, stroking her throat, squeezing her fingers into the tight pockets of her jeans.

"I received a letter," she said at last. "From Avis. I haven't shown it to anyone."

"Received it when?"

"The day after her accident. She mailed it that very day."

"What's it say?"

"I'll let you read it. That's why I wanted you to come. I trust you. You inspire trust, did you know that? At least in me." She leaned toward me. The first two buttons of her shirt were unfastened and I could see the tops of her breasts. Her teeth were very white against her tan.

"I'm glad. Did she talk to you about Joe?"

"He was Prince Charming. I used to envy her. He knew how to treat a woman, she said. In every way. Do you understand what I mean?"

"No, what do you mean?"

She bit her lip coyly. "You know. I envied her. We were close, close friends, but I must say, Avis was a bit . . . not slow, naive. Anyway, she aged very quickly. It was frightening. She told me she was seeing a doctor. She was worried about whether she could have children. I'd like to have children myself. But only with the right man."

"You're engaged, aren't you?"

She smiled a conspiratorial little smile. "Yes. But. Have you ever heard of free love?"

"Isn't that the way they do it in Russia?"

She compressed her lips for a second, then burst out laughing and ended by wagging her finger at me.

"How about looking at that letter?" I said.

"Yes. Yes, it's in my room."

It was hard to imagine her living in this manor house by herself. It struck me as a little girl's fantasy rather than a real home. A full suit of armor stood near the front entrance, looking as if it got dusted on a regular schedule. You could have walked into the fireplace without bumping your head. In the corner, a stuffed tiger was burning brightly in a ray of sun.

We climbed a wide oak staircase to the second floor and walked down a plushly carpeted corridor. Each wispy landscape painting along the wall was illuminated by a shaded light attached to the frame.

The room she took me to was part bedroom, part sitting room.

Tall windows let in a gush of sunlight. The severe family portraits contrasted with the light-blue chintz of the furniture.

"You have to promise that this will be our secret," she said.

"I wouldn't violate your confidence."

"Good. I know you wouldn't."

She pulled a small key from her pocket and unlocked the jewelry box on the dresser. She dug among the glitter of pearls and precious stones and came up with an envelope.

The letter inside was on a creamy notepaper, undated, the writing in a nun's hand.

It read: "Duchess— Don't know what's happening to me. Each day seems like a century. From bad to worse. I try. No good. I will soon go down the rabbit hole. If I do, I want you to know I tried. Always remember me. Don't show this to anyone, no matter what happens. —Red Queen"

"Anyone" was underlined three times.

"Did the police see this?"

"No. They asked me a few questions, but I didn't mention it. I didn't know what to do. I knew what it meant, of course. She took her own life. But there's such a stigma. And Duncan was so upset— he can be very emotional. I was afraid he'd be devastated, blame himself. I thought it would be better if he just believed it was an accident."

"What's this Red Queen business?"

She took back the letter and locked it in the box. "When we were girls we used to pretend we were characters from *Alice in Wonderland*. I was the Duchess. Avis was so lonely. That's something I'm an expert on." She flicked her eyes at me.

"I'm glad you showed me the letter," I said.

"I did right, didn't I?"

"Yes. It's helpful."

"You won't tell, will you?"

"Why shouldn't the family know?"

"Suicide is the ultimate disgrace to them. It's a sign of weakness, of failure. I don't think Duncan could handle it."

"Then why tell me?"

"Because I like you." She tittered over this. "Seriously, I just wanted you to know all the facts. As much as Duncan hates Joe, I didn't want to see the man accused of something he didn't do. He does have some redeeming qualities."

"Such as?"

"He's a wild man, I know that. But sometimes a girl, especially a girl like Avis, wants that."

"Then why did she kill herself?"

"Oh, she wasn't happy. But she wasn't happy before she met him, either. She was tortured. It would be terrible for her mother if she knew. You won't tell, will you?"

"I never reveal anything that's given to me in confidence."

"I knew I could rely on you. Now maybe you can help me." She flopped onto the big four-poster bed. "These boots are so hot."

I held the boot for her while she tugged her foot out of it.

"Sock, please."

I slid her pant leg up, took hold of the elastic of the white sock, and slipped it over her heel. Her toes were long, the nails painted a marigold color. As I took hold of the other boot, she positioned her bare foot on my thigh for leverage. She gave her toes a little wiggle.

When I tugged, her whole body slid on the bed. She slipped her hands behind her head and looked at me.

I looked at her. Her shirt had come untucked and in the gap above her jeans her bellybutton winked at me. Her chest was moving rapidly. The smile on her face was something to see.

Then she stopped smiling and her features softened and became grave. The ticking of a clock filled the warm room.

I grabbed hold of her knee and pulled the boot off quite roughly and threw it onto the floor. Then that sock. Then, to my own disappointment, I brushed her foot from my leg and held my hand out to help her up.

The next instant she was tucking in her shirt and chattering about her wedding plans. One thing I'll say about rich girls, they're always discreet.

Driving away, I congratulated myself on how well I'd had her pegged. An innocent playing innocent. Yet I had to wonder. Was she friendlier with Petrone than she was letting on? If I was fair game, her best friend's husband might be, too. Was this whole show something she had cooked up with him to throw me off the track?

Even if it was, my turning down the morsel of ecstasy she offered surprised me. Maybe she'd made it a little too easy. Maybe I was developing scruples that I didn't know about. Maybe a lot of reasons, but I was disappointed and I lectured myself about the missed opportunities I would regret on my deathbed. I couldn't think of any rebuttal and I fell into a funk.

I had to admit the suicide note, if that's what it was, made sense. It meant that the Bluebeard story was probably the fantasy that I had suspected all along. Young women turn sad and kill themselves. Married to Petrone, brought up against the hard surface of the world he lived in, Avis might have had good reason to drive off a cliff.

But it left me with nothing for Vicky to use against her husband. And the more I learned about Joe Petrone, the more I wanted to bring him down.

5

THE AFTERNOON WAS getting soiled around the edges when I drove out to a street behind the Stromberg-Carlson plant. Next to a dry cleaners, a storefront sign read CAVALIER REALTY.

I went inside. They had a fan pumping hot air straight down from the ceiling. Both of the desks were empty. On one wall snapshots of houses were thumbtacked to a corkboard and peppered with optimism. "Charming Cape." "Your dream come true." "Adorable split level on quiet street." "Close to stores." "Low taxes." "Affordable."

They had listings for commercial properties and city apartments. They advertised vacation cottages in the Finger Lakes, Sodus Point, Fair Haven, all the resort towns. Nathaniel Rochester, who founded the burg, had been a land speculator, and real estate was still a big game in town.

I heard a toilet flush. A woman emerged from a door at the back wiping her hands on brown paper.

"Fry an egg out there," she said. "Tomorrow we're supposed to set a record. You know how long the old record's stood?"

"I'm afraid I don't."

"Since 1887. Believe it? World's burning up. I read about it in *Popular Mechanics*. Fifty years, we'll all be Watusis. Won't wear no clothes. You'd like that, wouldn't you?"

Her laugh seemed to include the idea of herself in the altogether. She had flesh that reminded me of bread dough left to rise too long. Her curls were the washed-out color of gasoline.

"I'm glad you warned me," I said. "I think I'll apply for a Good Humor route."

"You'll be a millionaire before you can turn around. You'll be able to retire to the South Pole."

"Actually, I'm looking for a piece of income property right here."

"Those penguins are cute suckers."

"My uncle died, left me some cash. I can't afford much."

"Rest of us just gotta sweat it out."

"Maybe up in the old seventh. I hear you can get places cheap there."

"I wouldn't."

"Why?"

Her lipstick smiled at me independently of her mouth. "Dark side of town."

"Their money's green, isn't it?"

"If you can get your hands on it. Headaches, Mr. . . . what's your name?"

"Brant. Maybe you could show me what you've got out there. Or maybe the boss could take me around."

"Boss? I'm the boss. I run the show here."

"A friend of mine sold a house to you. He dealt with a heavyset fellow, he said."

She shook her head and chuckled.

I chuckled, but not at her. I had caught sight of a clipping on the bulletin board. "Realtor of the Month," the heading said. The face under it looked very much like the face of a certain Mr. Eddie Gill. EG. I remembered EG Management from the deeds office.

You form compartments in your mind. You have to keep the facts separate and distinct. But in a small city—I'd learned this before—you often stumble across connections. This one took me by surprise.

"I've got some really charming places in Brighton," she said.

"Where's Mr. Gill today, anyway?"

She put her hands over her ears, then over her eyes, finally over her mouth. She winked at me.

"It's too hot to fuss," she said pleasantly. "Understand? You want to see properties, I'll take you. You want to make trouble, go down to the city dump and chase rats. I hear they got 'em big as kangaroos down there. No end of fun."

"I understand you." I gave her my card. "Tell Gill to give me a call."

"You said you were Brant."

"I was joshing."

She nodded. "It's so hot. I think I'm going to go home and spritz myself with cologne."

I swung back west on Keeler Street and headed for the north end of the city. Maplewood Drive skirts a narrow park along the edge of the Genesee Gorge there. I had gotten the location from the police report, and I stopped to look.

At the place where Avis had gone off, the road took a couple of quick bends. A bad driver could have overcompensated, panicked, lost control. It struck me as an odd place to choose suicide.

I walked down along the fence and found where the iron palings had been rewelded. It was meant to keep pedestrians away from the edge, not to hold back a car.

The sumac and ash saplings had filled in the gap she'd made. I moved to a point where I could see the bottom through the undergrowth. I could hear the roar, the river taking its last drop to lake level. It would have been a hell of a plunge.

Some said that the river along there was paved with pure silver. Kodak had been dumping developing fluids in there for years. If you could get down and dig up the bottom, they said, you'd never have to work again.

I continued along Lake Avenue past the main film factory and Holy Sepulchre Cemetery. The garage that had hauled the car up was called Lockharts, almost out to Charlotte. It was a big place with a body shop attached and a junk lot in back.

A man in blue coveralls greeted me from the grease pit. I squatted. His name tag said "Billy."

"You brought a car in here last year, went over the gorge. Remember?"

He shrugged. I handed him my card, a folded five behind it.

"I'm with the insurance outfit," I said. "Just routine."

"You talking about the one, that girl was killed?"

"That's it."

"We had a hell of a time getting that one up."

"Pretty well banged in, I imagine."

"Hardly any good parts left on it. The radio was okay. Still worked, if you can believe that."

"You handled it yourself?"

"Sure. I would have earned some overtime, except the boss don't pay overtime."

"See any paint scrapes on it?"

His eyes lit up, but he said, "Hard to say."

I was going to give him another five, but I could see he was eager to talk. I waited him out. Finally he said, "It was the same color."

"What do you mean?"

"The car was dark blue. Prussian blue, they call it. There was paint laid on top of that, but it was almost exactly the same shade. I wouldn't have noticed it, except, like I said, I spent a lot of time with that car."

"The police have any interest?"

"I pointed it out to the detective who came around. He looked at it, made a note on his pad, that's it."

A mustached man in a white shirt caught sight of me from the glassed-in office. He hurried out.

"Help you?" he said to me.

I gave him the insurance story and told him what I was after.

"Well, the car was totaled, I can tell you that."

"Is it still on the premises?"

"Nope. Scrapped. What are you trying to prove?"

"Just tying up loose ends. Strictly routine. Thanks for your help."

6

IT WAS WELL AFTER six and I was late for my meeting with Angela Grecco. I continued on out toward the lake, crossed the Stutson Street Bridge, and drove over to Gleeland. The amusement park had drawn a crowd, but the folks seemed dispirited, dragging under the incessant heat.

Angela wasn't in her office. I sat on a bench beside the carousel and watched the brilliant horses and lions, the camels and zebras whirl past in their undulating arcs.

I had first brought Gloria to Gleeland years ago, "when I was little," as she put it now. The only ride that didn't scare her then was the merry-go-round. We rode it over and over. She had names for her favorite animals—the chicken was Moochie; the lion, whose fangs she loved to finger, was Flower; and the loopy camel she called, for some reason, Charles.

I remembered the names and I remembered those days when it seemed that life, too, would go around in the familiar groove forever. But things changed. Now she scorned the carousel as a kiddy ride.

One mother, a squat lady in a flowered dress, was holding her tiny son on the saddle of a blue stallion. The painted horse's eyes were rolling with ferocious excitement as he galloped through a four-year-old's imagination. The kid was clutching the reins, his mouth grim. The calliope was pouring out its breathless, slippery melodies.

I asked around and was finally told to check the house of horror. A sign on the front said CLOSED TEMPORARILY. I climbed over the chain and made my way inside along the narrow tracks that the cars ran on. After the first bend it was black as pitch and I had to grope.

As I felt my way forward, my skin went clammy and I started breathing too fast. I was, for an instant, back in Korea. You would awake there and it would be so dark you'd think you had gone blind. It was a dark that would sink into you. It would eat at guys until they cracked and filled that black void with their own screams. I was still sensitive to it. Pitch darkness seemed full of menace.

Every so often along the switchbacks I came to an alcove. In one I felt a large glass jar displayed on a stand. Because the lights were off, I could only guess what was inside. I imagined the old sideshows that displayed human fetuses and stillborn babies with two heads.

I heard sounds ahead and came around a turn into dim flashlight glow. Angela and a man in coveralls were both squatting beside an electrical panel bristling with switches and relays.

She greeted me with a smile.

"Put a new socket in there and try it," she told the workman. "If it keeps blowing, we'll have to trace the whole circuit."

She stood and wiped her hands on a yellow rag.

"We've gotta hurry," she told me. "Forlini's expecting us."

I followed her through a door in back into the bright light. Her summer dress with the tiny polka dots complimented her figure and made me think again of Moonbeam McSwine. A tiny smear of grease on the left side of her neck added to the impression. The silver lamé hat she settled on her head, with its *Sputnik* theme, also looked as if it belonged in a comic strip.

"This weather, huh? Let's go in mine, it's a ragtop."

She drove a brand-new pink Cadillac with white upholstery. The breeze felt good.

"Everybody has a Joe Petrone story," she told me on the way. "They say back in the forties he still had a crew making rotgut brandy from concord grapes. This farmer out in Wayne County thought he was slick, started shorting Joe, selling part of his crop to another bootlegger down in Clyde. Joe found out, cooked the guy. They tied him up with wire, put him in there with the purple mash, and lit the fire. It heated up nice and slow, hotter and hotter. Till it was boiling. Cooked the flesh right off him. Of course, that's ancient history. He's gotten civilized since."

We fought traffic back toward the center of the city. She parked in front of a big brick building half a mile from the public market.

Inside, the cold odor of raw meat hit us like a fist. I've never liked that smell—part iron, part flint, part north wind. We climbed a flight and checked the offices that opened off a gallery overlooking the plant. A secretary told us we could find our man in the killing room.

This was a tiled space in back that wasn't chilled. I could hear the hoarse complaints of hogs in pens outside. The floor was smeared with clotting blood.

The man in the rubber apron gave the impression of being big, though he was neither especially tall nor particularly fat. He filled his skin, you might say, bulged it. His head was massive and bony, his hands thick. His habit of moving his mouth from side to side, the way a cow does when it chews, emphasized his granite jaw. He squinted from time to time as if to prevent his protruding eyeballs from flying out of his head.

He was pointing a device that looked something like an automatic pistol to the head of a pig, which was held in a tight metal chute. The pig squealed. The gun made a flat sound like a .22 shot. The squeal went up the scale and abruptly ceased. The pig slumped. The man turned and flashed us a Sergeant Bilko grin.

The man hooked a clamp to the pig's hind leg and hoisted him up on a cable.

"You bleed him while the heart's still beating, so it pumps the blood out," he said, slightly out of breath. He jabbed a narrow knife into the throat and raked it across. "Always pull the knife out, don't try to slice in."

Blood began to gush down a drain. Little ripples of tremors ran through the flesh.

"A hog, you can cut up right away," he said, wiping his hands on his apron. "We age our beef, a week at least. That's where your flavor comes. Places sell green beef, it's tough and tastes like nothing. You gotta age. Right, Angie?" His laugh mimicked the grunt of a hog.

Angela introduced me. "Ike is interested in Viola, Leo. He wants to know about her."

"A saint, that woman. Married wrong, whaddaya gonna do?"

He stared at me as if I might have an answer.

Angela, jerking her thumb at me, said, "He's going to put it to Joe."

He muttered something that might have been Italian. He invited us to his office.

A pale, blue-jawed man was carving into the hanging hog now, splitting the carcass and delicately spilling the innards. The thick air, the smell, and the heat were combining to gag me. I didn't mind going back into the iced plant.

Forlini hung up his apron and we proceeded to his office. He sat behind a littered desk and poured liquor into three impossibly delicate glasses.

"Grappa," he said. "Good."

It burned going down and made me feel even hotter.

"I don't like to talk about it," he started. "She's dead, so rest in peace."

"You think Petrone killed your sister?"

He squinted. His big jaw swung back and forth, scraping his teeth. He glanced at Angela and said, "Know he did."

"How?"

"Easy. Hold her head underwater."

"I mean, how do you know?"

"I talk to a guy, knew the guy who did it. I was out drinking with this pal of mine, he's a gypsy, but honest. He says, I don't like to tell you this, Leo, but I met the douche bag who killed your sister. He says, This guy lives down there on Eagle Street in Utica, by the brewery. Petrone offered him two thousand and said make it look like an accident. So he did. My sister, he saw her naked."

"What about the radio, the electrocution?"

"Dropped it in after—that was the accident part. Clever." He shook his head as if in begrudging admiration.

"Who was the killer?"

"Whaddaya think I asked him? He didn't know. A guy he met in a roadhouse outside Herkimer, Zodiak Mongoose Club, Route Five. It's a strip joint. I been there. I mean, they take it down to the buff, believe me. I saw this one broad, I swear to God."

"So he met this guy."

"I'm telling you, she made Jayne Mansfield look like a boy. Right, he meets this guy, the guy's joking, he did a cute piece of work. Bragging. Mentioned the radio, the bath. It didn't take two and two to figure he killed my goddamn sister."

"What did you do about it?"

"What can I do? A guy like Petrone we call 'connected.' You know what that means?"

"He has friends."

"Friends, you think? Politicians? It's more. You know that guy Kennedy, that's in the news?"

"The senator they say the smart money's on for president?"

"His papa is tied in. Made a bundle, bought some foofoos. But he's still tied in. The son's tied in. See?"

"No. You mean Joe Petrone is friendly with Kennedy?"

"Not pals, but it goes that high. A guy who could be president. You don't understand the reach of these guys. It goes high, it goes low. I'm a law-abiding citizen. I pay taxes. But I have to respect the syndicate."

"What syndicate are you talking about?"

He laughed. "Not the one you're thinking of." He liked mysteries. Downstairs I could hear another pig give out that last squeal. At this distance, it sounded like a child's screech, an odd mixture of anguish and joy.

"Do you do business with Petrone?" I asked him.

"No. Me? This is my business. But I know Petrone's got support. The old guys in Rochester, they got this idea, we call it *rispètto*. They like a big man, a guy who runs things. They think he brought some order, some whaddayacall, discipline. They like that."

"You mean he shaped up the rackets?"

"Hey, buddy, everything's a racket. Doctors, lawyers? Don't make me laugh. Politicians. Priests. I'm a Catholic, but those guys got their pious bull and their palm out. Private detectives even." He grinned. "One big racket."

He wrinkled his nose and looked toward Angela, back to me.

"Thanks, Leo," she said. "I think Viola deserves to be remembered. This guy's sharp as a tack. If anybody can find out about it, he can."

He told me it had been a pleasure. "Forlini, best sausage in Rochester. You remember that."

7

DRIVING THROUGH THE CITY in her car that warm dusk was like a dream. A smoldering crimson sun floated in a sky gone pastel. Swallows were sweeping low, turning the air dizzy. Angela took off the silly hat and the breeze got in her hair and brought it to life. She pushed her skirt up when she drove, baring her sleek thighs.

The place where she stopped on Elm Street looked like a hole-in-the-wall tavern. ADOLPH'S was all the sign said.

"You had an Adolph's porterhouse?" she asked me. I must try an Adolph's porterhouse.

They all knew her. We settled into a corner table and ordered porterhouse and a couple of Ox Head ales. A huge nicotine-stained American flag covered the wall behind us.

"Leo telling the truth?" I asked.

"Why not?"

"Seems like you and him are stirring up trouble for Petrone. Maybe you've got a reason."

"What reason?"

"Petrone's a six-hundred-pound gorilla. He throws his weight around, everybody resents it. If you think it's worth your while to rattle Joe's cage and you're using me to do it, I'm concerned. I don't like being played for a fool."

"I was honest with you, Ike. No, I don't like Petrone. But yes, I truly believe Vicky's in trouble. You came to me, remember?"

"But you know more than you're telling."

"I hope to God I always know more than I'm telling."

"And what makes you the expert on this stuff?"

"Hey, my grandpa was from Trapani, in Sicily. Came over here and got a job in a shoe factory. The cobbler sitting at his bench, right? Let me tell you, that was hard work. Ten-hour days, six days a week. He hired out as a slugger for the unions back in the thirties. He knew how to make a bomb. Companies put the squeeze on, a shop would blow. Of course, now and then he broke bones for the bosses, too. He was no red." She laughed. She was the type of woman, you never know what's around the next corner.

"So he ended up in the rackets," I said.

"Ended up? He invented a few. It was the life he knew. It's all right to have ideals if you're driving a new car and eating tenderloin. Try to feed a family on a workman's wage, you'll see things different. He never backed Mussolini," she added.

"So that's your grandfather. What about you?"

"Me?" She laughed. "I went into the family business."

The waiter was laying before each of us a huge slab of loin, striped with black, a rim of crackling fat, pink juices flowing into the mound of cottage fries. "What do you know about a guy named Melvin Slade?"

She gave me a curious look and said, "Hey, get a load of that meat." She sliced eagerly into hers, sawed off a big chunk, slipped it between her lips, and chewed. She closed her eyes. A smile spread across her mobile mouth.

For a time we just ate. Good steak feeds the soul as well as the body. Watching her eat made it taste even better. She filled her mouth and rolled her eyes and smacked her lips.

She took a swallow of ale and said, "Slade? That name rings a bell."

"He's a fighter."

"I love the fights. I don't know anything about them, but I adore watching. What's the connection?"

"Vicky Petrone was seen with this guy."

"Colored?"

"Is it possible? You know her."

She looked toward her bangs and said, "A woman in her position, who knows? If she is, it's because Joe drove her to it."

"Doesn't it seem funny, she's so afraid of her husband, yet she does the one thing most likely to provoke him to homicide?"

"Think he doesn't run around?"

"That's a different story and you know it."

"So if he caps her, it's perfectly justifiable—says you."

"It might well be, the unwritten law. Besides, integration hasn't gotten that far yet."

"What's she say?"

"I haven't asked her about it. I thought I'd scope out Slade first. He's fighting at the Armory tonight."

"Take me with you. We'll see the fights, then go out for some drinks and dancing. I've been wanting to do the frog shuffle with you since I first laid eyes on you."

She darted her tongue along her greasy lips. Eagerness flooded her face.

"I was just going to invite you."

She finished her steak and decided to top it with a slice of cheese-cake—Adolph's cheesecake was food for the gods.

"Then coffee, a nice glass of Benedictine, off to the fights, a little rhumba, two or three highballs—this could turn into an evening."

8

AN ENTHUSIASTIC CROWD HAD packed the Armory before we arrived. Our seats were about nine rows back. The air was already thick with blue smoke and the sweet smell of rosin and leather and sweat. We watched a couple of lightweights mix it up in a four-rounder.

"I'll go see if I can find Slade," I told her.

"Hurry back. And bring me a beer, how about?"

I found a dark corridor and one of the sweepers pointed me to a door. Inside was a bare room with a rubdown table, some lockers, and a couple of shower stalls. Over in the corner they'd stacked pasteboard figures that they must have hauled out when the circus came to town. The one on top was a baby chick eleven feet high. Its beak was open wide and it had a hungry look in its eye.

A tall mulatto was holding up hand pads for his fighter to jab at. He kept moving them, and Slade kept hitting them with loud leather slaps. Slade's sleek body was already glistening. They didn't pay any attention to me.

As soon as he finished, Slade took up a jump rope and began to work to an easy rhythm.

The manager turned to me with a wary smile. "Help you?"

"I need to talk to your boy."

"About what?"

"Personal."

"He's gotta keep his mind on the fight."

"Tell him it's about a traffic stop a week or so ago. Won't take a minute."

"You police?" He ran his teeth along his lip, trying to read my stare. "He owe a ticket?"

"No, something else. Somebody who was with him."

I knew Slade was listening, though he never looked in our direction.

"That's all right, Willie," he said now. "I'll see the man. I'm warmed up good."

Willie hesitated. "You from them?" he asked me.

"I'm from myself."

"And who the hell is yourself?" the fighter asked, slipping on a dirty white robe and draping a towel over his head.

"I used to be a cop. Vicky Petrone sent me. You know who I'm talking about?"

"Petrone? I've heard the name."

"Don't say nothing," Willie advised.

"You know Joe has a wife, don't you?"

"I don't usually look at the society page. All them weddings, make me cry."

"Never laid eyes on her?"

"I didn't say that. I think I seen her at the Tic Tac one night. Yellow hair."

"You noticed her."

"Any woman, looks like that, a man's going to notice. Her husband, he's got a manny-cure. Any fella, a manny-cure, I gotta wonder about him."

"Think that's smart?"

"Brother, the ladies come to me. I ain't saying she's one of them, but they do come, don't they, Willie?"

"What do I know about it?"

"You seen me squiring some admirable tunafish around this town, haven't you?"

"Any lady gonna help you knock out Blik tonight?"

"They come on their hands and knees. What am I supposed to do, run away?"

"If you're smart," I said.

"Maybe you're jealous."

I said, "A guy like Petrone can punch your ticket before you can say boo."

"Boo." He showed me a gold incisor.

"Have it your way."

Maybe he was as stupid as he let on. Maybe inflating his rep as a ladies' man was a habit he couldn't break, even when it put him in line to get his head taken off.

Back in the auditorium the bell was just sounding. Our seats were both empty and I watched the last round of the prelim alone.

"Got tired of waiting," Angela said when she returned. "Went for beer and ran into some people I knew. What did you find out from your man?"

"He's playing it close to the vest."

"I don't blame him. That boy's walking around with a stick of dynamite between his teeth."

While we were talking, people around us started rising to their feet. We did the same, following the crowd.

"There he is," she said. "And with look who."

Marciano had entered the arena and was making his way down the aisle toward a front-row seat. I recognized the face, all right, the lopsided grin and the rubber sausage of a nose, but the body had swelled with fat. He wore a toupee that made him look like a Fuller Brush man. But he wasn't the only one to catch my attention.

Vicky Petrone held a white-gloved hand wrapped around Marciano's forearm. Her pastel dress, with its belt of shiny white leather, seemed to glow from within. She held her mouth tensed against a smile.

"The lady gets around," I observed.

"I wonder where Joe is."

An entourage of about eight men and four or five women followed the former champ. Bobo Palermo, a top spear carrier for Petrone, strode along at the champ's other elbow and appeared to be whispering in his ear. I recognized Frankie Delmonico, a slender lawyer who was a sweetheart of the racket boys. Morty Petrocelli, Dan Maloney, and a couple of other local promoters were with them. Bobby Lo Cicero, a Henrietta boy who had been a ranked bantamweight a few years back, followed in the wake.

"Looks like the Petrones are in with old Rocky," Angela said.

A few people from the crowd reached out to shake Marciano's hand, as if he were a politician. He nodded and smiled as he took his seat. Vicky settled on one side of him, Palermo on the other.

I was one of the last to stop applauding.

"You like this guy," she said.

"Listen, when Marciano got hit, he didn't flinch. When he got knocked down, he got up. When the other guy was fresh, he hammered him until he wasn't fresh. When the other guy dropped his guard, he punched his head off. He never backed up and he never lost a pro fight. To me, that's a class act. That's a champion."

Seeing Vicky there made me wonder what kind of game she was playing. Maybe it meant nothing, but the idea of Slade fighting and her sitting at ringside made my brain start clicking over like a Univac.

Maybe I would pick up some sense of it as the evening wore on. They were in the glare down front and we were lost back in the crowd, so I didn't have to worry about her seeing us, even if she'd been looking.

During the intermission between fights, Vicky carried on an animated conversation with Marciano. Occasionally she tossed a word to Palermo or over her shoulder to Delmonico. All three men leaned to listen. It was as if she sent out lines of force the way a magnet does, bending and attracting those around her.

They dimmed the house lights and put a spot on the aisle. Slade entered, still wrapped in the robe and swathed in towels. All you could see were a pair of mean-looking eyes. He bounced as he came down toward the ring, his gloved hands held near his chin.

After a few minutes the bright light followed Kid Blik into the auditorium. His silk gown hung open as he sauntered along the aisle. He waved to well-wishers. He was almost good looking, like an art student's sketch of a marble face.

They brought out a woman whose red hair drooped with the humidity. A spot lit the flag hanging from the rafters. The girl opened her mouth, closed her eyes, and emitted an "O-oh!" that twisted into a lewd moan before she went on with the anthem. A couple of jokers opposite us moved their hands from their hearts to their groins. I guess I have a sense of humor, but I don't like to see anybody disrespect the flag.

She was sweating before she finished. They held the ropes so she could climb out and the ring announcer, a wavy-haired man with a voice bigger than he was, began the formalities.

He never finished introducing Marciano. Everybody was already up and applauding. The ovation went on and on, people cheering for an already bygone era. Rocky wore his cherubic grin as he bounced up the steps and slid nimbly between the ropes. He held up the massive fist that had battered men's skulls. The crowd roared.

The champ wished the two gladiators well. We clapped him out of the ring and back to his seat.

Slade finally unwrapped and stood in his corner sweating. Blik threw some fancy combinations at imaginary gnats while his opponent watched. They took the instructions and the gong sounded.

Blik had muscles that looked like cocked pistols. Slade's arms were so sleek they were almost skinny. Blik bobbed back and forth as he moved in, not slipping punches but just trying to get into a rhythm. Slade tossed off a couple of jabs and a right that the Kid easily picked off, then repeated the same combination, only twice as fast, stinging Blik's cheek and hammering him hard enough in the spleen to make his eyes come open wide. Blik scowled and drew his right back to throw it, leaving himself open for a hard hook to the ear that tangled him in his own feet and made him stumble into the ropes.

Blik turned into a buzzsaw and battered Slade across the ring without hurting him. The crowd loved it. The fight was barely thirty seconds old.

Everybody who watches sees a different fight. To me, it's always a contest of wills. The guy who can take the punishment, who can suck it up and go on after he's run out of gas, who can grab on to a shred of hope floating in a sea of pain, he's the guy who wins it.

Marciano, I was sure, saw something else, the professional's view. To him, boxing was superior to life because in boxing there are no accidents. He saw the missed chances, the blatant setups, the inexpert feints. He saw it the way we might if it had been slowed down to a tenth the speed. He was inside time, more even than the fighters themselves, enclosed in another dimension.

Angela saw naked skin and a display of wanton and provocative violence. The sight awakened something primitive in her, as it did in many, and she was frank enough to admit it.

Vicky saw what? Maybe blows falling on a lover, whose nearness, given the circumstances, must have been arousing in ways I could only imagine. If that was the case, she hid it well. Like many who've seen the fights mainly on television, she flinched at the brutality of real punches smacking into real flesh. But she reacted as much when Blik was on the receiving end as when Slade got tattooed.

Bobo Palermo and his buddies probably saw a money contest, all the juice of it, like the juice of a horse race, depending on who you were backing.

"I love it!" Angela said after the first round. Her lips were parted and she was panting. "I want to see'm cream'm."

"Who?"

"I don't give a flying fig. I want blood."

She wasn't the only one. Take a look at the crowd and you see the action reflected in the faces. Eyes move. Mouths twitch and shape silent words and draw back to grimace. Arms wave mimicking punches. No sport sucks you up and makes you forget yourself as much as boxing.

The fight provided just about enough action to keep the crowd satisfied. But not quite. It was a hot night and they'd seen a card of mediocre preliminaries; they wanted pyrotechnics.

In the ring, a fighter once told me, you go through all the emotions known to man, and a few that nobody's ever put a name on. They don't mean a thing and they don't change a thing. Feel whatever way you want, you still have to knock the other guy silly.

The most dangerous, he said, is anger. Because anger gives you a charge. You see it a lot in the amateurs. Guys paw at each other until one of them, for whatever reason, gets mad. Suddenly, he's full of ginger. He hauls off and swarms over his man, maybe battering him to the canvas.

In the pros it's a different story. You get mad, you get careless. The other guy, if he's any good, lets you throw as many angry punches as you want. You either leave yourself open or punch yourself out. The anger's spent and you're spent. That's a dangerous place to be.

What made Kid Blik angry was a low blow in the seventh. It wasn't intentional. Slade was throwing an uppercut and the Kid shifted his weight and caught the punch partly in the hip and partly in the groin. The ref didn't see it, but Blik's face turned white.

He stepped back. He curled his lips. He raised his right hand as if it were a club. He ran at Slade and began to pummel him. Slade retreated, covering up. Blik's punches either missed or found only leather. The Kid took one step too many and Slade struck him with a hard jab.

The punch straightened him up. He was facing us and I saw his eyes look up, over Slade's head, as if he'd just recognized his mother in the back row.

Slade cocked his right hand. Blik was open. You could see Slade set himself for once, put his shoulder into position, and then skip to the side without throwing the punch. It happened in a fraction of a second and maybe I hadn't seen what I had seen.

Blik stumbled around while his head cleared. A hurt fighter is a dangerous fighter, the saying goes. Slade gave him room.

The crowd was up now. Marciano was on his feet, too, but not to cheer. He was walking. Vicky watched him, caught between the action in the ring and this sudden desertion.

The fight continued. Blik proved his gameness. He waded in, swinging his fists like mattocks. Slade seemed to fend these blows off easily, but when one of them caught the side of his head, he staggered. The arena became one great roar.

Then Slade was down. Blik was raising his bulgy arms in victory.

Angela was gripping my arm and talking a mile a minute, her words lost in the buzz.

9

THE AIR OUTSIDE WAS no cooler than the air inside. The sky was a dark gunmetal blue.

"So why did Marciano leave?" Angela asked.

"He smelled something."

"A fix?"

"Blik is a payday. It's pretty clear Petrone has an interest. Slade is an opponent. Nothing wrong with an exhibition, unless you've paid to see a prize fight. Some of us might have guessed. Rocky knew. He knows how things work."

"What did you make of Vicky being there?" she asked as we walked away from the crowd.

"Hard to say. She didn't kiss Slade after the fight, but she looked pretty sad when he got hammered. Maybe it meant something, maybe not."

"Would you go in the water if they paid you?"

"I wouldn't step into the ring in the first place. I'm a pacifist."

"You look like you could handle yourself."

She held her two fists level with her eyes and began to punch at me. I put up my guard and showed her some moves I had learned in the army. She came at me. I caught her wrist under my elbow and held. I socked her with a mock right, pressing into the softness of her belly. She slung her free arm around my neck and kissed me, flicking her tongue.

"Let's go somewhere," she said. "I'm itching to dance."

At her suggestion, we drove to the Tic Tac. I'd been inside a couple of times. The place was always full of sophisticated inebriates. The upholstery was zebra stripes and half the women were wearing fishnet stockings. The band was playing a syrupy version of "Strange Are the Ways of Love."

We sat at a table and ordered gin collinses. We drank and talked for half an hour. She still had the smudge on her neck, and it some- how illuminated a grace that I hadn't noticed at first.

The band shifted gears and blasted out a galloping version of "The One O'Clock Jump."

"Hey, did we come here to wear out our backsides?" she said. "Let's hit it."

She took me by the hand and pulled me onto the dance floor. Her summer dress wasn't right for a nightclub, and it had a little tear opening up in one of the seams. Her lipstick had worn off, her hair was all over the place, and she was sweaty around the edges. But, man, could she dance. Every part of her went in a different direction as she jitterbugged across the floor. She spun and dipped and jumped and twisted, keeping time to three beats at once.

My joints were not as well oiled as hers, but I managed to let loose and throw my hips around. She was the kind of woman who made you oblivious of what you did or who saw you doing it.

Then the musicians slowed it down and poured out a languid version of "Misty." The sax player stood and began to make his in- strument bleed, the drummer sanded his traps, and the bassman strummed a heartbeat. We held on to each other, a couple of fighters in the late rounds, punch-drunk and getting along on nothing but instinct. We clinched and swayed. I breathed her scent and felt her

moving beneath the thin dress. Angela's raucous voice and flamboy-
ant gestures had made me think of her as a big woman, but she felt
surprisingly fragile in my arms.

She had a way of casually brushing my thighs with hers, of making little countermovements to my lead so that her body crushed into
me voluptuously. It was intended to inflame and it did. I did some
things intended to inflame her, too. She leaned her head back and
shaped silent words with her mouth.

We were grinding each other to dust when I caught sight of a
short, pudgy man moving along the opposite wall. Was it? The roll
at the neck, the bulbous head splayed with strands of hair, it looked
a lot like Eddie Gill. He was leading a girl by the hand. A couple of
times, he stopped and seemed to be introducing her. I saw them
talking with one of the Petrone men, Delmonico. But by the time
the music stopped, they were gone.

Was it Sandy? What was her name? Mink? She looked older in
a dark cocktail dress. She had never called me, never returned to the
office. Maybe she'd made the decision on her own. Dresses and
nightclubs make a convincing argument when you're used to wearing
hand-me-downs and working for chump change.

It was like seeing something nasty through a clearing in the fog.
The memory of his mincing, fat man's gait and his clutching paws
gave me the urge to run after them.

"What?" she said, sensing my distraction.

"Somebody I thought I knew."

The band played another number before taking a break. We returned to our seats.

I felt like a caveman at a tea table. I paid the check and we left.
We crossed the Broad Street Bridge in her open car, and I noticed
the way the light of the moon skidded across the nervous black sheen
of the water. It was a pleasure to be with a woman who knew the
score. With Eileen there had always been complications. Complications can be a kick in themselves, but Eileen kept me guessing and
sometimes you get tired of guessing.

On the corner of Clinton and Main two beat cops were rousting a car of teenagers in an old green De Soto. Three or four people had come out of Neisner's Cafeteria to watch.

"Don't let 'em push you around!" Angela yelled. The cops looked. One of them took a couple of steps toward us, but the light changed and she made the car surge. To me she said, "I was a juvenile delinquent myself. I hate cops."

We slipped through the railroad underpass and when we came up, I started to see the glow in the sky. Next I heard sirens and bells. Then smoke, lots of it, and sparks jumping into the night sky. It was coming from the same area of the old seventh where I had wandered around the day before.

A big hook and ladder turned just ahead of us. Angela speeded up and went through red lights just behind it.

"Why don't we swing by, find out what's happening?" I suggested.

"You serious? I thought we'd light our own fire back at my place."

"I'm working an arson case out here. I need to see this."

"Oh, you need to see it."

She turned down Flower Street behind the engine. Now we could see flames. The fire had gotten hold of more than one building and it was still out of control.

Three blocks away a police barrier brought us to a halt. The cops swung the sawhorse out of the way for the truck but wouldn't let us pass. Curiosity seekers were streaming down the sidewalks, some of them running.

As soon as we stopped, a group of Negro youths closed in to look at the car. A man on the sidewalk was ranting at the police or the firemen or the powers of heaven.

"People dyin'! People cryin'! People burnin' for their sins!" Shouts of assent rose from a little pack of listeners. No white faces were to be seen.

"I'm getting out of here," Angela said. "I'm not leaving my car."

"I'll meet you later."

"None of that. If you're coming, you're coming. I don't wait up."

"I have to do this."

"Whatever you say, Jeremiah."

"Another time."

"Another time is another time. You can't dip your toe in the same stream twice, you know."

"Very true, I guess. Sweet dreams." I got out.

10

PEOPLE WERE RUNNING TO get there, running to see. I found myself running. The fire lit a panic inside us, ignited our rational thoughts. Why do moths flit toward the flame, embrace it?

The houses on that block, a lot of them two-family jobs, were packed cheek to jowl. You could literally reach out of your kitchen window and touch your neighbor's back porch. Most were old clapboard places, tinderboxes.

Three buildings were engulfed, and the fire was already licking up the side of another house. A guy across the street had his garden hose out and was trying to get the stream to carry to his own roof. Red cinders were leaping, dancing high to take the places of stars.

A distinctive expression infected the faces of the onlookers, some of them still in their pajamas. Not just the gawkers' usual mixture of curiosity and fascination. There was an older look, too, a raw, helpless grief. I suppose it afflicted my face, too, as soon as I understood the wails and whispers. Children. Their grandmother. Four little kids. No hope. Gone.

Snakes of smoke began to wriggle from the shingles of a fourth house. Its upper windows flickerred to life in rosy blinks. A fireman with a white helmet urged the hoseman to concentrate their attack there.

Moving along the sidewalk I caught a glimpse of a familiar face. Up on the lawn of one of the houses across the street, glowing orange with reflected light, was Orlo Zanek. I dodged through the crowd, but when I reached the spot, he was gone.

A scuffle broke out in the middle of the street, an argument. I pushed my way into the middle of it.

"Paddy!" I grabbed Doyle's shoulder and shouted to be heard over the cacophony.

He looked at me, dazed. When he recognized me his eyebrows crashed down and an eruption of curses spewed from his mouth. He pounded his fist into his palm, screaming about how much he'd paid me. I could smell liquor on his breath. His brain had short-circuited.

I started to explain what I had found out that afternoon. Oblivious, he turned and moved away from me. He caught up with a fire captain and grabbed him by his rubberized coat. The man spun and pointed to the other side of the street. Two cops descended on Doyle, and when he didn't move fast enough, one of them slammed his shin with a billy. Paddy fell into a gutter that was running with sooty water. I helped him up and dragged him down the sidewalk.

"Those are your houses?" I shouted at him.

"Fuck yes! I swear, Van Savage, they're not going to get away with this. Why didn't you get me the goods on those Italians? This wouldn't of happened."

"If this is arson, it's murder now. The cops will be all over it. We'll tell them your suspicions."

"Suspicions?" he wailed. "I know who's behind this. I told you and you wouldn't goddamn listen. I'm going to kill them dead."

"Take it easy. This isn't the place."

People had gathered around to stare at the apoplectic madman. Some of them knew him. I could hear them talking. The word "landlord" kept rising to the surface.

"He put Claude and his family on the *street*!" a man said.

"That's him! He owns them buildings."

"Fuck you!" Doyle snarled back. "Think I burn down my own property? You're crazy."

"Called the sheriff down on me once," an old man was saying.

"He ain't crying!" a woman screamed. "This man ain't crying over them babies dead. This landlord!"

"You're all nuts!" Doyle said. "I know who did this."

"Paddy," I said, close to his ear. "You're in a situation here."

It began to dawn on him. We were surrounded by angry faces and wild-looking eyes.

Paddy took a step back and ran up against a big man wearing greasy mechanic's clothes who looked like he'd been frowning since he was born.

"I know who torched those buildings," Paddy yelled. "I'll tell you who."

"Landlord!" came the cries.

A guy broke through and punched Doyle in the back of the skull. Paddy spun around. His assailant grabbed his own hand and winced. I jumped between them. Paddy tried to throw a punch around me.

Not a smart move. Four or five men converged on him. Somebody shoved me and I started to fall. I grabbed desperately at clothes. I didn't want to go under those feet.

I took a couple of rabbit punches and fended off some more blows with my forearms. I turned to see what was happening to Paddy.

They had him down. Several of them were trying to stomp him. Doyle's wild flailing was keeping them off for the moment.

I could hear police whistles, shouting, and the sick sound of nightsticks connecting with flesh. But the assailants were piling on Doyle faster than the cops could drag them off. An order was given and an instant later we were all hit with the full force of a fire hose.

People were knocked in every direction. Doyle himself took a shot of the water in his face. It bounced his head right off the concrete sidewalk. But it also pried loose the maniacs who had been beating on him.

Before the soggy crowd could descend on him again, I rushed

over, yanked him to his feet, and dragged him down the block, weaving in and out among the fire engines.

He muttered and swore to himself, turning back every few steps to curse at the fire.

As we walked away in our wet clothes, the night, still warm, began to seem refreshingly cool. The sounds faded. Glancing over my shoulder, I still saw smoke drifting into the sky, but the fury and the ominous glow had subsided.

"Do you have a car?" I asked him.

"A car? Sure, of course."

"Where is it?"

"Goddamn bastards. I'll show 'em. Show 'em something."

"Where's your car, Paddy? Where did you leave it?"

"I'll show them Italians some tricks. I'll teach them." He was starting to rant again.

I had a strong urge to leave him to his own devices. He'd gotten this far in life without me. But I felt an obligation, if only because the man was paying me.

I pulled him forward. Forget the car. We plodded two more blocks before I spotted a phone booth on the corner. I propped Paddy against an entryway and called for a Checker. He sank into a kind of stupor while we waited for the cab.

Doyle lived way out on the far west end of the city, off of Chili Avenue. The houses on his street seemed too big—each had to hunch its shoulders to fit into its lot.

I told the driver to wait. I could hear a baby crying before I shut the door of the cab.

Now Paddy, who had seemed more shellshocked than plastered, started acting the prodigal drunk, as if it were a role he knew well. He reeled as we walked up the short cement path, balanced precariously on each tread of the stair.

The porch light came on before we reached the door. Through the screen I saw the bulky figure of a woman. The sleeves of her bathrobe were rolled back to reveal fleshy forearms, which she held crossed on her chest.

"What is it now? Have you been swimming, or what is it?" she said, plenty of peat bog in her voice.

"They got my places on Flower Street," he said. "The goddamn dagos burnt 'em up. Oh, mother, they burnt 'em." He burst out weeping, a flood of tears pouring down his face.

"Look at yourself," she said. She didn't uncross her arms.

"My whole life, up in smoke," he wailed. He sank into a beat-up wicker chair on the porch and pounded his temples with his fists.

Now two small faces were peeking from behind the woman's solid hips. More appeared in the front window. What could the little ones be doing, up at this hour? I wondered.

"And who might you be?" she said to me, stepping onto the porch.

She eyed me suspiciously while I explained. I gave her a brief rundown of what had happened. As I was detailing the altercation at the fire, a noise interrupted me. It was Paddy, his head thrown back at an impossible angle, snoring loudly.

"Go to bed!" she snapped at one of the pajamaed youngsters, who was trying to ease himself through the door.

She stood staring at her husband while a solitary cricket took the pulse of night.

"His dreams were all so small," she said to me. "It's hard to think that there's not room for them in this world. But it's always been one forward, two back with Paddy. We're not having an easy time of it, I can assure you of that fact."

"I told him, you have to bend sometimes," I said. "When you're up against it, you have to give in. Maybe you can get the message across."

"Oh, he'll not give in. They can kill him dead, he won't budge. He'll leave a widow with seven mouths and a pocketful of debts, sure enough. But he'll not give in. It's not in him."

She looked at him again with an expression that suggested equal parts pride and irritation. A hint of a smile flickered across her thin lips. Her eyes softened. "You had better get on home yourself," she said. "You'll catch your death."

I gave the taxi driver the address of my apartment, but a half mile away from it, I told him to stop. I paid him and set out walking. I needed to unwind.

I had always liked to walk in the city at night. Even when I was married I often hiked across town, walking past the dark houses, past those others with their furtive, fevered lights, on and on, until dawn.

As I walked, I played a game of solitaire in my mind. On one card a spot of grease marked a woman's neck. On another, a navel winked through the gap in a shirt. I turned up a teenager's body draped in a womanly shift, then the hard face of a gangster's showpiece wife. Dying hogs and glass jars with pickled monstrosities. Seething flames and a placid lake and a cheap blue ashtray. I kept turning them over until I had gone through the deck three or four times without making any plays.

Then I climbed the stairs to my empty apartment and lay down and stared at the pattern the Venetian blinds made on the ceiling until I fell asleep.

SATURDAY

1

THE FIRST THREE WEEKS after I arrived in Korea, my outfit drew duty hacking underbrush away from fire zones and repairing roads near Panmunjon. Grunt work. We griped about it. We wanted action. We wanted to mix it up. We all felt the need to make a show of our eagerness, and we all went to sleep at night hugging our doubts.

I had grown up hating. Too young for the army, bubbling with the energy and confusion of puberty, I had embraced the diatribes, waged war in my mind against Japs and Jerries, dagos, slopes, and krauts. I'd had the taste of hate in my mouth, I'd been a connoisseur of its flavors and nuances. On V-J Day I'd celebrated with a hard piece of gristle lodged in my throat, the disappointment of not having had the chance to serve, to see action, to kill.

I'd thought I had missed the opportunity of a lifetime. But there would always be another war. When our boys were pushed back to Pusan, I couldn't wait to sign up, even though I was married and had a daughter creeping on the carpet.

Then we were ordered up to the front. No amount of training can help you get your mind around the strange idea that a bunch of

men with guns are about to descend on you and try to kill you. You're
too used to order, to sanity. Your brain recoils. We joked and
laughed. We didn't believe the time had finally come. Our stomachs
churned froth.

Three nights after we took up our position, the Chinese launched
an attack. It turned out to be a probe, but to us it was hell unleashed.
You hear about the so-called human waves, but the Chinks never
wasted men in hopeless charges. Infiltration was their specialty,
sneaking around your strong points and wreaking havoc in the rear.

Artillery shells drop at random. Waiting for them, you get more
tense than you've ever been, as if being tense would save your life.
Heavy machine-gun rounds tear up the air in a way that you can feel
in your bones. Mortar bombs drop out of the sky and fill the world
with a blizzard of shrapnel. You fire your M-1 into the darkness.
You're not hot, but you sweat constantly. You try to hook your mind
onto one thing, anything, in order to keep your thoughts from scud-
ding away before a squall of terror.

That night our lieutenant ordered four of us out of our holes.
The enemy were shooting up our right flank. I knew my legs were
carrying me, but it seemed as if the landscape was moving around
me. My heart was pounding in a way I'd never known before.

It was like being in a movie, a world filled with cruelty. We
scrambled into foxholes and started firing into the darkness. I never
saw an enemy soldier.

When that attack was over, when the tepid winter sun returned
after the longest night of my life, I wept. Our company had taken a
few casualties, nobody I knew well. As a unit, we had held our position and acquitted ourselves pretty well. But I couldn't help crying.
I bawled for close to an hour, completely out of control. Then it
passed and I pulled myself together and cleaned my weapon and
settled down to wait for the next one.

I saw a lot worse as the fighting wore on, a lot of things that I
had not imagined I would ever see, but I never cried again. Not
during the war, not after. Not once. My palate would grow hard.

Bitterness would fill my throat. My eyes would burn. But I was out of tears.

No tears dropped onto the newspaper that morning, onto the headline that screamed TRAGEDY. Not even when I came to the odd coincidence that Clarissa Morgan's birthday would have been today, the same as Gloria's. Clarissa would have been seven.

I simply lit a cigarette and read on. I read about Mrs. Isabelle Preston, age sixty-two, who had spent her life as a domestic. She had cared for her grandchildren while their mother took classes to become a practical nurse. I did not cry when I read about Yolanda Morgan, age thirteen, who a neighbor said had won trophies as a majorette. I could see her in a shiny satin uniform, strutting, twirling a baton. I could see her funeral, the closed coffin, the photograph propped on the cover showing her dimples.

Who was I? A guy with some connections and some instincts and a line of patter. These children and this hardworking woman had been murdered as part of a plot whose shape, if it had a shape, I had not been able to pick out of the fog. They'd been murdered while I was dreaming my life away at the Tic Tac. Who the hell was I?

The police would get right on it now, I had told Doyle. Sure. They used to have an expression down at the station house. *Orangutan*. It didn't mean any one thing, it was what they would say when an incident involved Negroes or Puerto Ricans or anybody who didn't fit the mold. Ease off. Don't sweat it. Orangutan, baby.

I bought a tin of Anacin on the way out of the Empire. I was feeling last night's high jinks in the form of a tungsten headache and a throbbing knee. A bright abrasion decorated my cheek.

I got into my car and headed out to Orlo Zanek's apartment. I would have bet a beer he had already beat it to Gainesville, where he was originally from, or Tampico, for that matter. Orlo could be as loopy as a rabid bat, but this thing had escalated into something that could put somebody in the chair, and I didn't think he was crazy enough to stick around.

I had busted Orlo the first time because he liked pie.

A battle royal had erupted among some truck farmers out on the muckland between Rochester and Syracuse. Years before, they had drained part of the Montezuma swamp out there, and the resulting black earth was great for onions and potatoes.

Some of the farmers had broken away from a market organization and were undercutting prices. Six of them had already had their barns burned. A couple of others had seen tractors or harvest equipment go up. Everybody was carrying shotguns, and the situation had gotten pretty tense.

The sheriff was short of manpower, so he put out word and a bunch of city cops went out there to patrol at night. It wasn't a lot of money, but in those days I was looking for anything that smelled of action.

Just on a hunch, any time I was in a bean wagon I would ask had they seen any strangers, anybody acting odd. Everybody, it turned out, has seen something strange in the last week if you ask them—a guy wearing a raincoat, the sun out; some slit-eyed fellow paying for a cup of coffee with a fifty; a man in a plaid suit asking too many questions about bicycle seats. None of it meant anything. Except, two waitresses told me a customer had eaten recently and had ordered three helpings of pie. Those places prided themselves on their pies. He had a twitch, one told me. The other agreed. A twitch and something about his eyes, he never looked right at you. Something about his eyes and not anybody they had seen before.

I started asking around about pie eaters. The third place I stopped at, the girl said, yeah, I just served that man over there his fourth slice. He really loves that banana cream.

I slipped into the booth opposite Orlo, flipped my badge, and said, "I know you did it."

He wasn't ready. His face gave it away and he knew it. "How?" he said.

"You'll have to take a rap. But you give up a name, I'll make sure they treat you like a citizen. You don't have to worry about a comeback from these clodeaters and you know it. Don't do hard time for a hick. It's just barns."

"Can I finish my pie?"

And that was it. I found naphthalene in his car. He ate the cheese. Three big growers went to jail.

Funny thing, four farmers remembered seeing Orlo among the crowd watching their barns burn. At one place he even pitched in dragging hose for the understaffed fire brigade.

That humid morning a bum was sitting on Orlo's front steps.

"How aboud gimme a cuppa coffee, huh?" he said, holding out his hand. "Ya wanna?"

Instead of the dime he hoped for, I held out a dollar bill folded lengthwise. "Seen a guy come in or out of here, third floor? Small, bird-faced, tick in the right eye?"

His face cleared. He was glad to have somebody take him seriously. "Know that jasper," he said. "Smokes."

"That's him."

"About four, he come in. I live over there." He pointed to a dilapidated residential hotel across the street. "Was sitting out."

"Act funny?"

He nodded. "In a hurry."

"See him leave?"

"No. I went to bed. Tried to sleep. Can't sleep. Ever since Hiroshima, the big eye. Know what that's like?"

"Sure, I know." I gave him the buck and went upstairs.

I knocked a couple of times on Zanek's door and waited. I took out a length of spring steel I carry in my coat and worked it into the doorjamb. It was only locked on the latch, and that made me suspicious. I pushed it all the way open and looked before I entered.

Orlo's apartment was set so that it caught the morning sun. Acrid light was pouring through the dirty glass, illuminating the stacks of newspapers, the open carton of Chesterfields, the glass with an inch of flat beer, the soiled T-shirt draped over a chair, the Timex watch and wadded handkerchief on the table, the pair of taped-up glasses. Orlo himself was silhouetted. The air was alive with buzzing.

In our day, the idea of honor has been so smeared by windbags and politicians that it's lost most of its meaning. But in that instant it occurred to me that Orlo Zanek had discovered at least a scrap of honor in himself, a fragment that his feeble brain had converted to shame.

When I was a cop, I used to hate suicide calls. They were never pleasant. A guy would take pills, go to bed, and a month later when they'd find him he'd give off a smell that would stay on your clothes even after they'd been through the laundry. Or he would eat a shotgun and you would have to help the coroner scrape brain and bone for an hour.

But it wasn't just the mess. You get used to unpleasantness. It was the ideas these cases had given me. Here were people—some of them respectable citizens, a guy with a family, a guy taking down a higher salary than I would ever see, a pretty young woman facing a life of possibility—people who had gone off to another land. Had they defeated their demons or been defeated by them? Sometimes in the wee hours that question grabbed me and wouldn't let go.

For me, suicide was the coward's solution. Or, I sensed, no solution. Kill yourself, you're letting your stone roll back to the bottom of the mountain when you don't have any idea how close to the top you are.

Still, the sights I saw flavored my nightmares, I can tell you.

I've seen them hanging by belts and rope and wire and bedsheets. One had gone off with a cigarette stuck to his lip—it had burned down and left a neat column of ash. Sometimes they take their dentures out and leave them in a plastic container in the bathroom. Sometimes they shave and dab the nicks with styptic pencil. I've heard of them wearing handcuffs. They climb up, place the noose, snap the cuffs, and kick the chair away. Then if they have second thoughts, or some reflex to save themselves, too late.

Orlo was just hanging, a double strand of clothesline running up to the heat pipe that crossed the ceiling, hands by his side, whites of his eyes showing, tongue protruding in a childish, mocking expression. These features were barely visible behind the shimmering, iridescent mask of flies that covered his face.

My instinct was not to touch a thing. This was a crime scene. A cop is careful to keep a crime scene intact. But I wasn't a cop.

I searched. He didn't have much. A First Genesee Valley pass-book stamped "Account Closed." A hundred and twenty dollars was the most he'd ever managed to save.

A diploma from a technical school, framed and hanging on the wall over his bed, declared him to be qualified as a refrigeration mechanic.

Boxes of light-anywhere kitchen matches—they filled a whole shelf in his cupboard. An early edition of today's *Democrat*—it was still neatly folded and looked unread. A stack of *Playboys* and the kind of lewd comic books guys used to read in the service. A lot of empty White Tower hamburger bags. Some containers like take-out Chinese food comes in. A butane torch. I turned the knob, but it was out of gas.

I wondered if I should call the cops. I decided the wino down-stairs was unlikely to point them toward me. I had parked my car around the corner, so he'd only have a description of my person, and with a dollar in his hand, he was probably off erasing that right now with a jug of Thunderbird.

I was just closing the door when I thought of something. I went back into the room. Using my handkerchief, I tipped up the chair that was lying on its side beneath Orlo's feet. It fit under him nicely, fit with nearly an inch to spare. And clothesline stretches.

2

I WAS ANXIOUS TO turn my mind in other directions. I drove out Lyell Avenue to Hartmann's Bakery. It was a place that had been in business since 1888. I knew the owner, a myopic German named Heinz Hartmann, whose kazoolike voice reminded me of Lawrence Welk. I had done him a favor years ago when he'd had some trouble with a gang of kids up the block.

You learn to shift gears fast. Orlo Zanek's corpse was one thing, my little girl's birthday was happening on a different planet in another solar system.

Heinz had made me the Red Wings' emblem, a baseball with wings, in devil's food, frosted with the team colors. It was decorated all over with squiggles and blossoms of icing. Spelled out in the center was HAPY BIRTHDAY GLORIA. When she'd been learning to read, we used to play a game where I would misspell a word and she would act the miniature schoolmarm. Every year I continued the gag on her cake and she would break up laughing at my foolishness.

"So how do you like that?" he asked me, wiping his hands on his apron.

"Another masterpiece, Henry."

"Devil's food. We're all devils inside, we need our food, huh?"

He pressed me to sample some fresh chocolate truffles. They were so rich they made my teeth ache, but I complimented him.

"Lookit this, Ike," he said. "I made up something very special for your little girl. Boy, will she love this."

Inside the box was an entire baseball team made of marzipan. He'd done the uniforms, the numbers, the gloves. One held a miniature sugar bat. And in the middle was a little girl, also wearing a baseball uniform, with the number 10 on the back.

"For ten years old," he said.

I smiled at him. He bounced his eyebrows.

"She'll like it, all right," I told him. "She'll go wild."

"Good. Kids should go wild on their birthday. Should have something to remember, hey?"

"Thanks, Henry."

"Bah." He waved his hand at me and went back to his oven.

On the way to Eileen's I noticed the trees turning up the white undersides of their leaves. Great pillars of clouds were building in the west. Whitecaps would be skimming Lake Ontario. Small-craft warnings would be up.

At the house, Gloria was already bouncing with excitement. "I wanna see, I wanna see!"

"No!" Eileen snapped. "Go out and play."

"Daddy, you're going to sit here. And when I tell you, you have to help me blow out the candles."

"Ten little candles, you can blow them out yourself."

"No, ten's a lot. I want you to help, because if I don't get them all, my wish won't come true. Promise?"

I made an X over my heart.

Eileen said, "What happened to you?"

"This?" I reached toward my cheek. "I was helping a guy in a fight."

"Ike, Jesus."

"With boxing gloves?" Gloria asked.

"No, sweetie, it was on the street. Some people got mad at this man and I had to help him out."

"Did you beat them up?"

"I didn't have to. The police came and calmed everybody down."

"Did you get me a present?"

I shrugged and looked innocent.

"And not clothes!" she insisted. "I want something fun."

I said, "You like bubble gum, right? Baseball cards?"

"I've got millions of cards." She wasn't exaggerating. Her enormous pack included three Warren Spahns and seven Yogi Berras.

"Go on now," Eileen said. "Your father and I have to make plans."

"Gum is not a present," she emphasized on her way out.

The battle plan was set: a dozen kids, balloons, food, plenty of pop, games, party favors, when to have the cake. Eileen worried these things into the ground. I reassured her, said it sounded ready to go. She needed ice; I agreed to pick that up on my way.

"Five sharp, Ike. It's going to be a madhouse. I'm counting on you."

"It's going to be fun. You should see the cake."

"And those things, poppers? I couldn't find them. Do you know anywhere? She loves those."

"I'll pick them up."

"Thanks." She jutted her lower lip and blew to lift her bangs and smiled. "She's so excited. Can you believe ten already?"

I shook my head. I had to fight off a reflex to kiss her good-bye. I took my leave and hurried to my car. Outside, the hot wind was running its fingers through the grass.

Events like this brought out the best of both of us, and suddenly the dead coals of our marriage weren't so dead. Twice we had tried to find some common ground. Twice it had soured and left Gloria with dashed hopes.

3

IN FRONT OF THE TIGER, Vicky had told me. I stood by thick wire mesh, my jacket over my arm, peering at the heap of plush stripes lolling in the shade. On no schedule, the animal flowed to his feet, stretched, and began to wander catty-corner across the cage.

The zoo was bustling with the Saturday crowd. Gusts of wind picked up a spiral of dust and twirled a handful of mustard-smeared napkins. Enough sun dodged through the towers of clouds to turn the air steamy. The wind muted the sounds of kids' excited babble and the tropical screeches from the bird pavilion; the heat intensified the jungle punk, the warm smell of popcorn and sawdust.

"You can never meet their eyes," she said. She was standing beside me suddenly, leaning on the black-painted railing. "They look at you, but they're always looking beyond. They're trying to remember freedom."

It was something she'd probably read in *National Geographic.* Her voice, it suddenly occurred to me, was laced, at all times, with an easy growl, a throatiness.

"I don't think so. Safety and effortless eating, that's paradise for a wild animal."

"In a cage?" In her poplin dress, she looked younger than she had in the Anaconda the other night, almost girlish. White-rimmed cat-eye sunglasses hid her eyes.

"There's no world outside for him. He carries his world with him. Not like you or me. If he has a mind, we can't fathom it."

"He's dreaming of the plains," she insisted.

I shook my head, unwilling to let it go. "We're the ones who worry about the past. You don't see animals shaking the bars."

"Still, he's beautiful." The big cat hesitated, twitched an ear, then stretched open his bristling jaws to yawn.

"If you haven't got your head in his mouth."

"You're hurt," she said. She instinctively reached a cool finger toward my bruised cheek. The touch hurt and felt good.

I shrugged off the question her eyebrows asked and said, "Any change?"

"I'm more and more afraid every day," she said. "He's been walking around on eggshells, snaps at me any time I open my mouth. I'm afraid he'll just haul off and break my neck. I can't sleep."

"Nobody can sleep. It's the heat. Has he had a tail on you?"

"Not today. I said I was going shopping. I was very careful. What have you found out? I need something to make him think twice. I have to have it, Ike, and it has to be good."

I watched the tiger lift a huge paw and lick it, the way a kitten does. "I spoke to Angela Grecco, some others."

"She knows what she's talking about, doesn't she? My husband killed those two women in cold blood."

I've never understood that expression, cold blood. "What she has is her suspicions. Others have their suspicions. Except for a speck of paint on Avis's fender, it's all guesswork."

"Guesswork is no good to me. I need to be able to threaten him and have it stick."

"I wish every mystery had a solution, like in the books."

"Either he killed them or he didn't."

"You say. But in the end, the truth is what you can find out. If it's beyond finding out, it's just an unknown. Let's get a cup, I want to talk to you."

We circled around the big cage where they kept the vultures. Two Andean condors with fluffy white collars stared at infinity. I bought a couple of coffees at the refreshment stand. We sat in the shade of red maples on either side of a wrought-iron table.

I gave her a rundown of my meeting with the Kerrs, Ceecee's idea it was suicide, Forlini's rumors, the other tidbits I had found out about Mrs. Petrone one and two.

"You can put it together any way you want," I said. "Call it Bluebeard. But life is no fairy tale."

"It can be. Monsters do stalk this world, Ike. I know that."

"Sure, and most of them live in here." I tapped my temple.

I planned to leave it at that. I was doing the job the client wanted done and she was paying me money to do it. Joe Petrone might have been a bully, but a wife killer?

Leave it at that. Yet I heard someone with my voice say, "I've gotta wonder, Mrs. Petrone."

"Please. Vicky."

"Vicky, you asked me to be discreet about this. Of course I'm going to be, it makes sense. But what about you? How discreet are you being?"

"I don't understand."

"Night Train Slade."

Her look was blank except for a tiny tightening of her mouth. The dark glasses made her hard to read.

"He's a Negro fighter. Know him?"

"I think I've heard the name. Joe likes boxing. He talks about it a lot."

"I understand you went out for a little joy ride with Slade a while back."

"What? Are you joking?"

"I don't think of it as a joke. To me it's very serious."

"What are you getting at? What makes you think . . . Are you implying that I have been friendly with this man?"

"People are saying you have a thing going with him."

"A thing?"

"Do I have to spell it out?"

"Yes, spell it out."

"Night baseball," I said. "Sex job."

Her nostrils flared and narrowed.

I said, "I'm just telling you what they say."

"What they say? People say things all the time. Most of it is lies. I didn't think I was paying you to tell me what people say."

"I guess that wasn't you watching him fight last night."

"You were spying on me?"

"I happened to be there. I saw what I saw. You tell me you think you've heard the name."

She squinted. "So what? My husband has an interest in boxing. He was supposed to be there himself last night. I went in order to sit beside the heavyweight champion of the world, not to watch a couple of morons punch each other's face in. The champ—didn't you see him? It's one of the bonuses of being Joe Petrone's wife."

"I saw."

"I cannot believe this. I can't believe I trusted you." She had a capacity for outrage that surprised me. It had me wishing that I had kept my mouth shut.

I said, "It seems to me somebody who's pushing the panic button about her mate's violent moods might want to be a little more careful."

"What the hell do you know about it?"

"What I see."

"I didn't hire you to investigate me."

"No, you were scared to death Joe Petrone was going to do away with you. If I run into a reason why he might want to, it makes sense I'm going to look at it."

"So I deserve to be killed? Is that what you're saying? Because of rumors? Because of lies?"

"You don't deserve it. But you hired an eye, sweetheart. An eye looks."

"Don't you sweetheart me! I paid you because my husband is a murdering bastard. I thought somebody might be able to help me. I was wrong. Did he get to you, too?"

"Look, I'm not judging you. I just think that—"

"Not judging? In your mind you've got me stripped naked so that that black buck can have his sweet way with me. Isn't that the movie that's playing inside your pinhead? Huh? Wham bam, jing jang, good night?" Her anger seemed genuine, but anger's an easy emotion to fake.

"You hired me to protect you. I do my job as I see it."

"Your job," she spit. "And when I'm dead—some accident, some rumor—you'll be sorry for about two seconds before you go out and buy yourself a drink with my money. You're like every man I've ever met. You know what you know and you'll never know what you don't know."

Anybody as edgy as she was should have been in a cold sweat to find out the world knew about her and Slade. Maybe this was her way of getting it off her chest. But she wasn't finished.

"You're not working for me anymore. I don't want to see you again." She leaned close and almost whispered, "If I do, I'll tell my husband that you tried to do me, that you diddled Joe Petrone's wife. See how long you live after that."

She scraped back her chair and walked away.

I sat there for a while over a second cup and watched the dappled light playing over the paving stones as I listened to the unearthly calls of the tropical birds. The atmosphere was as oppressive as the air in a cathedral. Gigantic white clouds climbed toward heaven. Static electricity prickled my skin.

Before I left, I stopped at a booth and dialed Angela Grecco's number. "I want to see you," I said.

"Likewise, pal."

"I made a wrong turn with your friend. I need to talk to you about it."

"How about dinner?"

"I can't. It has to be later."

"Meet me over at the Tic Tac. Say ten?"

"See you."

4

I STOPPED IN AT a luncheonette on a little downtown dead end
called Climax Alley. Earl Clear referred to the joint as his "office."
He spent a lot of time in a booth at the back, sipping coffee and
perusing the *Racing Form.*

It was the café of no illusions. The gray people who circulated
through there survived on coffee, cigarettes, Fleischmann's Blended,
and inside knowledge. They were city people, content with a world
of concrete, steel, and macadam. Physically, they all seemed to be
damaged—one had an empty eye socket, puckered like a navel; another was missing an ear; the face of a third had been torn in half
and sewn together seemingly without much effort to align the two
parts.

The management had installed a phone jack by Earl's table. He
sat with the receiver to his ear. I slipped in across from him and
waited.

"Two dimes on the seven," he said. "How's it moving on Malone's
Dream, the sixth? Okay. Hinky-dinky, parlay-voo."

He hung up, took a sip of coffee.

"Hot tip?"

"It's not the horse," he explained, "it's the price. You figure a price for a nag, then watch the odds. When he's a bargain, you bet him. A six-to-one colt going off at ten to one, I'm on him. I lose four out of five, but when I win, it's big money."

"So that's your system," I said. "And I didn't even have to torture you to get it."

"The hard part's not figuring the system. Any sucker can look at two or three years of performances, to see what's important. The hard part's not mixing up luck with God Almighty. Luck is just luck. You win five grand, that doesn't make you Saint Michael the Archangel. Start thinking you're the chosen people, you'll throw your money away chasing dreams of glory."

"How's it going today?"

He shrugged. "I'm down big on Panegyric, a golden filly in a six-board claimer at Belmont. I like the price on that animal."

The counterman put a heavy ceramic mug in front of me without my asking. The coffee tasted of scrap iron.

"Put Petrone on the back burner," I told Earl. "The guy I'm interested in now is Eddie Gill."

"I thought you wrapped that one."

"His name's come up from another angle. I think he's working a pimp operation. Plus, he has this place he calls Cavalier Realty—it's a front for something."

"Something, huh?"

"Okay, I'm groping. Ask around, see if you can get any word on him."

"Gill. I'll look into it."

I decided to drop into my own office and sort out some paperwork on a couple of background checks I was doing for a bond company.

The phone was ringing as I walked in the door. It was Duncan Kerr. He told me he had some information for me, would I meet him for lunch? Why not? I had lost a client that morning, maybe I could pick up a new one. We agreed to meet in an hour at his club.

I tried to get back to work, but in twenty minutes my sweat was smearing the ink and I was blinking to keep my eyes open. I decided to pack it in, have a drink in a cool bar before meeting Kerr. I was just going out the door when Paddy Doyle came storming up the hallway.

The beating he'd taken the night before had left him looking like an uncooked pot roast.

"I'm glad to see you're working on Saturday, Van Savage. What have you got for me?"

"An arsonist committed suicide last night. Or maybe he was murdered. I have a pretty good idea he was the one who lit your places. Who hired him and why, that's what I'm looking at now."

"Who? Why? You're fiddling, man."

"Does the name Eddie Gill mean anything to you?"

"Gill? You're fiddling while my places are burning. I've got the colored after me now. I can't walk over and look at my own property. Rents are gone to hell. Everybody thinks they can screw Paddy Doyle. Do you think you can screw Paddy Doyle, too?"

"No," I said. "And I don't want to."

"Then why in hell don't you do something for me?"

"You hired me to handle this. I'm doing everything—"

"Handle it? All you're giving me is a bunch of talk, it seems to me. Do you have one solid piece of information about who's behind this? Have you done one goddamn thing for me, all the dough I give you?"

"I kept you from getting your head beat in last night."

"Did you? Or were you there egging them on?"

"You were drunk, you were acting like a madman."

"I was the madman? Me? How many times do I have to tell you, it's the goddamn Italians?"

"You've told me. I'm on your side, remember?"

"Then why the hell don't you do something? I'm paying you to do something besides sitting around smelling your own farts."

"You have your suspicions. Even if they're correct, you need to have a plan. These guys aren't Boy Scouts you're dealing with."

"I've got a plan." He reached into his coat and pulled a revolver that glinted blue in a ray of dusty sun.

With his hand around the butt of that gun, he thought he had the world by the tail. But even the hoodlums, the smart ones, had learned that being pals with a politician makes you a bigger man than a six-shooter does. Doyle was a boy who had picked nickels off the ground until he had enough to make him feel he was somebody. He wasn't giving it up without a fight, even if it meant losing his life.

At the sight of the gun, I suddenly felt the heat.

"Put it away," I said. "You want to play that game, you play alone."

"Damn right I'll play alone. You gotta talk the language they understand."

"You're dreaming."

"The hell with you. I come to you because I wanted results, not a load of bullshit. You take my money and you give me nothing."

"You know something, Doyle? You're a pain in the butt. I've had it with you."

"You've had it? *I've* fucking had it. You understand me? I've had it with you and with all these dagos and all the cops that do their bidding. I ain't giving you another cent. And the boys in the back room are going to be looking out their asses before I'm through."

He rushed out, the gun still in his hand, slamming the door behind him.

Okay, fine. I'd lost two clients in one day. There were other clients. There were plenty of wives whose husbands were eyeing their secretaries' backsides. There were plenty of bookkeepers salivating over the petty cash. I had nothing to worry about.

Anyway, I suspected that I hadn't come to the end of this. There were too many threads hanging. Angela Grecco was one of them, and Duncan Kerr was another. And why did somebody mention the name Joe Petrone every time I turned around?

Just then, I was too tired to figure it out. I left the office, locked the door, and headed across the city through air so humid you felt you were underwater.

The Union League Club occupied a big air-conditioned mausoleum of a building off of Alexander. Duncan Kerr rose from a leather easy chair and greeted me cordially. His manner shared something with the quiet elegance of the building's interior.

In the bar, the walnut paneling and beamed ceiling whispered privilege. Billiard balls gave out quiet, expensive clicks as they rolled across the tables. A man in a white coat served us generous shots of expensive Scotch over ice. It was, I imagined, very high-quality ice.

"After you left yesterday I remembered something that might be important," he started. "It's about my sister's estate. There was a dispute."

He proceeded to give me a long-winded explanation of the trust fund that his father had set up for Avis, the provisions in the event of her death, the claims made by Petrone's lawyers, the legal finagling, the impudence, sheer impudence of the man.

Maybe I was a little thick, but I didn't see the relevance of it all. The fund had reverted to his parents, Petrone had pursued the matter no further. I guess for Kerr, money questions were always at the front of his mind. I was pretty sure that if Joe Petrone had killed his wife, it hadn't been for the money.

But maybe that wasn't the point. We moved into the dining room, where the ceiling was four stories high and the silverware polished to a brilliant gleam. The waiters, all of them black, wore white gloves and picked a warm roll out of a basket for you with tongs. Maybe he wanted to show off for me, give me a view of what money and position could buy.

Maybe he suspected that his fiancée was in the habit of taking to horseback in the hot sun in tight Levi's, that she would invite a private dick to watch and to pull her boots off afterward. He was the type whose nerves lay close to the surface. Perhaps it was her that he wanted to feel me out about, but this good taste kept him from raising the topic. Maybe he knew more than he let on. Maybe he was rich enough to hire detectives to follow detectives he hired—I imagined a whole pack of gumshoes, each one spying on another.

We often envy the rich, I suppose, but they pay for their privileges. When your money talks, you lose your voice. When your bank account clears a path for you, you lose your feel for the jungle.

As we ate our lunch, Kerr pumped me about my investigation. I didn't mention that my original client had kissed me off that morning. He was very interested in the parties I planned to talk to, how I would go about ferreting out the facts. He gave me the names of some of Avis's friends, ones who might have insights. He was very interested in the paint on her car—a definite clue, he thought. What did it prove? I told him it was too early to say.

"I must admit," he said, "I've always seen myself as something of a sleuth, Sherlock Holmes and all. How does your business work, Mr. Van Savage? I'm very curious."

"I talk to people. I listen. I watch. If their eyes drift up to the left, they're trying to remember. If they drift to the right, they're dreaming it up."

"Interesting."

"I always tell the truth myself, because the truth rattles people. Most people aren't used to hearing the truth."

"What is the truth about my sister? Forget all that we've said, all the innuendo. What do you think?"

"For lack of anything better, you go with the odds. Auto accidents happen every day. Murder almost never. Anything's possible. But anything isn't probable."

"I would like to believe that's true. A nagging suspicion is the worst. I can't disentangle the whole matter from my hatred of Joe Petrone. It's so easy for me to believe the worst about him."

"Do you know him well?"

He speared a hunk of chicken salad. "He would have liked to have gotten cozy. He even proposed that I put him up for membership here. Asked me point-blank."

"Did you?"

He laughed. "Can you imagine?"

"They say he's friends with important people."

"Not friends. Tolerated. Business is one thing. Can you imagine him at the next table? The people he would bring in? No. Things in this country are sliding downhill, but they haven't gone that far. Not yet."

5

MY APARTMENT CAME WITH a sleeping porch off the bedroom. I lowered the awning, took off my clothes, and lay down on
the cot.

Delicate. I kept thinking about that word. On the police force,
you learn: Don't let fear in the door, even a little fear. Because if
you do, he's going to invite his friends. And he's got a lot of friends.
And pretty soon, you're hiding under the covers and crying for your
mama.

I was working for a mobster's wife—or I had been. I felt like a
man walking through a pitch-black room. You never know when
you're going to bark your shin against the coffee table.

Tired as I was, I couldn't sleep. I lay there thinking and my
thoughts kept coming around to Angela Grecco. I'd had a few sweet-
hearts since Eileen, but I'd been careful with them. I had only been
wading. Now suddenly I felt as if I were in over my head. But hell,
one kiss? The way she drove a car with her skirt pushed up? The
way she laughed?

A fly was buzzing against the screen and some kids must have
been playing ball in the vacant lot on the next street. Their game

patter drifted over on a waft of breeze and sank like a pebble of memory into my consciousness. While the ripples were still spreading, I fell asleep.

Dreams, on a hot afternoon like that, don't stay inside your head. They seep out and haunt you, more real than the ominous clouds. You wake up with a distinct feeling that a gear has slipped somewhere.

I plodded into the house and poured myself some ice water from the pitcher in the refrigerator. It was later than I had thought. I needed to get ready and hustle over to Eileen's. I was looking forward to it and dreading it. I loved to spend time with Gloria, but when a dozen fourth graders got together, they inevitably turned into imps. I would be climbing the walls before the thing was half over, with Eileen shooting me daggers and the little ones whining with the heat.

At the same time, I anticipated with childish pleasure the look that would appear on Gloria's face when I presented her with the signed mitt. I figured if I took a quick cold shower I would make it over there—not on time but not late enough for Eileen to yap.

The icy spray had just blasted away the last cobwebs of sleep when an insistent hammering began on my door. Why not ring the bell? I wrapped the towel around my waist and went to answer it.

I knew one of them, Teddy Coates, a detective in the property crimes unit. The other was about six-two and must have spent time practicing blank looks in the mirror because he had the expression down pat.

"Keeping busy in burglary, Teddy?"

"I did such a good job, they moved me over to the persons unit. Now I get the juicy stuff."

"I'm glad for you."

"Want to take a ride?"

"No, I don't."

"We got orders," the younger cop said.

"You ready to back them up?"

"If you kick," he said, "we'll handcuff you and take you in on suspicion."

"You might need a riot squad for that one, sonny."

The guy puffed himself up but couldn't help glancing at Coates, who laughed.

"Do us a favor, will you, Ike?"

"Who's running the investigation?"

"Cahoon."

"I guess I have no choice, but let's get it over with, I'm in a hurry."

I sat in a windowless room at headquarters for almost an hour. I heard distant thunder, then the drumming of rain. Even in that box, I could smell the change in the air.

When I went to ask about the holdup, I found the door locked. I pounded on it until a uniformed officer opened up. He said he would pass the message on to Lieutenant Cahoon.

"I used to be on the job here," I told him.

"I know."

It was close to six when Cahoon finally showed.

Outside I could hear thunder like a distant artillery barrage.

"Sorry to keep you waiting, Ike. Paperwork, it's a disgrace. You know about that, correct?"

I told him about Gloria's birthday party.

"You know how this business is. Smoke?" He opened a box of long olive-colored cigars. I refused. He picked one and ran it under his nose. "Life's been hectic around here lately. A real madhouse. I'm hoping you can point us in the right direction on this case. It's a nasty one."

"Who's dead?"

His cheeks moved in and out as he set fire to the stogie.

"I want you to look," he said when he had it going.

Sheets of water were pouring from the sky with a demonic hiss. We took his car over to the morgue. It was in the basement—the rain splashing against the narrow windows near the ceiling gave it the ambience of a fish tank. They had three tables of cream-colored enameled steel where they did the autopsies. A row of metal drawers pulled out from the cooler.

"Cats and dogs, hey, Lieutenant?" a pudgy, mustached man said.

"The farmers need it, I guess. Number four, Carl."

I knew Orlo's face would be black and bloated, the skin a ceramic glaze. You tend to steel yourself for a sight like that by tightening the muscles across your stomach and pressing your tongue into the roof of your mouth.

"Yeah, it's good for the crops," the little man said. A draft of frigid air tainted with a sharp disinfectant seeped from the cooler as he pulled open the drawer.

Lightning sent a shiver of blue light through the narrow, barred windows.

Being a cop, being in war, it builds a delay into your reactions. When you're on sentry, you learn not to jump at every sound. You can be alert and still take your time. You learn how to keep cool when the shit hits.

When he rolled the drawer out, I thought he had grabbed the wrong one. They don't cover the corpses with sheets the way they do in the movies. It was a woman's face, not the gargoyle I expected. She was staring at the ceiling through milky eyes—it was Sandy Mink.

I glanced involuntarily at Cahoon, who was looking at his cigar as if it had spoken to him. His eyes came up to take in my reaction.

I turned back to the naked corpse. Her relaxed lips uncovered her teeth, giving her a knowing, slightly amused look. The hint of a smile was caricatured in the arc inscribed deeply into her throat.

Cops will tell you they can look at anything. They've seen the worst and whatever comes along is cold fish. It's not true. You may have seen brains splattered, or a body mangled in a wreck. But then the simple slit across a girl's throat blindsides you. I felt my stomach heave.

In an instant, the world became too small for me. I wanted to run out of that stifling basement and keep on running. I wanted to run all the way to the lake and dive in. I wanted to swim out and never stop.

Instead, I took out a cigarette, lit it, and examined the corpse in front of me. She appeared younger than she had in life. Her nose hadn't quite taken on adult proportions. Her bones were slender, the skin stretched taut over the points of her hips. Her breasts puckered into little smiles at their tips. A gossamer of foxlike hairs licked up her belly. Her thighs were long, knees bony, toes pudgy like a child's.

She seemed impossibly young to me, maybe because she had no future. Gloria would be eighteen the day after tomorrow and a young mother of twenty-five next week. Sandy would never experience those ages. Her life would be a child's, an adolescent's, then nothing.

There can be beauty in death. The skin takes on a white translucence. The peace that settles on the features transforms them. The stillness invites your gaze to linger, to notice the complex curve on a lip or an ear, the mild extension of a fingertip.

A flash of lightning squeezed in again, washed her fragile limbs. An angry clap and roar followed almost immediately.

"Know her?"

"Her name's Sandy Mink." My voice sounded hollow, as if I were speaking in an empty gymnasium.

"We found your card in her brassiere. What's the story?"

I told him about Gill, her date with him, my surveillance. I mentioned that I had talked to her at the hot dog stand.

"What about the wife?"

"She came in yesterday. I gave her the report."

"How did she take it?"

"She was interested in saving the marriage."

"Upset?"

"No more than you'd expect. What happened?"

He stroked his chin while he studied me for a second. "She lived in a slum, over on Cicero Street with her mother. But the mother was in the habit of staying out late, sometimes a couple of days late. She says she came home this morning, made herself some toast. Rye toast, with butter and sugar. She was eating this toast and drinking a Hires when she wandered into the living room and found the girl and a lot of blood. She knows nothing from nothing."

"That throat's the cause?"

"Most likely. We'll know more when they cut her, which will be when, Carl?"

"We've been up to our ears, Lieutenant. They're out to supper now, planning to get at this one tonight."

"A shame," I said. The word came out a little twisted.

"It's always a shame," Cahoon said. He took some time relighting his cigar.

I didn't want them to close the drawer. I didn't want to think of her in the dark, in the cold. But they did, and it slid to rest with the impersonal sound of a cash register.

As we drove back to headquarters, Cahoon smoked in silence. I spent the time thinking about Sandy, her laugh, how she had joked with Gloria and how she had sized me up, ultimately deciding to trust me.

In his office, Cahoon asked me more questions. I told him what I knew about Gill.

"I saw them last night."

"Where?"

"I think it was him. I can't be sure. And the girl. The Tic Tac. I should have . . ."

"When was this?"

"Two-thirty maybe, a little later."

"We've already talked to Gill's wife. Funny, she didn't mention your name."

"What did she say?"

"That he was home last night. Closed up his business and got in about one and went to bed."

"That's his story?"

"We haven't located him yet. Checked the stand, they haven't seen him. There's something wrong, that guy."

"How do you mean?"

"Just some connections we're trying to run down. He's on the fringe. Can you give us a definite statement, seeing him at the club?"

I shook my head. "I never saw his face."

"You know what the girl's mother said? 'These kids today. Noth-

ing but trouble.' She finds her daughter with her throat sliced, nothing but trouble."

"Thanks, Mom."

"On top of that arson job, too. I'm getting too old for this."

He took a sip of smoke and said, "Anybody with you last night?"

"For an alibi?"

"For my information."

"A woman named Angela Grecco."

The cigar had gone out again. He took the chewed stump from
his mouth and looked it over meditatively. "Grecco? Who runs Gleeland? What's your business with her?"

"That concern you?"

"Not if you know what you're into."

"I know what I'm into."

"Do you? You know she operates a vice racket outta there? One
you took a strong interest in at one time."

"What are you getting at?"

"The Lucky MacAdoo thing." He smiled. "You didn't know, did
you? She had you busted off the force. If bygones are bygones, fine.
But I gotta wonder."

"Where'd you get the dope on it?"

He shook his head. "You should have asked me back then. You
didn't. You were on the glory train. Okay. Now I'm telling you. That
dame has clout. First you're messing with Joe Petrone, now you're
sniffing after Angela Grecco. Yeah, I gotta wonder about you, Ike."

6

IT WAS DARK BY the time Cahoon enlisted a patrolman to take me back to my office. Streetlights were smeared across the pavement. I picked up the mitt, which I had wrapped in blue tissue paper and a pink ribbon. The card said "For a teenage slugger. Love, Daddy."

The main part of the storm had passed, but heat lightning was still making the sky nervous. Fireflies reacted to it, flashing frantically in the trees. The steamy air was clogged with the perfume of electricity, maple leaves, and wet asphalt.

I knew there was no reason to hurry now. But I did hurry. I almost skidded off the slick road halfway to Eileen's.

"Well," Eileen said. She crossed her arms. "Well, look who's . . . Hey!"

I pushed the door out of her hand and went inside. There was no sign of a party. The Hoover stood in the middle of the living room.

Eileen liked to clean things up. When we were younger, we would throw parties, lots of people, lots of drinking. She had fun, though it was always too easy for her to take a step back and see a mob of drunken yahoos. She would get this look on her face. Anyway, by the end I'd be ready to hit the sack or I'd be singing sea chanteys on a rolling ship. She would always stay up and clean. No sign of debauchery would ever be left at dawn.

"Don't." I held up my palm as if fending off a blow. "Start."

"You don't want to hear?"

"Where is she?"

"In bed, where did you think she'd be at this hour?"

I turned toward the stairs.

"Ike, you can't . . . She's sick!"

I stopped halfway up.

"Four of them," she said. "They ate that marzipan after big slices of devil's food and upchucked all over the place. I had to explain to the mothers. It was nice. We couldn't go outside because of the rain. She kept asking Where's Daddy? You didn't call. No word, nothing. I was half worried something terrible had happened. I couldn't imagine you would just forget. Then those Miller twins got into a hairpull, I thought they were going to kill each other. Judy Pensler knocked over my mother's Dresden unicorn. The horn's broken off. Two hundred years old. Somebody poured grape soda on the living room rug. Oh, it was a load of fun. Too bad you couldn't make it."

On another level she was trying to read my face. I don't know what it looked like, but it felt pretty raw. I continued up the stairs.

Gloria wasn't sleeping. By the night-light I could see that her eyes were open. They didn't look at me. They stared at the ceiling, just the way Sandy's had.

"Hi, sweetheart. Happy birthday." I switched on the bedside lamp. My hand was shaking. "I brought you your present. I know you're disappointed I wasn't there. I had to do something."

"You promised."

"I know I did. I'm sorry. But you know how, sometimes, you want to do something but you can't? I wanted to be here but I couldn't. Look."

She moved only her eyes.

"Look. Don't you want to open it? I'll do it for you. Wait till you see."

I started on the wrapping. When the ribbon wouldn't untie, I ripped it with my teeth. I tore the paper.

"See," I said, "it's a MacGregor. And look who signed it. Look what he wrote. Right there. See?"

"I don't want it. You said you'd help me blow out my candles. I didn't get my wish and I threw up."

"Luke Easter signed this especially for you. Look what it says. I'll help you break it in. We'll rub it with neat's-foot oil. That's the thing for a glove, neat's foot. Makes it nice and soft. Neat's foot. Okay?"

"I hate you."

"Look at that stitching. Real rawhide. Look at that pocket."

"Where were you?"

"I had to work, darling."

"You always have to work. Mom cried."

"I'll make it up to you. We'll go out to a ball game."

"I'm ten now."

I held my breath. A decade suddenly loomed in front of me.

"Don't," I whispered. "I know you're mad at me. But don't. Please."

Her lower lip was trembling and she refused to look at me again. A thick silence filled the room. I put out the light. I went to kiss her forehead, but she jerked away.

Eileen was watching from the doorway. We exchanged a glance as I left the room.

"She'll get a kick out of that glove," she told me downstairs. "You know she will. She's just feeling low. You know how birthday parties never match our expectations."

"What does?"

She shrugged. Her eyes were rimmed with red. "What happened to you, Ike?"

You see a woman's face in a passing car. She looks at you, looks into you, and your heart leaps with a yearning you can't explain.

For a second my gaze connected with Eileen's. I wanted to tell her. I wanted to embrace the mother of my child. I wanted to hold the woman who had been my lover and my best friend. I wanted to hide under the covers of her sympathy.

The car moves on, the face is gone.

"Good night," I said.

"Are you okay, Ike?"

"Sure, I'm okay."

7

A ROUGH-EDGED WIND WAS still blowing raindrops around outside. I climbed into my car, swallowed a couple of bennies dry, and headed for the Tic Tac Club.

I knew it was past ten and I hoped Angela wasn't waiting for me. I hoped she was. I wanted to see her, I didn't want to see her. I felt like strangling her, I felt like making love to her.

Mostly I needed some drinks. I needed to see people having a good time, dancing and turning their backs on the darkness. I needed to wipe away the image of a dead girl, an image that kept tangling with the image of my cruel, hurt daughter.

I stood in the raised entryway of the club for a long time scanning the raucous revelers. Smiles and laughter, perky bosoms and flounced skirts, the tinkle of ice, the happy thump of the jazz band, the slow shuffle of bodies on the dance floor. Nowhere a familiar face. Nobody waiting for Ike Van Savage.

I pushed across to the bar and settled onto a thickly padded stool. The mirror behind the ranks of bottles was not clear but tinted with pink bronze and decorated with chrome spangles. The whole place was reflected there, an image of heaven as a dreamy nightclub.

God made problems and God made booze to drown 'em in, the saying goes, or should go. I had the man in the white coat pour me a double shot of Old Grand-Dad and draw a glass of Genesee lager. Heaven and earth shall fail, but a boilermaker never faileth.

Maybe at the morgue they were weighing Sandy Mink's brain. Or scraping under her fingernails. Or examining her heart. They would sew her up afterward, but she wouldn't be pretty any-more.

The beer jacked the bourbon right to my brain. The bourbon set fire to the Benzedrine. Colors became softer and brighter. The music flowed like honey. Ice cubes turned to jewels.

The band was playing a whimsical version of "Glow Worm," which the Mills Brothers had been singing when I shipped out to Korea. For some reason, it made eight years seem like a long, long time.

"If you'd stood me up again, I would of killed you."

I turned toward her tight smile. She fingered a strand of her unruly hair and put it back in place, a flirty little gesture.

The smile slowly faded. "What is it?" she said with alarm.

"I missed my little girl's birthday party."

She tented her eyebrows. "Aw."

"A teenager who came to me for help is lying on a stainless steel tray. Somebody cut her throat."

Her face became all concern. "God, Ike."

"I think she was being roped into a chippy scheme."

"That's terrible."

"You should know." I caught the bartender's attention and pointed to my glass. "Drink?" I asked her.

"What are you talking about, I should know?"

"When I was on the police I was laying for a pimp by the name of Lucky MacAdoo. I knew he was just a straw boss. I didn't know that the operation he worked for had juice up to the top. So I got set up and busted off the force."

I showed her my teeth.

She stared at me for a second, as if she didn't understand. Then she burst out laughing. "You didn't know? My God, Ike. And you're supposed to be a detective?"

"You think it's funny," I said flatly.

She stopped laughing. "What did you expect me to do, close down? Serve time? Join the rosary altar society? I was handing out the payola and I expected to be left alone. It was nothing personal."

"It was to me."

"We should have talked. We could have come to an arrangement."

"I wanted to send you to jail."

She barked a laugh. "That's the problem. But why should we crab over it now? I said no hard feelings. It was business."

"Peddling human flesh? That's what you call a business?"

"Get off your damn high horse. I didn't even know you. Now you come around here, accuse me of killing somebody. Who the hell do you think you are?"

"Was Gill pimping for you?"

"Who?"

"Eddie Gill. He's a regular here. You've never heard of him?"

"Gill? Yeah, I know who he is, a wannabe, a loser."

"He may have been a loser, but he got girls for you, didn't he? Huh? Turned out underage snatch?"

"You're outta your gourd. He never got me nobody. I remember him hiring girls *from* me a couple of times. They didn't like the blubber, but he always handed out enough coin to make up for it."

"I thought you ran a kiddie park."

"Are you joking? That place has been in the red for years. You can't make money in legitimate business, Ike. Didn't they teach you that in second grade?"

"So you make your money from the sex trade."

"What did you think, I took in laundry on the side?"

I spit on the floor.

"I'm not ashamed of what I do," she said.

"Why should you be?"

"That's right, why should I be? All the company men, the big shots, they're the ones who should be ashamed. All those Kodak men with the wife and kiddies, their house in the suburbs, going to church on Sunday. Damn hypocrites, coming slinking around looking for a good time after dark."

"Who cares if you're breaking the law."

"Listen," she said, "I don't have to justify what I do to you or anybody else in the world. They keep it illegal just so they can put the squeeze on me. Talk to the preachers and politicians if you don't like it."

"Listen to you. Why don't you go peddle your line of bullshit to someone who's buying? I've had enough of it. I've had enough of you and your racket friends and their wives. There's a big lake out there. Go take a running jump."

She looked at me for a long moment, her eyes active and her mouth poised. She shook her head once, then turned and walked away.

Of course, even as I was chewing her out I knew she was right. She hadn't done me wrong. Both of us were just wheels in the big machine. It wasn't personal. Nothing's personal about a machine.

Benzedrine opens space inside you for booze, burns it up as fast as you can put it away. I was more sober than I'd been in a long time, I thought.

"Whaddaya know, Van Savage?" a voice said behind me.

He slipped onto the padded stool beside mine and snapped his fingers at the bartender, who said, "Of course, Mr. Delmonico."

Another shot, another beer appeared in front of me, a glass of vermouth for him.

He reminded me of Sinatra. I don't know why, he didn't look like Sinatra. Maybe it was the Wildroot hair and the sharpness of the eyes. Maybe it was just the fact that his name was Frank. He adjusted his cuffs before he said anything else.

"What is it about women?" he asked. "You think you have them figured, and Jesus."

I lifted the glass in his direction. He mimicked the gesture.

Frankie Delmonico was a guy in the know. He had a law degree from Fordham. He knew lots of people in New York City, knew all the state pols in Albany, knew the movers in Rochester. He had been associated with the Petrones for years. He knew who to talk to and who not to talk to. He knew dirt. People were afraid of him. He could place articles in the papers at will.

"You know they say curiosity killed the cat? Women are a lot like cats, I guess. They can't leave well enough alone. They have to find out what's inside the box. That the way you see it?"

I said, "I remember a woman, she'd been in a couple of movies. She had a real sweet face. You might even say beautiful, except that word's kind of overworked these days. Blonde, natural even. Her husband owned a tavern on Driving Park. He was the jealous type."

"You know what I learned a long time ago?" His mouth turned up on one end and down on the other. "I used to be kind of a dreamy guy, believe it or not. When I was in college I used to torture myself, who am I, all that. First year of law school, a professor I had—he'd been a very tough prosecutor, worked with Dewey—he said, 'Francis, introspection is overrated.' That's been my motto ever since. And I think it applies to a marriage, too. I should know, I'm on my third." He chuckled.

"The real jealous type," I went on. "He didn't like it that men looked at his wife, even though he'd married her for her looks. He suspected her, the old two-time. So he hired a guy. The guy got hold of some hydrochloric acid. You know how it feels, when that stuff starts working on your skin? Your eyes?"

"Did you hear about Mickey Rooney? He got hitched again. The headline was PINT MARRIES FIFTH. Good, huh?"

"The pain, they say, is really memorable. Of course, it was hard to get acting jobs afterward. Men still looked, but not for the same reason."

"Women get so curious," he said, "they hire private detectives. Hit this man again, Sid."

"Give us a round," I said. "And take it out of here."

"You're putting it away tonight, Van Savage. I don't know if I can keep up with you."

"The acid thrower confesses. He points the finger at the husband, even produces the cash he's been paid. So what happens?"

"Everybody deserves a fair trial, it's the American way. Or don't you agree?"

"He gets a lawyer who knows which strings to pull and he walks. And divorces the wife on top of it, he can't bear to look at her. American way?"

"Let's talk some raw meat here, okay? That Petrone broad is nuts. You keep poking your schnoz into places it don't belong, you're going to be wishing all they'd done to you was throw a little acid. Okay?"

"I get it. You're the guy who squats behind the guy."

"Now, be nice. Joe likes the ladies. His heart pulls the strings in his head. That's his only problem. He doesn't kill them. Just the opposite. But he can't abide somebody digging into his business. Why? Not because it would embarrass him. *Others* would be embarrassed. They trust him and Joe can't let them get egg on their faces."

"You are full of shit."

"She's paying you, right? You're a businessman. I'm willing, right now, to make up for any losses. See this?"

His hand, below the level of the bar, held a fan of bills. They were clean, no wrinkles, and bore designs and portraits I didn't see that often—Grant and Franklin.

I don't think I had cold-cocked a guy since a free-for-all in fourth grade. The stool gave me no leverage—Delmonico swiveled with the blow, which probably saved me from a broken hand. He went down, the money scattered. For an instant the band hesitated. The hum of conversation wavered expectantly.

Delmonico rolled into a fetal position. I planted my feet on the floor and drew my leg back to kick him. I felt a blow to my chest. I landed on my back and somebody suddenly sucked all the air out of the room.

I recognized Bobo Palermo. He'd grown half a foot since last night and had put on forty pounds.

But he had two legs. Two legs, they taught us in basic, is not a stable platform. You can always topple a guy if you push in the right direction. I thrust my own leg straight out and caught him in the right knee. His head slammed the edge of a table as he fell.

He lay there dazed for a second. Before he could regain his feet, a couple more guys, also big, were on the scene. They worked for the place and talked with the soothing menace of professional bouncers.

Then the clarinet player stood up and gave out with a wild tood-leoo, the boys picked up the beat, and everyone went back to Saturday night. The whole thing lasted probably five seconds.

Frankie Delmonico was rubbing his jaw and smiling. Palermo ordered a hooligan even bigger than he was to get down on all fours and retrieve the money that had scattered under tables. He didn't like having to do it, and he glowered at me when he finally stood.

Bobo touched his arm and said something that calmed him down. Then Delmonico came over and stood next to me, the bouncer mediating between us.

"It never occurred to me you might be fucking Joe Petrone's wife," he murmured. "I hope she's worth it."

He was readjusting his cuffs as he walked away.

8

I WAS NO LONGER in the mood for the forced gaiety of the Tic Tac Club. I was tired of tough guys and gangsters and gangters' wives. I climbed into my car and started driving, no destination in mind.

As usual, I headed for the lake. I drove to Charlotte and walked onto the pier and watched lightning irradiating the insides of thunderclouds. I imagined every flash pouring down cold light onto Sandy Mink's skin, illuminating her white teeth, her questioning eyes. The vision, charged by the bennies I'd swallowed, began to rattle me.

I drove back downtown along Lake Avenue. The area around Mill Street, on the west bank of the Genesee, was not a place where most people would choose to live. It was just above the high falls and it had been industrial since the days when they diverted water to run the sawmills, the machine works, and the old trip-hammer forge. Rats lived in the gorge and sometimes would come out by the thousands to soak up the moonlight. A damp malty smell drifted from the breweries across the river. The few houses that backed up to the precipice were unpainted relics of another era.

It must have been well after midnight. I found myself climbing

the staircase that ran along the outside of one of the houses. It led
to an attic apartment.

I knocked. No light showed from inside. I hesitated. Go home,
Van Savage. I knocked again. I couldn't face having to trudge back
down those stairs. I couldn't face being alone. I stood watching the
water go over the falls and thinking no thoughts.

Finally the lock clicked and the door came open a crack and an
eye looked at me.

"Hi, boss," Penny said.

"That girl is dead, Penny. Gloria hates me and I'm half drunk."

She answered with a sympathetic smile. She let her door swing
back. She was barefoot, all legs in her baby-doll pajamas. "Come
on in."

Her apartment was under the pitch. The ceiling sloped to the
height of a chair back and a big gable projected out the back toward
the river. The windows let in the angled glow of the downtown lights.
A couple of candles burned on a battered trunk that served as a
coffee table.

"Tell me about it," she said.

"Drink first."

"Black Velvet's all I got."

I nodded. She poured half a tumbler of it over ice and cut it
with a shot of 7-Up. She made a weaker one for herself. We sat at
the table in her little kitchenette. The oilcloth was printed with she-
loves-me-not daisies.

"I was over at that fire last night," I said.

"Oh, God, I read about it."

"This is no joke, Penny."

"I know."

"This whole thing is no goddamn joke. The man hired me. I
started wondering if it was really arson, he had so many violations. I
couldn't find the answers quick enough. Somebody's children died.
Somebody's daughters."

Her cool fingers patted my hand. "I was going to go out to Sodus
for the weekend," she said. "A couple of girlfriends and I went in on

a cottage at the Point and they're having a big festival out there, their sesquicentennial. But I read about those kids and I couldn't go. I was too sad."

"Sometimes the world turns queer," I said. "It's happened to me before. Nothing sits right, nothing fits."

"Because you're human. Tell me what happened."

I talked for quite a while. I rambled. I talked about sides of beef, giant chicks, Night Train Slade. When I told her about finding Zanek, the flies, Penny grimaced. When I described Sandy in the morgue, she pressed her fingers to her lips and closed her eyes.

"I was the only one for her," I said. "Her one hope. The one person who could have helped. And I was careless about that, too."

"You did care. You would have helped her."

"What I have never gotten into my head, Penny, is how urgent, how really urgent, life is. It's a lesson I never, never learn."

"You couldn't know. It's fate, Ike. The cards are stacked a certain way, no matter how many times you shuffle them."

I got up and I stepped to the window. "If I really believed in fate, I would walk out of here right now and go over that cliff."

"You're so poetic. Let me cool that down for you."

On the sink a candle burned in a wine bottle covered with layers of colored wax. As she stood in front of it cracking ice out of the freezer tray, the light penetrated the gauzy fabric of her top and outlined her shape.

Below, two ropes ran to a telephone pole. Laundry was hanging out, in spite of the evening's rain. I could hear the rumble of the falls. She handed me my glass.

"Just like Sam Patch," I said. "He stepped off."

"Who?"

"They don't teach you in school anymore? The famous daredevil who challenged the Genesee. Friday the thirteenth, eighteen-something. He jumped from right over there."

Penny stepped close to me and rested her hand on the small of my back.

"A cold wind was blowing," I said. "Maybe he thought about it too long, I don't know. Maybe he was drunk. But goddamn it, the man stepped off. A hundred and twenty feet down. That took guts."

She raised herself on her toes and leaned to look out.

"It went all wrong," I continued. "He flailed his arms, hit flat. They waited and waited. They said it was a trick. But next St. Patrick's Day a man broke the ice down at Charlotte to water his horses. Found Sam frozen in a block. The preachers said Patch was a fool. 'Some things can be done as well as others.' That was his motto."

"It's a foolish motto." She padded over to the couch and folded her legs under her. I sat beside her.

"You're right," I said. "Foolish."

"Look, Gloria loves you. You've gotta let her have her moods. In her heart she loves you."

"I should have worked it out with Eileen. Broken home, what's that do to a kid? Long term, what's it do?"

"Never think about the long term in the wee hours," she said. "You could use a little of this." She held up a cigarette wrapped in paper the color of wheat straw. She put it to her lips, leaned toward the candle, inhaled deeply, held her breath. An exotic, weedy aroma filled the room with ideas.

She offered it to me, I drew in the pungent smoke. I was no reefer addict, but that night I would have tried anything.

We passed the stick back and forth in silence. In my head I began to feel a sensation that was like a chord played on a pipe organ.

"There are nights when this stuff gets me through," she said. "It's the trapeze that lets me swing over the rough spots."

"You? Rough spots?"

"Sure. World War III, Little Rock, gray-flannel men running the world. We've both looked behind the scenery, my friend."

She took one more puff and deposited the remaining scrap in a glass ashtray, grinding it out for what seemed like half an hour.

As the quiet deepened I closed my eyes and listened to the cascade, letting the sound merge with the whisper of blood rushing through my veins. I could feel the exact dimensions of my skull etched in a prickle of electricity. My head started to tumble the slow tumble of the tumbling tumbleweed.

I opened my eyes to watch Penny putting a record on her phonograph. The sound of a jazz combo drifted into the room, little snatches of simple melody repeated and twisted and reflected. I sank back into darkness—the music carried me. It formed and erased itself.

"What's left?" she said, her voice music, too. "What you do and what you are, Captain Midnight. You care about Gloria, about that girl, about Eileen. Caring's painful. You walk down the street, you tell the truth, you stand up for people. That's what's real. Everything else, one big dream. As the actress said to the bishop."

Her smile brought a smile to my face. Some of my anxious thoughts had evaporated and I felt better. I patted her knee.

"She knew something," I heard myself say.

"Who knew?"

"Avis. Petrone's second. She found out something."

"Let it go, Ike. For tonight, let it go. Listen to Monk." She pointed to the record player. "The world is coming apart and Monk knows it, feels it."

She was right. Every note was a beautiful omen, a child skipping rope through a graveyard.

"Once, after a concert," she said, "Monk sat at the piano, on stage, for half an hour. The audience didn't know what to do. Sat there listening to the silence. There's hope, he's saying. Hope is small and common and easy to mix up with the coins in your pocket. It's easy to drop in a jukebox by mistake. Or a parking meter. Or something." She smiled a honey-coated smile. Her eyes were drooping to half-mast.

She stretched along the couch with her head in my lap. Her hair felt like fine silk to my fingers.

"It's 'Straight, No Chaser.' Can you dig that?"

"She knew something," I said. "But what? What was it?"

"Listen." She was making tiny movements with her shoulders,

her bare thighs, her hands. She was dancing minutely to the staggering, inebriated music.

I put my glass down and closed my eyes. "There's hope," I said, repeating her sentiment.

For an instant, before I drifted off, I believed it.

SUNDAY

1

THE SUN HIT ME in the face early. I was stretched on the couch under a blanket. Penny danced out of the bathroom in bra and panties, drying her hair.

"I hope you don't mind using a Lady Schick."

"Coffee," I croaked.

"Coming up, boss."

I washed and shaved and drank the cup of Turkish java she made in a complicated brass contraption. It was thick and left a powdery taste in my mouth but it jolted me awake.

I could see now why she wanted to live in this godforsaken section. Her apartment caught the morning sun and came alive. Outside, the falls was making a clean hiss and throwing up rainbows.

On top of that, Penny had read a lot of philosophy and might have had some communist sympathies, for all I knew. Her notion of solidarity with the masses might have included living among the poor. Plus anything exotic appealed to her.

We went to a clattery short-order restaurant around the corner for breakfast.

"I appreciate your taking me in last night," I said, breaking the yolks of my poached eggs. "I needed a port in a storm."

"I know a little about storms. How do you feel?"

"I've felt worse. Did I tell you I punched out Frankie Delmonico at the Tic Tac last night?"

"Are you bragging, or warning me to get out of town?"

"Just letting you know life is likely to get complicated."

"Complicated? I'm all grown up now, Ike."

"I'll say." I bounced my eyebrows.

"Such a romantic." She sipped her fresh-squeezed and winked.

We talked about Sandy Mink and what might have happened to her.

"When I went to work for you," she said, "I told my friends I'd be solving murders. It was going to be a groove, like on *Peter Gunn*. But Christ, Ike, I can't stop thinking about that kid."

"How did she seem when she came in?"

"It's hard, knowing what happened, not to make all kinds of judgments. Why didn't I see it? Why didn't I care about her more, do something for her? I feel like it was my fault."

"You did just what you should have. Anyway, that's then."

"But Sandy was so haunted. I should have interrogated her on the spot. I should have pulled it out of her what was the matter."

"No regrets. That's something you better get through your head or you'll never last in this business."

"You think it was that guy Gill?"

"I saw the two of them at the Tic Tac—*thought* I saw. Her mother found the body around nine, at ten the coroner judged she'd been dead six hours, that puts the murder at maybe four. Gill's the type—at least I can imagine him being the type. Plus, this link with the rackets."

"What rackets?"

I told her about the real estate company.

"I've got Earl digging up background on him," I said. "I think the wife had an inkling. She didn't say so, but I got the sense she was afraid of him, afraid of what he might do."

"There's no end to it, is there?"

"The evil that lurks in the hearts of men? Nope."

I stood up, took her face in my hands, and told her I loved her, which I did. More and more. "Thanks for everything."

"You mean, nothing. I'll tell you one thing, after church, I'm going back to bed with the funnies."

2

THE GILLS LIVED IN a new housing development off of Latta Road in the town of Greece, northwest of the city.

The streets of the development were laid out in graceful curves without sidewalks, the way the suburbanites liked them. The houses, one after another, were identical in every respect: split level, big picture window, two-car garage, neat foundation shrubbery, blank lawn with one anemic sapling, fake gaslight on a pole by the black-topped driveway. They were all painted pale yellow or washed-out salmon or pastel blue. Occasionally somebody got really daring and added a plaster deer out front or a little cast-iron Negro holding an invisible horse.

I wouldn't be surprised if half-crocked husbands came home from work, walked into the wrong house, and were halfway through dinner before anybody noticed.

I found the number I wanted and saw Mrs. Gill watching me as I came up the brick walk. I pushed the flesh-colored button that made gongs sound inside. Her hair was in crimpers and she still wore a bathrobe.

She invited me in and offered coffee. The living room furniture was hard and square, one of those sets you buy at Sears—everything matches, including the *Autumn Sunset* on the wall opposite the television set. She had that tuned to Bishop Sheen, who left off rubbing his hands together and gave his silken cape a swish. He continued his wheedling murmur as we talked.

"I have been bothered," she said. "Police. You know?"

The coffee cup she offered was fragile china with a handle that I couldn't get a finger through. It rattled a little as I picked it up.

"Of course I know. I was the one who sent them. Are you aware of what happened? Do you know what your husband did?"

"My husband? What you talk?"

"That girl is dead."

"I don't believe you. Better you mind your own business. I don't know nothing."

"You know your husband was fooling around with a young girl. You know what happened to her. The police told you that, didn't they? How somebody cut her throat?"

She shrugged, bent her mouth down on both ends.

"Where is your husband, Mrs. Gill?"

"Gone. He's gone away. The police, they asked me."

"I'll bet they asked. You know, it doesn't look good for him to disappear if he is innocent. It's evidence they can present to the jury. Guilty flight."

"Guilty of what? Of course he's innocent. Do nothing. He don't know the girl who die. Never seen her."

"I watched him grope her. I took pictures of it. Remember? What are you, crazy?"

"No, you crazy. I paid you, watch him, not talk to police."

"That girl was murdered, Mrs. Gill. I saw the two of them together just before it happened."

She shook her head. "Eddie was here."

"You're lying."

"What you calling me, my own home? You don't know. My husband was here. He sleep that night, all night. Never go out."

"Of course he went out. I saw him." Or did I?

"You lie! Liar, you don't know nothing."

"I know a person is dead."

"Person? Slut?" She spit the word.

"Did you confront him? Did you show him the pictures I gave you?"

"What pictures? I burn pictures."

"You told him you knew about him? Yes or no?"

"He is my husband. I don't have to say nothing. That is the law. A wife don't have to say nothing against husband. You understand? The law of the land. My husband did not know this girl, did not see this girl, did not touch this girl."

I returned my cup and saucer to the tray. In the quiet I noticed Bishop Sheen writing on a chalkboard and saying in his flighty whisper: ". . . and they said, 'Ye men of Galilee, why stand ye gazing up into heaven?' "

I said, "Of course he knew her. She worked for him. He took her out. I have copies of those photographs."

"Took her out, so what? For fun."

"To a motel."

"For fun. Means nothing. You are a sick man, Mr. Savage. You look at through keyholes. Sick."

"I get it. Deny the nose on your face and you won't smell the stink."

"What you talking, nose? Go home. My husband was here that night. Wearing pajamas. Nowhere else. Pajamas. You go home."

"You're not doing him any good, you know. The longer he hides, the worse it is for him."

"Worse? Okay, good-bye. See you in hell."

She was standing now, opening the front door for me.

Driving away along those loopy streets I thought of something. Many of the houses had a basketball hoop over the garage, or a swing set in back, a kiddie pool, bicycles, toys. And I saw kids here and there, playing war in their side yards.

But at the Gills' I had not seen a child or a single sign of a child. She had told me they had four. Something wrong there. What the hell else had I missed?

3

I TURNED BACK EAST and swung out toward the lake. Gill's hot dog stand had just opened. The young man who had waited on Gloria and me was unwrapping sausages and slicing each one with a knife. They curled as they cooked, and he had to keep pressing them with a spatula.

The man did not have an appetizing face. Years of acne had left his skin pocked. The pimples stubbornly persisted on his neck and nose, some flaming red, about to erupt. Behind this stormy mask, his features were actually fragile, like those of a librarian. But the blemishes were what you saw first, and his awareness of his appearance imbued his eyes with a permanent sadness.

His name was Ronny. Assistant manager. He said Gill hadn't been in, that he didn't know when he might be around.

"If ever," he added, bitterly.

"Did you know Sandy Mink?"

"You going to ask about that? The police came to my house. Got me out of bed. Just like *Dragnet*. They wanted answers. Where was I, this time, that time? Mr. Gill. What had I seen? When did I see it? Who? Why? Where? I was still in my pajamas. It was a pain."

"How do you feel about the whole thing?"

"Too bad."

"Did Gill kill her?"

First he laughed. Then he shook his head violently. "Why would he? He could get all he wanted. He wouldn't do anything like that."

He told me Sandy had worked there since Memorial Day.

"Did you know Gill was plowing her?"

He gave me a furtive glance and swallowed. "Sure," he said, jutting his meager chin. "She was like that."

"Like what?"

"She was always twitching her ass around. She was hot for it. I can tell."

"How do you tell?"

He sniggered. "You can tell. You can smell it."

"Gill smelled it?"

"They go for him. All the girls. Why?" A little smile came over his features, as if the idea gave him hope. He wanted badly to believe that you could win prizes in this world with something other than good looks.

"I don't know, why?"

"He's got money and he don't mind spending it. He's got a flashy car, a gun. He knows people."

"He carries a gun?"

"Sure. He handles a lot of money, he needs one." He continued to lay hot dogs on the grill.

"Did you like Sandy?"

"Me?" It stopped him, as if he'd never thought about it. "I guess, why not? But I never. I told the cops that. I never."

"You sorry she's dead?"

"Sure, I'm sorry as hell." He looked at me with desperate eyes that told me the tough-guy act was wearing thin. In two seconds his tears would be sizzling on the grill. It was a sight I wanted to avoid, so I decided to leave it at that.

I drove over to Cicero Street. A bunch of rail lines that served the factories on the northwest edge of the city crisscrossed out there. Blocks were short, houses grimy. The whole area smelled of ash, pig iron, and whatever chemicals Kodak happened to be dumping out the back door. A dirty blanket of clouds creeping in off the lake made it that much gloomier.

I climbed out of my car and approached a group of women seated on chrome and vinyl kitchen chairs a couple of houses down from the place where I had watched Sandy climb the stairs to a house at dawn.

"Any of you know Sandy Mink?"

They hummed a variety of tunes as they looked at each other.

"Her mother around?"

"She's gone to her brother, lives out in Brockport somewheres." The woman who spoke wore a dirty housedress and beat-up bunny slippers. "Cops got after her, leavin' that kid alone."

"Sandy was a good girl," an iron-haired lady offered.

The others nodded in agreement.

"Her mama shouldn'ta left her alone so much," the first woman said. "You invite bad in the door, it's gonna sit down at your table."

"You can bet it was somebody she knew," said a woman whose young cheek bore a raspberry birthmark.

"Why's that?" I asked.

She shrugged. "Who would it be?"

I asked if Sandy had any close friends in the neighborhood. Rhonda, one of them said. Was she Sandy's friend? Some thought yes, some no. They threw the question around for a few minutes. I let them talk.

Where could I find Rhonda? They looked around as if she might be hiding in one of the windows or on the roof.

Finally they told me she might be at the playground, where the kids hung out. A carrot top, one said.

I walked the three blocks. A dozen children of all ages were idling about the dirt playground. A stiff-armed girl passed me, roller skating precariously.

I approached the redhead who was stretched out on the center of a teeter-totter, perfectly balanced, hands propped behind her head, staring at the sky.

When I said her name she shifted her weight so that her feet slowly descended and her head rose. She looked at me with red-rimmed eyes.

"You police?" she said.

"No. Have they talked to you?"

"No." She sat up all the way, the board came to rest on the ground, and she straddled it. "I thought they would, but they didn't. I wouldn't have told them anything anyway."

"I spoke with Sandy, talked about helping her. I'm a private detective. She needed help, didn't she?"

"I can't stand it, what happened to her. She was good. She didn't deserve that. Bad people deserve that. Why did it happen to her?" She fished a crumpled pack of Larks from her shorts and put one in her mouth. I lit it for her.

She might have been the same age as Sandy, but her knobby knees and big eyes made her look younger. Her face was wild with freckles, her hair a bright orange mass of curls.

"She was afraid of something, wasn't she?"

"Yes! That man."

"Gill? Her boss?"

"Yes. He gave her a lot of money. A lot."

"What did she tell you?"

"They ate bamboo shoots. It's Hawaiian or something. Then he took her to this place, like a bar. She said it was just like being in the movies, everybody dancing and laughing, a real orchestra. He ordered her a liquor drink. She said it was sweet and had cherries in it. It tasted like candy. She drank a lot. She got tanked. Everything was going around and around. He put her in his car. She woke up in this room, a motel. She didn't want to go there with him. Then she got sick on her dress. He told her to take it off. He'd bought it for her and said she had to."

She stopped and chewed on her lip.

"Then what?"

"She felt like she was going to puke again and she had to lie down. Then he was on top of her and he pulled her underwear down and he did it."

The idea seemed to strike her as both horrific and exciting.

"She never wanted him to," she added.

A little posse of younger girls came sprinting past. They were dragging a plastic snake on a string, screaming as if it were chasing them.

"Was that all of it?"

"No. The money. He gave her money and she didn't know what to do. He wanted her to go with his friends. He said they would give her money, too. All she had to do—you know."

"Did she go out with him the night she died?"

She shrugged and held her hands up as if feeling for rain.

I asked her about boyfriends, enemies Sandy might have had. Sandy didn't neck or anything, she told me. Everybody liked her, pretty much. She didn't know why they had to do what they did.

"I should have helped her," she said.

"What could you have done?"

She wiped her nose on her sleeve. "Killed him."

She gave me a ferocious look. As if all you had to do was get a gun and shoot all the evil-looking men in the world. Any fool could do it, anybody with enough guts.

She told me Sandy's mother's name was Peets, not Mink. Her father never came around and Sandy had thought he'd gone to Texas, which was where he was from, or Alaska.

"Could you do me a favor, Rhonda?"

She nodded. A sob was closing down her throat now.

"I want you to buy a bouquet of flowers for me," I said. I handed her a twenty from my wallet. "Nice ones. For the funeral. Whatever's left, you keep."

Sucking in shallow breaths, she looked at me with her big, suspicious eyes. Finally she nodded and took the money. I turned once to look back. She was stretched out again on the battered board, tilted to a point of equilibrium, and staring at the mournful clouds.

4

THE NIGHT BEFORE, I'd read in the paper, a pitcher for the Pirates, a little journeyman hurler by the name of Harry Haddix, had walked to the mound at County Stadium in Milwaukee and had held the mighty Braves hitless for twelve innings. No walks, no errors, not a single man had reached first base. In the history of baseball, no pitcher had ever thrown twelve perfect innings. The game went scoreless into the bottom of the thirteenth, and even the opposing crowd gave him a standing ovation.

Then an error, a man on. He walked Aaron on purpose. The next man up hit a home run. Haddix lost the game. He was thirty-three and must have known he would never pitch so well again. It was, according to the paper, the most heartbreaking loss in baseball history.

Heartbreak, it seemed, was in the air.

Gloria was waiting on the front steps, chewing on a jelly doughnut and looking as glum as a rainy day. When she saw my car, though, her face brightened in a way that made my own spirits soar.

"You ready?" I asked her.

"Let's play catch first," she said.

"We haven't got much time."

"Please?"

"I'll throw you a few."

"Hard ones."

She put on the glove I had given her and pounded her fist into the pocket. She scooped up the grounders and pegged them back to me, not always on target but not out of my reach. I threw her a fly ball.

"Higher!"

Another one. She caught it.

"Higher."

I heaved one as high as I could. It shrank in the afternoon sky, traced a bit of an arc, and began to descend. I winced as she stood under it, looking up, her glove wavering. I had a vision of the speeding ball slamming into her nose. That would finish me. She staggered back, her eyes closed, and the ball slapped into the web of her mitt. She looked at it, yelped her pleasure. She threw it back and demanded it still higher, but we had to go.

"Wait!" she said. She ran to the porch and grabbed a handful of wilted dandelions.

When we were moving, she said, "I picked you flowers."

I thanked her and told her to grab my jacket and put one in the lapel button. We were friends again.

Being an adult, though, I couldn't leave it alone.

I said, "You see, honey, the things you look forward to, that you think are going to be wonderful, a lot of times they aren't as fun as you think they'll be. But other things, like playing catch together, they can be great."

"I know," she said dismissively, her serious mouth rimmed with confectioners' sugar. She never mentioned the birthday fiasco and never said thanks for the mitt.

We reached the stadium on Norton Street just before the anthem.

The Red Wings had been a St. Louis affiliate for years and had fielded some decent teams in the early fifties. Then the Cardinals decided to sell off a lot of their farm teams and the Wings almost folded. Some community people got together to sell stock to the public and buy the team so they could keep baseball in town—one of Rochester's better moments.

That afternoon they were facing Richmond, a club we loved to hate because they were allied with the mighty Yankees.

"Do you know the names of the two dogs and a rabbit?" Gloria asked me. The pitcher, Howie Nunn, was popping the ball past the first Ohio batters and seemed to have his control problems in hand.

"Lassie?" I guessed. "Bugs?"

"No, I mean the ones they sent into space, the Russian ones."

"You've got me there."

"They were Courageous, Snowflake—I like her the best—and the bunny was Marshoo, Marshfoosh, something like that. Only, we sent up two little monkeys that were so tiny, they were like this, Dad. You could hold them in your hand. Baker and Able were their names. They were cute. But which one was which?"

She looked cute herself in her pink pedal pushers and her red Wings shirt. It was still hot, but the sky had cleared, the grass was emerald, we were in the heart of summer, and the sound of the ball couldn't have been cleaner.

"They rode in a Jupiter rocket," Gloria said. She knew all the rockets. "Did they have a window, do you think?"

"I think they must have."

"So they could look out and see the earth from space. I wish I could. Would you be scared? I wouldn't. I want to do it because it would be like going to heaven. Do they let girls be astronauts?"

"They might later."

"They should."

In the middle of the fourth inning, with the Wings a run down, Earl Clear slipped into the empty seat beside Gloria.

"Pluck your magic twanger, froggie!" he said.

"Hi, Mr. Clear."

"Secret message from headquarters," he said out the side of his mouth. "Got your decoder ring?"

"No," Gloria said. "I don't need it, I'm in disguise. Tell me the secret."

"They're on the beach."

"Who are?"

"Little green men. They're taking over. Over and out."

"You silly! You know who I am?"

He looked at her gravely, picking the remnant of a cigarette off his lip. "Ida Lupino?"

She spurt laughter. "I'm Fury! And now I know your secret! I can conquer the world."

"Sure you can. Do me a favor." He handed her a five. "Some dogs and a drink."

She looked at me. I nodded.

"Will you keep score?" she asked me.

I told her I would try. I always bought her a scorecard, and she filled it in with little pictures and symbols that she made up. By the late innings she was drawing portraits of women with eyelashes and Veronica Lake hair.

She took the money and said thanks and ran up the steps toward the tunnel.

"Nice day for a game," he said. "Howie's got the curve working."

"He can throw when he wants to."

"I got something on Gill. Talked to Penny, she said you were out here. Thought I'd drop around and give it to you."

"I talked to the wife," I told him. "She's covering up for him, but I think it's a matter of time before the cops run him down."

"Don't count on it. I heard from a couple of Arabs over on Plymouth Avenue. This Gill is not all hot dogs."

"I know." I mentioned the real estate connection.

"The word I'm getting, he's some kind of foxhole buddy of Joe Petrone. Done some gun work for them."

"Interesting. You think the dead girl might have found out?"

He shrugged. "Maybe it's why he thought he could douse her, no questions asked. I don't need to tell you, that crowd has a pipeline straight into the police. I wouldn't count on them turning Gill out.

That girl's gonna be off the front pages tomorrow and forgotten by the end of the week. She sure don't rate rousting a friend of the big man."

"I guess we'll have to do it ourselves."

"What about Petrone's wife? I thought she was sweating bullets."

I gave him the story in a nutshell, Slade, Vicky's pique, the run-in with Delmonico.

"I don't like it, Ike. We're bumping up against Petrone from too many directions."

Gloria came down the steps loaded with hot dogs and drinks. I quickly picked up the program and scratched in some commentary on the inning, which had consisted of a walk, a single, a liner back to the pitcher, and a double play.

"I got you a hot dog, Mr. Clear," she said, "but I didn't know if you liked sauerkraut so I didn't get it because I don't like it."

He thanked her and assured her he could take it or leave it alone. She handed me mine, which was heaped with kraut. She gave Earl back the change from his five. He said she could keep it, but she shook her head.

"And I got everybody orange pop. And Cracker Jacks for dessert." She pulled the box from her waistband.

I handed her back her scorecard and described what she'd missed.

"Think Gill's routine is Mann Act stuff?" I asked Earl.

"Those guys, anything's possible. That's why I thought you should know your man's not the Lone Ranger."

"Who's not the Lone Ranger?" Gloria asked.

"This jazzbo from Kokomo. We found out he's not the Lone Ranger. You know why?"

"He doesn't wear a mask?" she guessed.

"Right. And no silver bullets."

"Oh, yeah. Where's Kokomo?"

"Just outside of Timbuktu, about a half a mile from Kalamazoo."

"I like the zoo."

"So do I. I like to see the elephant's trunk and the camel's hump."

"I like the monkeys. Do you know the names—no, do you know who Baker and Able are?"

We ate our hot dogs. Earl stayed for a couple more innings. He told Gloria some fascinating stories about when he played semipro ball before the war. That was news to me, if it was true.

During the seventh-inning stretch, he took off. The Wings looked sharp that afternoon, for a change. They'd given up a run in the fifth but played good defensive ball to keep the score tied. In the bottom of the eighth Luke Easter launched a homer that must have made it into Irondequoit Bay. Gloria jumped up and down and screamed, "Luke!"

The crowd buzzed about it right through the top half of the ninth when Al Pehanick set them down in order. We left, satisfied that we'd seen some good ball.

5

I THOUGHT I COULD save some time cutting through the back streets. But north of Andrews we found ourselves caught in thick traffic. Up ahead, we could see whirling yellow lights and necklaces of helium balloons strung over the roadway.

"Look!" Gloria cried, as if she'd caught sight of Oz. "Let's go see!"

I knew it must be the St. Francis of Assisi festival. Rochester's Italian population had filled in this area around the turn of the century when it was still known as Sleepy Hollow. Eventually they melted into the rest of the population and after the war began to escape to the suburbs along with everybody else.

The festivals still drew crowds back to the old neighborhoods. The St. Francis of Assisi parish church was a large rococo building where one priest would still hear confessions in Italian. Every summer they turned the block into a bazaar and set up kiddie rides in the parking lot. Third-generation managers at Bausch & Lomb danced the tarantella in the street and politicians fell all over themselves to see who could eat the most Italian sausages.

Gloria loved festivals like this. I couldn't deny her. We paid a little boy in a crew cut a dollar to park in his family's front yard, and set out walking toward the action.

Warm weather, huge crowd. They were trying to hold a parade down the middle of the clogged block. A band and a bunch of teen-agers holding flags were pushing slowly along the street. They were all dressed in yellow satin shirts and black pants, with bright purple sashes. The flags were all colors, with insignia of lions and castles.

The trumpets and the trombones were both playing "Funiculi, Funicula," but at two different tempos. It got to be like a frenzied race, with the tubas plodding along in the rear. The saxophones had gone completely off the reservation and were wailing what sounded like "That's Amore." Dancers formed a conga line and snaked be-tween the rows of musicians, who were marching stoically in place.

We crossed the street behind the band to get to the rides. We had to cut in front of an open Caddy carrying Miss St. Francis. Perched on the back deck, she was a pretty Italian girl in a strapless gown that she kept tugging up. Her enthusiasm knew no bounds—she waved so frantically you expected her hand to fall off. The swirl of the crowd brought us up against the car, which had come to a standstill. I turned. The beauty queen, her eyes glittering, leaned over and planted a kiss on my cheek. That spontaneous act gave me a welcome little boost.

Behind her, a coughing cub tractor pulled an enormous horn of plenty. Mixed with the crêpe-paper fruit was a television set, lawn-mower, stereophonic record player, and other goodies you could have on the installment plan. Little girls in crinoline were flinging hard candies at the masses in self-defense.

I looked around for Gloria and didn't see her. Normally, I wouldn't have thought much of it. I would find her a few minutes later by the cotton candy concession or watching the man who made butterflies out of molten glass.

For some reason, though, I was gripped by a strange urgency. Too much had happened in the last few days. The crowd was too boisterous. Maybe my nerves were stretched too thin.

I made my way down the line of booths constructed from two-by-fours and canvas. They sold gobs of fried dough, and paper bowls overflowing with spaghetti, and plates of squid sloshing in black ink. Forlini had the biggest stand, offering fragrant Italian sausages or enormous meatballs on crusty bread with fried peppers. Patrons crowded to buy.

Farther down the line, red and black and white wheels spun with a ferocious ratcheting sound, and players leaned to take chances on dolls in wedding dresses or bottles of liqueur or homemade cakes. Sweaty faces crowded the Under-and-Over table, the Chuck-a-Luck. The shooting parlor rang with the snaps of .22 rifles as men tried to obliterate clay trolls.

My eyes kept scanning the faces, kept swiveling toward every child's voice. Bodies pressed against me, breathed wine into my face. I climbed the steps of the church to get a better view.

No good. My eyes were growing frantic—I wanted to look everywhere at once. I plunged back into the crowd.

In the center of the block, multicolored lights crisscrossed above the street. They glowed brighter now as the sky faded toward evening. They gave the place a feverish Christmas air, tawdry and full of forced merriment. To me the scene was becoming a nightmare.

Another band, this one beefed up with three accordion players and a couple of gondoliers with fiddles, was blasting "Lady of Spain" from a platform in the park across from a row of dirty brick apartment houses. Normally it was a place where old men gathered to play bocce and talk about city politics. Now a cyclone of dancers swirled in the little square. Men were hooking elbows indiscriminately with women, giving each other a fast turn and flying apart to latch onto new partners.

As I moved through the crowd, a large, no-neck woman in a peasant costume took my hands and tried to spin me. I shook my head at her. She opened her mouth to laugh. She leaned backward and I stumbled trying to keep her from toppling. I pulled violently away.

They kept picking up the tempo until the musicians couldn't play any faster. The clapping and shouting of the crowd kept pace. A point came when they all just blew a final note and stopped. Everyone laughed.

The dignitaries were taking their places on the front part of the stage. I spotted Vicky Petrone. She sat down on a folding wooden chair and looked bored in her white gloves and pillbox hat.

In the relative quiet that followed, I heard faint lilting music. On the edge of the park, the throng had opened a space in front of a bronze statue of a World War I doughboy. I clawed my way through the spectators and caught sight of an organ grinder and his little monkey.

The machine had a maroon fringed apron hanging down and was giving out "Stranger in Paradise" as the grinder turned the crank. He wore a peasant shirt and a whisk-broom mustache. His eyes kept rolling back in his head as if he were trying to remember the words. The monkey was mimicking soft-shoe steps in the clearing.

Gloria was squatting in front of the legs of the onlookers, her chin propped on her fists. When she saw me, she ran over. "Can I have a dime?"

"Where have you been?"

"Please?" She gritted her teeth with impatience.

I handed her a coin. She got down on her knees and waved it at the monkey, who sashayed over, now carrying a tin cup. Gloria dropped the dime into it. The monkey quickly removed his fez and gave her a little bow. Everyone laughed. Gloria held out her hand. The monkey took hold of her finger and shook it. More laughter.

The music ended and the little animal worked the crowd for more coins.

"Did you see?" Gloria said. "He liked me."

"I want you to stay with me," I said as casually as I could manage. "Don't go wandering off."

"Okay. Can you buy me a balloon? I saw a clown with balloons."

"Maybe later. I want to watch the speeches."

"Why?"

"Come on."

I moved near the front of the podium. Next to Vicky, a man had turned in his seat and was talking with two characters behind him. He turned back to the front and I took some time to study him.

So this was the mighty Joe Petrone. He wasn't as old as I had expected. He resembled a man who had thrust his head out the window of a fast-moving car. His plastered hair, wedge-shaped nose, and thin lips all made him look aerodynamic. He was dressed like a men's shop mannequin.

A couple of city councilmen sat on either side of him. The brassy buttons of the chief of police gleamed in the electric light. Miss St. Francis was still kissing people; her dress had slipped to reveal some unsaintly cleavage when she leaned. Bobo Palermo was seated two rows back, his arms crossed, his eyes cast upward as if wary of pigeons.

A man who looked like Jerry Lewis stepped to the microphone and adjusted the red, green, and white sash across his chest. He put his mouth too close—when he spoke a squeal of feedback drowned him out. He looked over his shoulder at a technician.

Then the loudspeakers began blasting his voice, echoing it from the buildings across the street.

"Wunnerful, wunnerful day. Isn't it? So glad to see all of you out here having fun, fun, fun. Let's hear it. Let's put 'em together."

Gloria was gripping my pinkie tightly. "Look," she said. "There's the clown. Can I get one?"

". . . our community. A tradition that really goes back to ancient Rome. That's right, Caesar, Nero, the great emperors of yesteryear. Makes you proud."

I saw them nodding on the platform. Bobo Palermo was nodding. Vicky rubbed her teeth across her top lip and let her eyes rake the crowd.

". . . whose contribution to making Rochester one of the finest, most wunnerful places on earth! Now . . . further ado . . . great pleasure . . . that son of Italy . . . Mister. Joseph. Anthony. Petrone."

They erupted into an applause that reverberated from the buildings. Petrone had appeared tall enough sitting, but when he was on his feet you noticed his bantam legs. He made up for his stature with a pronounced strut. He stood there nodding his head, waiting for the crowd to settle down.

"Come on, Dad. Please."

"Not now, honey."

"He's going away."

At that moment, my eyes connected with Vicky's. She was nervously crossing and recrossing her legs. She frowned when she saw me. She made a tiny gesture with her hand that could have meant "see me later" or maybe "stay away from me." She glanced at her husband with a look of impatience.

"Thank you, my very good friends!" Petrone's husky voice boomed through the P.A. "What a day for the Italians! Eh, cumpari! Huh? Eh, cumpari!"

That got them stirred up.

"Just hold your horses," I told Gloria. "I want to hear this."

"What horses? There he goes."

". . . to thank our wonderful mayor, our city manager, Bishop Kearney, all the wonderful people who . . ." Petrone spoke with a silky, professional voice.

The spider, I thought, can look quite innocuous. It's the web you have to worry about.

"When I look across this great city . . ."

Gloria tugged impatiently at my hand. A flock of pigeons leapt from the roof of the apartment building opposite. The air above the street split in half.

Joe Petrone took two scissors steps backward.

You learn to keep your head. Most people, in an emergency, can only see what's directly in front of them. They react wildly or not at all. Adrenaline takes over and they lose control of time.

I squatted, pulled Gloria between my knees, and held her head down. I began to waddle toward cover.

I saw guns come out. I heard two more shots at street level. Glass broke in windows across the street.

On the stage, Petrone began a reverent genuflection. Halfway down, he collapsed and fell heavily onto the plywood. Palermo bent down over him. He held a square automatic pistol and was cringing, his eyes frantically scanning the crowd. A uniformed police officer hunkered behind the wooden lectern for cover.

Chaos erupted. People shouted and pointed in ten directions. The crowd began to move like liquid in a sloshing tub, heaving this way and that.

Standing but still hunched, I swept Gloria forward and pressed against the side of the platform. Just above us, Vicky was down on her hands and knees, along with most of the band members and the dignitaries. I grabbed her arm. She gasped and clung to my neck. I eased her off the stage and set her down on the dirt.

More shots. I hauled Gloria and Vicky over a low iron railing and behind a thick sycamore.

They were jumping from the platform in all directions now. A man holding a trombone leapt. He fell, the bent horn went clattering. A priest put his arms out as if he could fly, jumped, and landed hard on his rump.

The bystanders were running, leaping, tripping, and shoving. Each shot sent a fresh spasm of panic through the crowd.

I picked Gloria up and held her in my arms. She buried her face against my shoulder.

"Daddy," she whispered. She pressed closer, gripping around my neck. "You be Captain Midnight."

"That's right, hon. Don't worry."

"Are they shooting?"

"Somebody is."

"Make 'em stop, okay?"

"The police will. We don't have to worry about anything."

Vicky was breathing rapidly, her eyes wild. The shooting stopped. I put Gloria down.

"Stay with the lady, okay, sweetheart?" To Vicky, I said, "Don't move. Hold on to her and don't move."

I moved back to where I could see the platform. Two men with guns were standing over Joe. They weren't tending to him. They knew he was dead and so did I.

A lot of shouting was coming from across the street. A dozen men were exiting the building directly opposite. Three of them in the center, all wearing windbreakers, were goose-walking Night Train Slade. He looked a lot more dazed than he had when Kid Blik had tagged him.

Bobo Palermo held his pistol jammed into the notch under Slade's jaw, causing him to walk with his head tilted to one side.

The crowd started to pull itself back together. They were yelling, waving fists. "Killer!" went the chant. "Get him!"

Slade's arms were pinned behind him. A gash along his left temple was spilling blood into his ear.

The hoods didn't seem to know what to do with him. He almost fell from their grip as they dragged him down the stairs.

I stepped back behind the tree.

"What is it?" Vicky demanded. "What's happening?"

"Slade. You still say he was nothing to you?"

"Yes! Are you crazy?"

I looked into her eyes. They steadied for a second. "Well, it's him and that don't look good for you."

"What are you talking about?" she said. "What's happening?"

"Let's get out of here. Now."

"What about Joe?"

I didn't answer that one. I picked up Gloria again and gripped Vicky by the arm. I started backing up so that I could keep an eye on the activity in front. In that instant, Palermo pulled the trigger.

In the movies, a man will convulse when he's been shot. If you've ever seen it in real life, you know it doesn't happen that way. A head shot drops a man instantly. He goes as loose as spaghetti all at once. It's a sight that can make you queasy.

Slade disappeared from sight.

Police whistles and sirens were mounting toward a crescendo. I led Vicky through the park and along a back street. Now that the shooting had died down, gawkers were rushing back to see what had happened.

I turned and we hurried out of the park on the other side. We

walked quickly down the sidewalk, turned a corner. I put Gloria
down.

"Were they playing a game, Daddy?"

"I don't know what they were doing."

"Can we look for that clown? I want a balloon."

"We have to go home."

"But I want one."

"You can't have everything you want. You know that."

"Yeah, but . . ."

We reached the car. Vicky got in back. Gloria sat beside me and
cried. She didn't know exactly why she was crying, so after a few
sobs she gave it up and knelt on the seat to look at Vicky. She told
her her name. They got acquainted while I maneuvered through the
chaotic traffic. We passed police cars and an ambulance going in the
opposite direction.

I shook a cigarette from my pack and pointed it over my shoulder
at Vicky. She reached for it with her lips. I took one myself and
punched the lighter.

"Let me!" Gloria said when it popped. She carefully held the
lighter for Vicky, then for me.

My eyes kept glancing at the rearview mirror as I cut across the
city.

"You know what I want to be when I get big?" Gloria asked Vicky.
She was desperate to make things normal, a trait she'd gotten from
her mother.

"Let me guess—a singer on television, like Dinah Shore? That's
what I wanted to be."

"No, a cowgirl. I love cows and you get to sleep out every night
and ride a horse. And I want to go scuba diving like on *Sea Hunt*.
But mostly, an astronaut. Because in space you just float around.
There's no . . . what is it, Dad?"

"Gravity."

"There's no gravity so everything just floats."

On the block where I used to live, quiet reigned. Katydids were
trading three-beat insults from their perches in the trees.

"Honey," I said to Gloria, "tell Mommy I'll call her up when I get home and explain about all the craziness and the shooting and all that, okay?"

"Okay."

"We don't want her to worry or anything, so don't—I mean, you can tell her, but don't make it seem too . . ."

"I know. I'll tell her about the monkey."

"Yeah, tell her you shook hands with a monkey."

"And Luke hit a homer. And we saw a parade. And Mr. Clear gave me money for hot dogs. And orange pop." Her eyes narrowed and she looked at me with a sly grin. I didn't want her to get in the habit of lying, but she loved conspiracies.

She said good-bye to Vicky, collected her scorecard, the glove, and her Wings pennant. She kissed my cheek and climbed out.

Vicky shifted to the front seat. We waved to Gloria and took off.

"I want to put you on ice until the dust settles. Knock off a guy like Petrone, there's bound to be fallout."

"Is he dead?"

"As vaudeville, baby."

She broke out crying. A guy she loathed. And she wasn't faking. You figure it out.

6

I DROVE UP GOODMAN and cut over to Oxford. I didn't ask her anything more until we were inside my apartment. Her sobs had quieted down by then. She went into the bathroom to freshen up.

First I called Eileen and gave her a sanitized version of the fracas at the St. Francis shindig. Funny, she said, Gloria hadn't even mentioned it. Next I telephoned Penny.

"Earl called," she said. "He tried to reach you. Rumors are flying. A blowup at a church festival. Get this—Joe Petrone got shot. They don't know—"

"I was there."

"You were? What happened?"

"They killed him. The shooter's dead, too."

"Earl says the cops are on the lookout for the wife. So are the racket boys."

"She's with me."

"Oh, that's lovely. What are you going to do?"

"Lie low for now. Anybody who sticks his head up is likely to get it blown off, this atmosphere. Earl pick up anything else?"

"Every hoodlum in town is walking around with a loaded gun and they all think she was behind it."

"That's good to know. I'll be here until I figure my next move. Maybe you'd better have Earl stop over when you hear from him again. I might need help."

"Be careful, Ike. The game's for keeps, you know."

"I know. Straight, no chaser. See you."

I fixed us a couple of CCs on the rocks. She thanked me, sipped her drink, and shuddered.

"They put you on the spot," I said.

"What do you mean?"

"Somebody wanted your husband dead. They spread stories about you and Slade so there'd be an easy trail to follow after they got him to do the deed. Hell, the rumor was issuing straight from the police bureau. They're going to nail you for the murder."

"That's absurd."

"If the mob doesn't get you first. Rule number one with those guys: You hit them, they hit you back in spades."

"Joe was going to kill *me*."

"Keep saying that. It's a good motive for popping him."

"You don't believe I did it, do you?"

I stared at her. Again, I got the feeling of eyes looking from behind a mask. I couldn't believe the mask, but I trusted the eyes.

"I need your help," she said. "I was wrong yesterday. I knew it afterward, but I was too proud to call you."

"If I'm going to help you, I'll have to find out who ordered the hit on your husband."

She wiped her palm across her forehead. "There are so many who hate him. He had to keep them all afraid."

"Are you sorry he's dead?"

"It's funny. You detest a person, but you can't get happy over him dying. What happened back there, anyway?"

"Slade was in a window across the street. Probably used a hunting rifle. He must have planned to run out the back, but they got to him before he made it. Odds are somebody was waiting for him."

"Why would he do it?"

"You put him up to it." I raised a hand to stop her protest. "You hated Joe. Divorce was not an option. You were afraid. A tough guy you were sleeping with told you he could solve your problems. You went for it."

"I need you to believe that's not true."

"What is true, you and Petrone?"

"The whole story?"

"Start from the beginning." I paced up and down the room.

"Where does anything begin? I didn't have it easy as a kid."

"Who does?"

"Okay, forget that part. I left home when I was fourteen. I got started on the wrong foot. I'd grown up in the southern tier, Elmira. I came up to Rochester, moved in with my cousin. I waited tables, married young. Gary was a handsome louse. I thought he was supposed to support me. It didn't work out that way. I had to keep working, plus I got a taste of this."

She showed me her clenched fist.

I grabbed the bottle and poured her a refill. We clinked glasses. I stepped over to glance out the front window.

"What happened to him?" I asked.

"He told me he was a welder when he worked. He liked to gamble. Sometimes he scored big at the track and we lived the high life for a while. He came home one day all hunched over and bleeding through bandages. He had drilled a hole in a finance company vault and had poured in two ounces of nitro—it blew before he was ready. He was a mess."

She noticed I was staring down at the street and stepped over beside me.

"Keep back."

"What is it?"

"Just a couple of guys talking. They pulled up in that Lincoln. Recognize them?"

She put her eye to a crack in the blinds. "Yes. That's Nick

LoQuasto, the one leaning on the fender. The other one I don't know."

"LoQuasto a friend of Joe's?"

"Sure."

I saw the other man lift his head. I snapped the blinds closed. I motioned her back to the couch and sat on the arm of the chair opposite her.

I said, "So that stuff about you being a spring chicken when you married Petrone was malarkey."

"I guess. I'd seen a few things. Gary went squirrelly after his little accident. He drank and he kept telling me men from Mars were putting wires in his teeth. He would get violent like that." She snapped her fingers. "I put up with it until I couldn't put up with it. Maybe I should have had more patience with him."

"What happened?"

"I killed him."

That made me sit up. She was staring at the cubes in her glass.

"The sweater girl," I said. I remembered the case from the papers. They'd been living in Lackawanna, south of Buffalo. The jury convicted her but recommended leniency. The Sweater Girl Murder, they called it, because of one shot of her in a tight pullover. I think she got four years.

"Gary could be a bastard, but he didn't deserve what I did to him. I don't know why I did it. I mean, I knew why at the time, but I shouldn't have. I wasn't so perfect." She fell silent. Her face had turned sad. Her beauty struck me as genuine for once, not a glamour mask.

"So you got out of jail," I prompted.

"I went back to what I knew. Hostess, this time. I used to sing with the piano some nights. I was determined not to make the same mistake twice. I wanted the cush, Ike. I wanted a man who wasn't afraid of himself. I wanted somebody who could keep me in the style I wasn't accustomed to. In prison down at Bedford I lost my romance. I wasn't in the market for fairy tales anymore."

"Then you met Joe Petrone."

"Yes."

"You understood just what you were doing."

"I thought I knew what deep water was all about. But, Jesus, I learned things. I always imagined there would be a way out if it turned sour. Then it turned sour and I realized the cage had no door."

I lifted a slat of the blinds and peeked out. The car, the wax job gleaming under streetlights, had not moved. The men were not visible.

"So you understand the position you're in now," I said.

"You're right, vengeance is their game. If they think I'm responsible for Joe getting it, I'm dead. It doesn't matter if you, or the police, or the goddamn Hundred and Third Infantry want to protect me."

She looked at me, looked around the apartment, covered her mouth with her palm, and began to cry. I sat down beside her and patted her gingerly on her shoulder.

I sympathized—fate rips off the top page of your life, wads it up, and throws it in your face, what are you supposed to do? But I'm not good at comforting. I can't make the warmth flow the way some can.

The tears fed on themselves and pretty soon she was deep into it. A knock sounded on the door.

She jammed a fist against her lips, shut up, and looked at me. I went to the closet and took my pistol from the shelf, an army Colt. It was a gun that could shoot through a door if necessary.

I turned out the light in my entryway and stood against the jamb. "Who is it?"

A long pause, then: "Cahoon, Ike."

I unlatched the door.

He came in followed by another detective, a hulking young man I didn't know. Tom said his name was Willis.

"Mrs. Petrone here?"

I glanced into the living room. She had stepped out of sight. "What's the deal?"

Willis said, "You better get rid of that gun before I make you eat it."

I dropped the pistol into my pocket.

"Right now, material witness," Cahoon said. "I think they plan to charge her."

"On the basis of what?"

"Slade confessed, named her."

"I saw them grease him."

"Four people heard it, they all agreed."

"Now he's conveniently dead."

"Accident. Citizen's arrest. Palermo even had a license for the cannon. They may slap his wrist, but Slade brought it on himself. Only, he had to have had a reason. She's it."

I shook my head. "Can't you see the setup, Tom?"

"I only see what's in front of me. Orders are, bring her in. She here? I'm not asking again."

"You guarantee her safety?"

"Don't give me that crap. Willis."

The big man moved past me. Cahoon and I followed him into the living room. Vicky came out of my bathroom looking fresh and hard.

The cops went through the formalities, asked her if there was anything she wanted to say.

"It's a hell of a way to treat a widow," she said.

"You have a lawyer?" I asked her.

She shook her head.

"I'll get you one. Don't say anything, is my advice."

"She don't need advice," Willis said. "She's got something on her conscience, that's her business."

"We're all gonna be nice here," Tom said. "This ain't a game. Let's go."

I phoned Keith Miller, a criminal lawyer I knew who was savvy to the way things operated over on Exchange Street. I filled him in on the basics and told him to head right down there.

I didn't have any reason to trust her, but I did. Maybe it was the lush sound of her voice as she told me her hard-luck story. Or maybe the drinks I had poured down my throat were skewing my judgment.

I was just tipping the Canadian Club bottle over my glass when the phone rang.

7

BECAUSE IT LIES BEYOND the Appalachian Mountains, Rochester really shares more with the Midwest than with the East Coast. Like the cities of the plains, the downtown core is surrounded by an expanse of frame houses, low-rise businesses, and, farther out, factories. The near suburbs are so densely populated that you never know when you're leaving the city limits.

As I drove out Ridge Road into the town of Irondequoit the complexion of the streets barely changed. I turned down a quiet residential block. The brick houses were small and neatly separated; the neighborhood gained a decided elegance from the median strip, where a row of locust trees lifted feathery leaves into the darkness.

The Colt was an awkward, comforting mass under my arm.

The man who answered the door had the solemn smile and solicitous eyes of a funeral director, the bulk of a left tackle. The small parlor opening off the entrance looked perfectly ordinary, or like a set designer's idea of ordinary. In the dining room, two elegantly dressed women who had not spared the eye shadow sat playing hearts. One was frowning at her cards, the other threw me a smile that sparkled with dollar signs.

"Upstairs," the doorkeeper told me. I followed him up around two landings.

"I like the heat," he added. "Don't mind it at all. I come from the South. South Bend."

I didn't get the joke, but he seemed amused.

There were four bedrooms upstairs. As we stepped down the hallway I glimpsed three women lounging on a couch, their faces washed by the blue light of a television that I could only hear. Arthur Godfrey was strumming his uke and singing "Chi-baba, chi-baba, my bambino go to sleep."

My guide pointed toward the next door. Inside, Angela was making notations in a book and a sharp-eyed middle-aged woman was talking on one of three telephones.

"See, I really do work for my money," Angela pointed out. "And after slaving all day at that damn amusement park."

"Nice work if you can get it."

"You know what I called you about, don't you?" she said.

"Sure, if it's what I think."

"Let's go somewhere and talk." She gave some instructions to the woman, who held her hand over the receiver and nodded. The big guy had waited in the hall and now followed us downstairs.

As I put my car in gear, she said, "I've got telephone lines coming into a house on the next block. They run out on wires you could never trace and come into here through the back. Everything's by referral, no rough clientele. All the girls are clean, they get a checkup every week. They work regular hours and they take home decent money, more than they can make pouring coffee for Haloid executives. And no taxes. Some of them have been with me two, three years. A couple of them have put themselves through college on what they made with me."

"The Chamber of Commerce give you your citizenship award yet?"

"You still wearing that chip on your shoulder?"

"Do I resent you making an ass of me? Why shouldn't I?"

"Because you ain't the type to hold a grudge and you ain't the type to trade twenty years of bullshit for a two-bit pension. Because you and I came within sight of each other and a spark flew, and you know it did. Because that don't happen often to any two people, and if you don't follow up on it you're a fool, and you ain't no fool. Because the way things are in this city right now, you want somebody who you can trust covering your ass and so do I."

We looked at each other, she tightened her eyes, and I knew she was talking truth. Whatever it was between us was roaring down the tracks and it knocked my bitterness out of the way like so much horsefeathers. I had known it was going to be like that before I went out to her place that night.

"I was there today," I said. "I saw Joe get it."

"Do tell."

"The cops are holding Vicky. They're planning to charge her with conspiracy."

"I've been hearing about it all evening."

"From who?"

"My customers aren't just salesmen from Cleveland. The girls are in touch with wrong guys on both sides of the law."

"That's why I wanted to see you."

"Oh, that's why."

"They've set Vicky up. I think she's in real danger."

"You're not the only one on pins and needles. If Petrone can get it, who's safe? There's not a racket guy in this city who isn't looking over his shoulder tonight."

"Who killed Petrone?"

"Word on the street says Vicky did it. She threw dream dust in the eyes of that fighter, convinced him to pull the trigger. The plan fell down on the getaway."

"What do you say?"

She shrugged. "I don't buy it. If she planned to kill him herself, she never would have made a stink about how he was going to bump her off. That gives it away. Hiring you, all that. Ask me, it has nothing to do with her."

"Why would they rope her into it?"

"They lay it on her, it avoids war. For these old Italians it's still *la vendetta*, blood washes blood. They remember *il mano nero*, all that voodoo. They can't let something like this lie without a St. Valentine's Day massacre. You put the blame on a guy's domestic problem, all you have to do is snuff her and it's business as usual."

"They plan to kill her?"

"I think so. It's blood."

I turned north on St. Paul Boulevard.

"Let's stop somewhere," she said. "I need a drink bad."

I pulled up in front of a liquor store just past Seneca Park Avenue. I went inside and bought a quart of rye.

"I don't want to go to a bar," I said, handing her the bottle. "I need fresh air."

She broke the tax stamp, took a big swallow, and passed it to me. There's something about a woman who drinks from the bottle, something I like.

I was still feeling the adrenaline left over from the Petrone shooting. The sweet liquor fumes perfumed my mind. "So who really killed Joe? Forlini?"

She took another long swig. "I don't think so. As much as he liked to gripe, he made money off of Petrone's political ins. He had suspicions about his sister, but that wouldn't have been enough. The only reason for him to knock the boss out of the box would be to take over himself, and he hasn't got the organization, the people, or the energy to do it. He's used up, Leo. Anyway, Joe was anointed by the powers that be."

"Who do you mean, John Foster Dulles?"

"The gang up in Buffalo. Behind them, the movers in New York. There's always somebody higher, somebody pulling strings. The old guys respect that. A guy gets canonized, they lie down. They might grumble, but they've got fear in their hearts. If I was a man, I might have taken care of Petrone myself. Only, I wouldn't have put his wife on the spot for it."

"What about Bobo Palermo?"

She tapped her fist against her chin a couple of times, then pointed her finger at me. "That could be it! That gazoony acts like a dope, but he's the one who stands to gain. He's Petrone's front man in the fight game. He promises Slade the moon, somehow sets him up with Vicky. After it's over, Bobo aces him to make sure he won't talk. He ends up by sliding into Joe's highchair."

"Anybody else out there with a grudge against Petrone?"

"They're legion, Ike. That's the problem. A guy like Joe operates on fear and friendship. It's a delicate balance. Even the people who like him hate him. I can't imagine how many in Rochester are celebrating tonight."

I thought about Paddy Doyle. He had his grievance and I knew that his bogtrotter act covered a level of cunning that just might let him pull off something like this.

A layer of dirty clouds held the heat close to the earth and soaked up the light of the stars. Sounds were magnified in the stillness. I put the car in gear. Insects swarmed in my headlights.

"On the other hand, it's possible Vicky did do it," I said. "She killed her first husband, did you know that? The sweater girl."

"You're kidding. That was her?"

"And if she didn't know Slade, how come he got picked up speeding and she was in the car?"

"So why side with her?"

"Sometimes the facts say one thing and your gut says another."

"She tell you she used to work for me?"

I looked at her, shook my head. "That lady is full of surprises."

"She was a hell of an earner. Men went cockeyed over her, that hair."

"She cross the color line?"

"If the dollars were there, sure. She didn't give a damn. Through me she made connections, met Joe."

"That wasn't part of her story."

"I'm not surprised. She made me swear I would never tell him she'd been on the game. Joe needed to think it was a casual acquaintance."

We turned down Lake Shore Boulevard. At Durand Eastman

Park the broad, rolling roadway divided the waterfront from the darkness of the trees beyond.

A gravel parking area lined the pavement. The beach was closed at this hour, the lights extinguished. The cars of lovers were parked at discreet distances. I stopped. We could smell the sweet fishy aroma of the lake.

Climbing out, she bent over to remove her shoes. She tossed them onto the seat. The neck of the bottle in her hand, she wandered over the bank and down one of the dirt trails that led to the sand. I left my coat in the car, stashed my gun under the seat, and followed.

The night was still warm and very close. Behind us, the low clouds glowed pinkish yellow from the lights of downtown.

When I caught up with her, she was crying. Her arms crossed, she squeezed herself and fought against each sob.

I hesitated for a moment, then put my hands on her shoulders from behind. She swayed back against me.

"What a world," she said. "What a goddamn world."

She lifted the bottle, took a big swallow. She sniffed a couple of times, wiped her nose with the back of her hand, and the squall was over. We continued to stand there, my arms around her.

"We used to come down here with my granddad," she said. "He loved fireworks. Made his own. He was a wild man. Every Fourth he used to set off a ton of fireworks on this beach."

She broke away and turned toward me and held up her hands. "What you people don't see, survival is the game we're playing. All of us. I was never a whore, Ike. Never. But I saw a chance and I took it. That's how I was brought up. You understand, don't you?"

"I understand."

She drank again. A trickle of rye ran down her chin.

"So many suckers out there chasing the dawn," she said. "And if they'd only wait twenty-four hours, the dawn would come back on its own. You scared?"

"Why should I be? Think I want to die in bed?"

Her laugh became unhinged. "You and I belong to the same club, Ike. We can kid the world, but we can't fool ourselves. We can't fool ourselves, and we can't run away. We've seen the dark side of the moon and we're stuck with it."

"Give me that bottle."

The hootch didn't taste raw anymore. It slid down my throat like honey and filled my insides with amber light. The taste swirled around my head. It swirled around my head again when I inhaled it from her mouth. Her fingernails raked my hair.

Sometimes we drink to enter the fog. Other times we drink to dissolve the layers of varnish that cover the wood grain of reality, to see things as they are. Tonight the booze was taking me somewhere. My mind was expanding to fill the great void over the lake. I couldn't have walked a straight line, but I could see.

And I could feel each breath she took.

"Let's go in," I said.

"I can't swim. Believe it? I never learned."

"I'll teach you."

Her face turned eagerly toward mine. The clinging fabric of my clothes suddenly became an insult in that muggy air. I popped a couple of buttons on my shirt. She beat me to it. A few lithe motions and her garments were lying limp on the sand.

She danced down to the water. Her bare limbs shone white above the blackness. When she was knee-deep, she simply sat down. She splashed her hands in the water the way a child does. She threw water on her face. Lights from up the shore drew long wavy lines along the surface.

I strode past her. The water lapped over my waist and I dove. I swam out, the way I had been wanting to for days, the way I had in so many dreams, stroking through the coolness, the eerie pale clouds hanging over my head. On and on. Not thinking.

I was swimming away from shame and sadness, away from loss, away from confusion. Away from dead young girls and poor people burned in their beds and my own child waking in terror of a world war. I was swimming away from a glimpse of the madness inside my own skull.

I didn't decide to turn back or want to. I simply found myself heading in the opposite direction, returning the way we return in dreams to the shores of morning.

Angela was still lounging in the shallows. She stood and smiled and said, "So teach me."

As we waded into deeper water, she clutched my hand tightly.

"Relax," I said. I put my palm on her soft slick belly and held her up. She tried a tenuous doggy paddle. I let her go. She moved a body length away, straining her neck to keep her head above the surface.

She stood and laughed. "I'm a fish."

She took water in her mouth and, coming near, spit it at me. It ran warm down my chest.

She was not beautiful, but the girlish curls plastered around her face suddenly struck me as beautiful. Her fragile wrists and round white shoulders struck me as beautiful, and more than beautiful. I put my hands on her waist and gently, gently, brought my lips against hers. The night turned to mother-of-pearl.

MONDAY

1

BIRDS DON'T WHISTLE THE way we do, they have no lips. They make their sounds with a gizmo in the throat. Usually they wait until the sky brightens before they start, so it was odd to hear one singing in the pitch dark, God knows what hour.

I didn't know where I was. In a room, in a bed, undressed, sweating on damp sheets, lost in a corner of night. I kept my eyes clenched as I danced on a razor's edge of vertigo. My headache shined a light at my eyes from behind. I tried and failed to assemble scattered fragments of thoughts into coherent notions.

The sound of that bird bored into my brain. What was it? A mockingbird? Some forlorn sparrow? The song started with a trill like a robin might make. But just when it got going it would break into an imitation of Woody Woodpecker's demented cackle.

Technicolor memories of the events of the previous day flashed into my head, but each was sealed in a glass museum case. I could see them but I couldn't get at them or draw them together into a story. They seemed real and at the same time phony, like a diorama, where the actual merges into a painted backdrop that recedes into a far distance, into snow-covered mountains and angelic skies. I couldn't tell where the event stopped and the illusion began.

I could see a painted plaster deer on a suburban lawn, a thousand deer before identical houses stretching beyond the horizon. All the doors of those houses opened at once. From each, a woman's anxious, mulish face looked out, the hair in crimpers.

I gritted my teeth against a glimpse of a smiling marble mannequin on a stainless steel tray. Her grin kept widening and I kept leaning closer to look and saw at last that her mouth was rimmed with powdered sugar and blood.

I could see Luke Easter's homer, could trace the exact arc of the ball, the sweet rainbow of it. It ended in a pot of gold, but just out of reach, just beyond the right field wall.

A vein was tap, tap, tapping on my temple. Only by holding my head absolutely still could I avoid the armor-plated hangover that awaited me.

A beauty queen stooped to kiss me. A tiger stretched his mouth wide, his teeth glistening. A monkey danced a cha-cha, balloons sailed into warm evening air, a stuck hog shuddered his amazement.

I was swimming. I was halfway to Canada, the water warm as a bath, far out, out of sight of land. Washed by the happy thought of escape.

Then I remembered the bewildered look on Joe Petrone's features as he watched the lights of the world dim. Was he dead? The black man, his head twisted to the side—the way he dropped.

At that my eyes opened on their own. I knew then, by the way the streetlight cast the Venetian blind pattern on the ceiling, by the right angle the shadows made where the ceiling met the wall, that I was home. I was in my own bed. The bird stopped singing—if it had been a bird and not my imagination whistling.

I heard a sound, a real sound, a careful footstep approaching. I closed my eyes and let a new collection of memories march into the theater behind my eyes.

My fingertips still felt the slickness of her belly as I held her afloat. They felt the smoothness, the roundness of her waist, the lazy flex of her buttocks. My tongue still tasted the lake water on her mouth.

I was kneeling in the shallow water washing sand and fish scales from her legs. I was splashing and laughing and barking like a trained seal. I was lying spent, breathing from that giant dome of air over the lake, the low ripples caressing the shore with a sound like whispering.

More dimly, I saw a deserted amusement park. I saw the two of us mounted on a maniac painted stallion. I saw close up the fiery pattern of his mane. We were riding a dark, silent carousel, our hips moving together as the animal rose and fell, rose and fell. Around and around in the night.

After that, only shreds. I must have brought her back here. She must be, at this instant, padding barefoot across my living room.

Booze will sometimes scour you, leave you feeling buoyant and clearheaded and lewd. I waited for her, not moving, expectant. My being was focused on hers. I drew a bead on the essence of her, trembled with anticipation.

It all came clear now. Not the details, but the sharp feeling of connection. I had been sleepwalking since the split with Eileen. No, since long before. Sleepwalking, going through the motions like a stiff-legged automaton. I had been on a long journey away from myself. Now I was back, cotton-mouthed, hung over, beaten up, and randy as a goat. Hello, world.

We all grope through the darkness. If we're lucky, we connect. We connect and for a little while we live with the glorious notion that we're not alone.

I imagined her approaching in the stillness, hair disheveled, lips parted, thighs brushing each other silently.

Why this one and not another? Why now? I didn't know. But if you feel yourself flooded with warmth, brother, grab on, cling for dear life. Time is an incorrigible thief, I knew that much.

The door made no sound, yet I felt it open, felt the acoustics change in the room. Her step made no sound, yet I sensed her approach. I lay still, feigning sleep. I waited for her moist lips to touch my forehead, her cool breasts to brush my bare chest.

She was creeping toward me with aching slowness. I couldn't wait. I looked.

A figure stood right beside the bed. One of the slats of light angling through the blinds glinted on the descending blade.

I struggled to reach. The sheet caught my hand and for a second I was paralyzed, back in a dream.

I jerked my head toward the wall. The blade caught and ripped. Feathers flew.

I swung my right hand. The steel slashed my forearm. My fist struck hard against her hip. She gave a little grunt.

She swept her arm down again. I deflected the blow. The blade sliced my palm.

Rolling, I pushed wildly against her. My elbows thumped onto the floor. My legs tangled in the sheet.

I rose to my knees. I met the knife again. It glanced along my back. A scream leapt from the bottom of my lungs. I threw my shoulder, all the weight I could gather, into a punch. My hand sank deep into her belly.

She fell.

I scrambled. I caught hold of the hand that still held the knife. Gripping the wrist, I took hold of a finger and bent it back. It cracked. I kept bending.

The knife clattered onto the floor.

I hit her. I raised my fist and slashed down with the side of it onto her face. I felt the nose break like a shingle. I punched her hard in the ribs. I hit her in the neck. With each blow, blood spattered hot and cold from my arm.

She rolled away from me, drew her knees up, and covered her head.

I climbed onto my unsteady feet. I kicked the knife away.

I staggered out to the hall, found my holster in a heap of clothing. I pulled the gun, cocked it. Blood ran down my hand, onto the barrel.

I rummaged in the closet where I kept a pair of handcuffs from my police days.

In the bedroom, she was moaning and retching. I laid the gun on the bed, twisted her arms behind her, and made the cuffs bite her flesh. A sick flood of saliva filled my mouth.

I raced to the bathroom and puked into the toilet bowl. I knelt there retching. I was making bloody handprints on the seat.

I found a roll of gauze in the medicine cabinet and wrapped my left palm. She had cut the meat to the bone. I was looking around for something to stanch my arm when I remembered the gun. I tore back to the bedroom.

She had gone for the knife. She'd crawled over and groped it out from under the bed. She held it in her cuffed hands and was struggling to regain her feet.

Someone laughed. I guess it was me. I kicked at her with my bare foot. She toppled, dropped the knife. I reached over her and picked it up by the blade with two fingers. I laid it on my bed.

I lifted her and pushed her into the easy chair in the corner. She slumped. In the moment of quiet that followed, that damn bird began to repeat his lunatic tune.

Only now did I turn on the light. I had to squint against the painful brightness. Mrs. Gill's Slavic features glared at me with a hatred shaped by centuries. Blood was gushing from her nose. It shaped a clown's mouth around her lips and continued down, dripping from her chin onto her bosom, disappearing between her breasts.

I was completely naked. I reached for the .45, my hand sticky with blood. I was going to shoot her. Where? In the head, end it? In the gut, make her suffer?

"You killed her!" I meant to say that, but the words that came out were just loud, shredded sounds.

I very deliberately clicked the safety off. The weight of the gun fought against the weakness of my wounded arm.

"I want you to say it," I said, restraining my voice.

"You. Bastard."

I flicked the barrel of the gun at her mouth, breaking teeth.

She closed her eyes and began to blubber, drooling blood and spit.

"Tell me what you did," I said, calm now. "You followed them? Huh? You found out where she lived? You were waiting? You took that little girl from behind? You pulled your knife across her throat? Is that what happened? Did she know? Did you surprise her? What?"

She dropped her head, forming a stack of compact chins. I took hold of a hank of hair and tilted her face toward the ceiling and pointed the gun right at her eye. She stared.

"Tell me."

"You are stupid," she muttered. "You are nothing. My husband, he is a good man. That girl . . ."

"She lured him? She seduced him? Is that what you think?"

"Whore!"

"You had to do it, correct? Point of honor?"

"She owe me. Owe me blood. I do nothing wrong."

"You had to kill her?"

"Is right. You don't know, mister. You don't know what is, to have everything gone. He save me. Eddie save my life. Is my life."

"And she was a threat and you had to get rid of her. You had to make her pay."

"She steal my Eddie, she die. Simple."

"So you cut her throat. Say it! You killed her!" I was pressing the gun barrel into her forehead now and screaming.

"Yes!" she hollered. "Yes, I kill!"

2

MY CLOTHES WERE DAMP and itchy with sand. Diluted light was beginning to define the windowpanes. I must have called the cops. A couple of prowl car boys arrived.

The professor from downstairs, in trousers and pajama top, wandered in through the door the cops had left open.

"Is everything all right?" His chin was peppered with gray stubble. "I heard a noise."

"I was dusting," I told him. A laugh escaped my throat. When you're alive, everything seems funny.

The poor guy just wanted to make sure everything was all right. He looked at my bloody arm. His mouth joined my laugh, but he frowned anxiously.

The dark half-moons under Tom Cahoon's eyes suggested he hadn't been sleeping much lately. I could imagine him trying to keep up with his caseload, carrying the weight of his wife going blind on top of it.

To him, Mrs. Gill freely admitted her crime. She had a knack for stealth, for breaking and entering. I had helped her out by failing to secure my deadbolt when I came home the night before.

Sandy Mink's place had been easy to crack. Mrs. Gill had gone there, found nobody home, and waited. In her mind, she had been completely justified. To her, a person who commits adultery steps across a line. In that territory, anything goes. You steal what's mine, I kill you. It was the Old World way. Simple, clear, and final.

As he listened, Cahoon kept brushing his lips meditatively along the length of the day's first cigar, savoring the aroma.

"My Eddie, wonderful man," she said.

He asked her to repeat. Between her accent and broken teeth, it was difficult to understand her. "Wonderful provider. These young girls, phew." She blew a spray of diluted blood.

Tom searched his pockets. I found him a box of kitchen matches.

"Did you intend to kill the girl when you went over there, Mrs. Gill?" he asked, puffing. It was the crucial question, premeditation.

"Intend?" she said.

"Did you plan it?"

"I plan. I see her face, I cut."

Tom finished lighting his cigar and said, "Let's take a ride."

They put me in an ambulance, which would take me to Strong Memorial. The attendant was a wiry young guy whose harelip scar gave him an angelic smile.

"Buddy, you gotta reach an accommodation," he honked. "Go easy. Keep away from the hullabaloo boomboom horseshit, you'll be all right. You know what I mean?"

"Sure, I know what you mean." He must have thought I was a suicide case.

"I've been around the block, not once but three times, count 'em." He held up fingers. "I know. The answer is, roll with the punches. That's the answer."

"You're so right."

The driver hit the siren to get us through an intersection.

"'At's a boy. Go easy on yourself. Think about Christmas. Think about Wonder bread."

An intern in the emergency room rinsed my wounds with iodine wash while humming the theme from *Mondo Cane*. He closed the incision on my arm with two dozen stitches, and put fourteen more in my hand. He said the wound on my back would heal okay without being sewn. He gave me a tetanus shot and a vial of pain pills. He told me to go home and lie in bed for a few days.

I called for a taxi and rode across the Court Street Bridge to police headquarters. Cahoon produced a cup of coffee. I had to will my left hand to stop shaking to avoid spilling it down my shirt.

He already had an affidavit drawn up based on what I had told him at the house. I looked it over and signed it.

"What about Gill?" I said. "He ever show?"

He shook his head. "We've had an APB out on him. I don't know why he's hiding. Unless she's covering for him."

"She spill?"

"Gave us the whole thing wrapped with a ribbon. Signed the statement. 'This keep my Eddie free?' Sure, I said. 'Is good man.' "

"She mention anything about kids? She told me they had four kids."

"Yeah, as a matter of fact. It bothered her bad she couldn't have any. 'Eddie heartbroken. Good man.' "

"Gill a pimp?"

"Nothing came up on his sheet except carrying concealed two years back and a bunch of health department violations on the hot dog stand."

I tapped a Lucky on his desk and lit it. "You know what gets me, don't you, Tom? I killed that girl."

"You?"

"I was the finger on this. If it hadn't been for me."

"I wouldn't look at it that way."

"I handed it to her. Who, where, what. I snapped the pictures, I wrote the report, I pointed her in the direction, and she did the rest."

"I said, don't wear it out. You did a job you were hired to do. The job was legal. She could have killed him instead, done the world a favor. You had no control."

"Except, the girl came to me for help."

"Okay, so go home and cry in your beer. I haven't got time for this. The milkmen are finding bodies after that Petrone mess."

"What bodies?"

"Mr. Vincenzo Palermo, for one."

"Bobo?"

"Neighbor discovered him draped over a yew bush by his house. Shotgun."

"What do you make of it?"

"Joe gone, the rackets are up for grabs."

"Slade definitely the shooter on Petrone?"

"We found a Remington thirty-thirty, his palm print. Paraffin on him came up positive."

"You don't really think Vicky put him up to it, do you?"

"Yes, I do. We've been pulling together all kinds of dope. She and Joe were on the rocks, he threatened her—that's motive. She was tight with Slade—that's opportunity. Slade pointed the finger at her—that's a dying man's testimony. She ran—that's guilty flight. I've seen thinner cases send a person to the chair."

"Take a whiff, Tom. Everything about it stinks."

"In this town, I'm surprised you've still got a sense of smell left. Go home, Ike. Go home and forget about it."

3

I SHOULD HAVE TAKEN his advice. I had no bottom to me as I walked onto Exchange Street. The heat had been toying with us for a week. Now it was coming on with a roar. It was still morning and I could already feel the burn of the pavement through my shoes.

I needed something to eat, but the idea of eating made my stomach do a half gainer. I needed a couple of bennies worse than food, but I hadn't brought any with me. I needed about twelve hours of uninterrupted sleep, but that would have to wait.

I walked down to a cab stand on Main and told the driver to turn up Joseph Avenue. He wanted to know where we were going. I told him just to roll slowly north.

We passed grocery stores where the owners had wheeled refrigerated chests outside to dispense snow cones and ice cream sandwiches, rib stations where the succulent aroma was already pouring out the ventilators. A crowd of black, shiny faces stared from in front of a funeral parlor, the sun gleaming off the polished coffin. People were coming out of their houses trying to find a breath of breeze. A fat lady still in her nightgown and slippers sat under a stunted sycamore, fanning herself with a newspaper. Everyone was staying in the shade.

I caught sight of a sign, a painted-over Coke advertisement, the crude lettering reading EMMANUEL BAR AND GRILL. I told the driver to pull over.

Climbing out and walking ten paces in the sun had me seeing spots. I was glad to make it through the door, but the dark inside didn't translate into cool. A ceiling fan revolved lethargically, moving no air. The sunlight that streamed in the front window dissolved into pure heat once it got through the glass.

Two men sat at the end of the bar, just out of the sun. Each fingered a half glass of beer. Farther down, a white woman in her twenties was poking a plastic swizzle into a rocks glass. Pretty, but on the downhill slope. A cigarette lay on the edge of the tray by her elbow, a blue arabesque dancing above it. Her short black curls had the celluloid look of a doll's hair. Her dress was unzipped six inches, baring an innocent nape.

She looked over her shoulder at me without expression and exhaled a stream of smoke. I gripped the edge of the bar to steady myself.

"Christmas," I said.

"You believe in Santy Claus?"

"Sure."

"I don't," she said glumly, and took a sip from her drink.

"Willie around?"

"Santy Claus never brought me what I wanted. I sent him a letter every year."

"That's too bad."

"That is too bad, buster. That is tragic. 'Cause now I'm grown up and it's too late. It too late for you?"

"I guess it is. I'm Santa now for my little girl."

Her eyes filled instantly with tears. They dissolved her mascara and traced a couple of inky paths down her cheeks.

"What is luck?" she asked me. "That's what I want to know."

"I guess it's what the other fella's got."

She looked at me for a moment, then sniffed, wiped her nose with the back of her hand, and called out, "Willie!" in a musical voice.

I heard footsteps. Willie Christmas climbed through the trapdoor behind the bar that gave access to the cellar.

He set a case of Genesee Cream Ale on the sink and started to transfer the bottles to a cooler.

"This man is from the North Pole," she told him.

"That right?" he asked me.

"I came to talk to you about a dead man."

"Who's dead?" the woman said. "Willie, another."

Without looking, he grabbed a bottle from the shelf behind him. For a dive, it had an elaborate back bar—the carved cupid poised along the top was smirking down at the drinkers, his bow cocked, his eyes on the lookout for a sure shot. A sign glued to the mirror said "Don't go away mad . . . just go away!"

Willie's other hand picked two ice cubes from the cooler. He dropped the ice into her glass, splashed Scotch over them, and picked out some coins from the change beside the ashtray, all with the movements of a sleepwalker.

"Melvin Slade," he said to her. "If you read the papers, you'd know."

"Who the hell? Wasn't he that wiseass used to be in here? I don't need to read no *Democrat* to know what's going on. What happened to him?"

"Shot."

Her hand trembled as she put another cigarette to her lips. Willie had the flame ready.

"Ask me am I surprised," she said.

To me he said, "So you are police."

"He ain't police," the girl said. "Can't you tell a cop, Willie? I can tell a cop a mile away. I can smell 'em."

"I don't doubt it," Willie said.

"What the hell do you mean, you don't doubt it? I got nothing to do with cops. What do I know? Maybe this guy *is* a cop. Are you a cop, buster? You gonna put poor Willie in the cooler for that crap game he runs back there?"

"Your mouth running away from you now, girl. Better hurry and catch up to it. It got nice teeth."

He finished drawing two glasses of draft beer and came around to the other side of the bar. I nodded to the woman.

"Copper!" She sneered.

I joined him at a table in back.

"I'm no cop," I said. "The mob's got Joe's wife targeted. I'm trying to help her out of a jam."

"And who's getting Melvin out of a jam?"

"He pulled the trigger on Petrone. Was he stupid, or what?"

"Melvin didn't think right. Too many bells ringing in his head. Plenty of fighters like that."

"Question is: Why did he do it? He played cat and mouse with me when I talked to him at the Armory. You know what was going on with him. If you cared about him, I'm sorry. Help me out, you'll find I'm a man worth knowing."

"Cared about him? He was a human being."

"How did he get off the track?"

"He had good in him. He had skills, not just in the ring. He had too much other stuff along with it. So the talent got lost. Maybe I brought him along wrong, too. I told him the fight game, it's give and take. Sometimes you gotta go in there, play a part."

"He was playing a part on Friday?"

"He hated that, the champ watching. Night Train hated it. But the deal was made and we had no choice. Afterward, I've never seen him so raggedy. He wanted to punch the world out."

"Was Petrone behind Kid Blik?"

"Him, friends of his. Building up a record so they can take him down to Cleveland or Pittsburgh and make some money on him. Melvin coulda used some money. He loved money."

"What about women?"

"He loved them, too. Loved running after tail. Couldn't leave it alone."

"He do Petrone's wife or didn't he?"

He shrugged. "I wouldn't doubt it. Always had a taste for angel food, taste for suicide."

"You ever see them together?"

"Once. Blonde, right? He'da killed for a blonde."

"He said that?"

"Something like it. I told him, You have got your grave dug. All's left is to fall in it."

"What did he say?"

"Look at me. I'm near fifty years old. You think I got anything to say a young man's going to listen to on that subject? I did my share of catting, believe me, my day. I got a razor scar here to here, some bitch's husband gave me."

"Was Slade in the rackets?"

"He knew everybody."

"Leo Forlini?"

"Sure. He did work for them."

"What kind of work?"

"I didn't ask that. Debts, I think. Melvin had a look he could give you, make you want to pay what you owed."

"You sorry he's dead?"

"Like I said, he was a human being. Live fast, die young, that was his motto—and a fighter gets old quick. No, sir, time was not on his side."

"Thanks for the beer."

"You're looking a little peaked. Maybe you better see that lady over there. She'll fix what ails you."

His mirthless laughter rang like a chime in my head. Walking past her, I noticed the careless zipper again and the way the light caught her neck. I had to make an effort to keep myself from reaching to zip it.

4

OUT IN THE BOOMING, blazing light, I spotted a bus grinding down Joseph Avenue. I hurried across the street and jumped on it. All the windows were open, but the inside was an oven. The whine of the engine seeped through the seat and soured my stomach. The procaine the doc had shot into my hand and arm was wearing off. Both were throbbing a mile a minute.

Sometimes, when you're operating on too little sleep, time moves in jumps. An hour will go on and on while the pressure builds behind it. Then the clock will surge forward and heave you into the future. I thought it should be about ten but my watch said twenty past twelve. I had the distinct feeling my clutch was slipping.

I swung off the bus when it reached Mortimer Street and walked up to my office.

"Where have you been?" Penny said. "I was worried. What happened to your hand?"

"I should have called. I had to—"

"You should have, all right. She's out."

"That Gill thing, Sandy? I pointed her. It was the wife. She cut that kid's throat. Broke into my place and tried her best to do the same to me."

"She's out, Ike. Vicky. She called here asking what she should do. I said I didn't know where you were, couldn't get you at home, hoped you would be here any minute. I told her to stay there. Was I right?"

"What do you mean, out?"

"The cops put her on the street."

"What?"

"It's not good, is it?"

"Good? The racket boys are hell-bent to kill her. When did she call?"

"Forty-five minutes ago, more."

"What happened?"

"She told me how you saved her life, all that. So this morning, an hour or so ago, they took her into city court, no lawyer or anything, the judge lowered her bail, they told her a bond had been posted, she could walk."

"Where is she?"

"She called from some diner over on Main, near Madison. She wanted to know if you had arranged it, pulled strings or something. She thought a couple of plainclothes coppers were following her. I told her you needed to talk to her and not to move until she heard from you."

"You have your car here?"

She nodded.

"Let's go."

The drop of the elevator made me queasy. That and the fact that I knew it was no civic generosity that had set Vicky free. The fix was in. If she disappeared while under indictment, the ones who had actually set Joe up would be able to rest easy. The case would come to a neat dead end.

The traffic was murder. Penny leaned on the horn of her '51 Chevy and took advantage of every opening to scoot forward, but it still took us a good fifteen minutes to cover the distance across the river and down Main.

The temperature was pushing a hundred degrees. The good-natured tolerance of the populace during the last few days was turning to alarm as citizens sweated through their talcum.

I spotted the railroad-car diner across the street, still a block away. The sun caught the aluminum skin and flared back at us.

I could see her, too. She was wearing the same sky-blue knit suit, the same square white hat. Her hair attracted sunlight. She was standing on the steps of the eatery, looking up Main.

The traffic light was against us. I told Penny to continue to the next corner, go around the block, and pick us up in front.

A couple of buses passed between us. I lost sight of her. Then I saw she had descended the steps and turned away from me. She was striding rapidly along the sidewalk.

I started to cut across the street, but I had to wait on the traffic.

Then the whole picture changed. Two men in dark suits came up on either side of her. Her head swiveled quickly from one to the other. She jerked away, but they already had a grip on her arms. They lifted her off her feet.

It was all happening very quickly. They boosted her across the sidewalk. They opened the door of a butter-yellow Imperial at the curb. She resisted. One of the men drew his arm back and punched her hard under the breast. She stumbled forward. Her high-heeled shoes came off.

I sprinted along the street, waiting for a gap in the traffic.

People were walking down the sidewalk but none of them came to her aid. Maybe they figured she was a drunk or a lunatic. Let the cops handle it. Don't get involved.

One of the men leaned over and grabbed Vicky under the armpits, his friend took hold of her ankles. They tossed her into the backseat of the Imperial. One piled in after her, the other scooted around to the driver's door. The car began to move.

By this time, I was in the middle of Main, waiting for a Sibley's delivery van to pass. The Imperial was fifty yards away, picking up speed toward me.

Brakes squealed. I felt myself lifted. I sprawled onto the hot hood of the car that had almost run me down from behind. I rolled backward over his fender and landed hard on the pavement.

Coming back to my feet, I was standing in the open lane and watching the Imperial move past me. I took a step and grabbed for the door handle. The car was already gaining momentum. I could see her face as she scrambled around to look at me, first through the side window, then the rear. Her mouth was open, her eyes wide.

Penny's green coupe swung out of the westbound traffic. The Imperial swerved, scraped against a parked truck. The two cars came together nearly head-on. A metallic crunch and a shattering of glass reverberated from the buildings.

I sprinted toward the wreck. The torpedo in back tumbled out of the car and ran. His pal climbed from behind the wheel and reached under his jacket. He drew a revolver, pointed it at me, let loose with a wild round. I wasn't stopping. He reached back into the car and fired again. Then he turned, raced two doors up the block, and ducked down an alleyway.

By the time I reached the cars, Vicky was picking herself up from the floor in back. The bullet had missed.

"You all right?"

"I twisted my arm."

"We'd better keep moving. You're a popular girl."

I helped her out of the car. Penny had pulled herself from behind the wheel of her car. She ran over to us, her eyes wide.

"Keep her on her feet," I said.

I went over to the first in the rapidly building line of cars behind us. The driver of the Mercury had the short-sleeved white shirt, clip-on bow tie, and earnest jaw of a Kodak engineer. I showed him the dime-store badge I kept in my wallet.

"Lady needs to get to a hospital quick," I said. "Pull up in the other lane."

I jumped in the backseat of the four-door. The guy was glad to follow orders, glad to do his bit. I swung the far door open. Penny helped Vicky inside beside me, then climbed in front.

"Step on it!" she ordered.

The car leapt and swerved, the driver sounding a continuous warning on his horn.

"I saw them grab her as I was coming up," Penny said. "My hands jerked the wheel before I knew what I was doing. Jeez-us!"

"You did good."

"My poor car." She laughed. She was getting her first taste of adrenaline and liking it.

The driver twisted his head and yelled, "St. Mary's is the closest. I think. But we'll have to turn around. Or Highland. We could cut down to Highland. That might be better."

"You decide," I said. "And slow down. We don't need a rough ride."

"What happened back there?"

"Accident. Car threw a tie rod."

That satisfied him. He continued to swerve around cars, cut into the wrong lane, and run lights with his horn going. He would be talking about this for years to come.

I said to Vicky, "How's your arm?"

She was holding the elbow. "A sprain, I think. I can move it. What was that all about?"

"I'll tell you later. Hey, buddy, pull up here," I said to the driver. "She's not having the baby after all."

"What?"

"She's going to go to her own doctor. Let us out. Thanks."

A frown of suspicion wrinkled the driver's brow but events were passing him by. I slammed the door and touched the brim of my hat and gave him as big a smile as I could manage.

The hot sidewalk burned Vicky's bare feet. We went into a lunch-eonette on Court Street. I called for a taxi while the two women ordered iced coffee to go. We sipped our brew on the ride over to my house. Penny was so excited she could hardly sit still.

"Your best bet is to lie low," I told Vicky. The driver was maneuvering through heavy midday traffic. "We'll find a place for you. They've laid Joe's death on you, and they've got clout downtown, which is how they sprung you."

"I can't take jail. I know what it's like and I'd rather die."

"Trust me, okay?"

She nodded.

"My God, Ike!" Penny said as we got out of the cab. "You're bleeding. It's coming right through your coat."

Suddenly I was feeling lightheaded, too. Penny held my arm as we mounted the stairs to my apartment. It was like climbing the Alps.

Inside, I turned on a fan and gave them an abbreviated rundown of my encounter with Mrs. Gill. The story seemed preposterous even to me, but the mess inside testified to its truth. The medics had left bloody swabs and bandage wrappers on the rug. I must have knocked over a lamp while I was scrambling around. A couple of blackened pools of blood stained my bedroom floor. And the smell of vomit tinted the warm air.

When I pulled my coat and shirt off I could see that the cut on my arm had opened; blood was seeping from the soaked bandage. Penny unwrapped it while Vicky cut one of my undershirts with a scissors.

"Thanks, Nurse," I said when Penny finished washing and rewrapping the wound.

"You should rest."

"She can't stay here," I said. "They were around last night and they'll be back."

"I'll be okay," Vicky said. "I'll go to a hotel."

"No good. You know yourself they've got informants. Any hotel in the city, they'd track you down."

"Who is it?" Penny said. "Who wants to kill her?"

"It's an organization," I said. "Like a colony of ants. The boys rub antennae and suddenly you've got a couple dozen bozos gunning for her. She had Joe bumped, there has to be payback."

Vicky said, "I swear I—"

"You didn't have anything to do with it. So what? You're on the spot for it and nothing else matters. Certainly not truth."

"Ike, listen," Penny said. "How about we drive out to that cottage I'm renting in Sodus? It's out of the way. We can relax out there until things cool down."

"I can't put you to that trouble," Vicky said. "Or danger. I'll deal with this my own way."

"What way is that?" I asked her.

She bit her lip and thought about it. "Give me a gun. I know how to shoot."

I shook my head. "What chance would you stand in a gunfight? I think Penny's idea is solid. Go out there and sit tight until the situation gels."

"And you should get to a doctor," Penny told me.

"You know what they say in the movies, only a flesh wound. Here are the keys to my car. Don't go home. Head straight there and stick to the back roads. What's the phone number out there?"

"No phone."

"Call me and let me know you're safe. Try the office if I'm not here. Keep trying."

"I owe you," Vicky said. "I won't forget."

"You don't owe me. Nobody owes me. Just go."

5

I STILL WASN'T HUNGRY, but I needed to put something into my stomach. I stepped into the hot exhalation outside. My rubbery legs carried me toward a delicatessen around the corner. I had to stop and lean against a tree while visions of a black sun went dancing through my head.

The ordinary short-order clamor sounded to me like the inside of a boiler factory. I let myself heavily onto a chrome stool and ordered a BLT, a side of macaroni salad, and a large iced tea. The patrons all seemed to be speaking Chinese.

I picked up a copy of the *Democrat* and read the accounts of the Petrone shooting while I ate. "Gangland" was a word they kept repeating. "Gangland slaying." "Gangland-style assassination." It was a place with its own rules, this gangland. They were the rules that govern fairy tales, where beanstalks grow to the sky, and witches get pushed into ovens, and virgins are sacrificed on the altars of lust. You wake up in a nightmare called gangland, and, buddy, watch out.

I looked at the account of the Red Wings game. Easter told a reporter about how sweet it felt to get the good wood on the ball. It made me think back to Gloria's little fists clenched and raised to heaven in celebration of yesterday's homer.

I came across a small story at the bottom of page five, "Highway Planned for Northeast." It only ran about five paragraphs. Unnamed sources had leaked word that the city would be approved for federal money to build yet another highway into the city. They were planning a "miracle mile" through the old seventh ward. Tenements would make way for shopping centers and parking lots. Montgomery Ward, Star Supermarkets, McCurdy's, Ott's Chevrolet—they were all expected to sign on. The project would revitalize an entire area of the city, the report claimed.

Miracle mile. The term had a ring to it. I needed a goddamn miracle myself.

Walking home, I felt revived and weary at the same time. The air, warm as blood, was making me drowsy. A silver airplane droning through the blue threatened to take my thoughts away.

I climbed the stairs and lay down on the couch. But I was too wired to sleep. Thirsty, I checked the refrigerator and found a can of V-8. I punched two holes in the top. The color of the liquid gave me the notion that it would make up for the blood I had lost. It tasted good. I poured another glassful and was livening it up with a jigger of Smirnoff and a lemon wedge when the phone jangled.

"Van Savage," I answered.

"We're here, boss." I was relieved to hear Penny's voice. "Everything's cool. We picked up a couple of bathing suits. All they had was a horrendous yellow and a mauve my grandmother wouldn't wear. Anyway, we're heading for the beach with a Thermos of whiskey sours and a stack of movie magazines."

"Think it's wise to go out?"

"We're certainly not going to sit in the house, this weather. We'd cook. Don't worry. The town is absolutely mobbed. This week is the festival."

"What festival?"

"I told you, the sesquicentennial. All the local merchants have grown beards. Parades, fireworks, the whole shebang. That and the heat, the place is swarming. It makes it better. We fit right in. A couple of carefree career girls looking for fun."

"Just keep your eyes open. I'm worried about somebody spotting the car."

"We can walk anywhere we need to go. How are things there? Are you in bed?"

"Just done eating lunch."

"Take it easy. Those cuts open up, you'll be a drained turnip."

"Don't worry about me."

"I like this gal, Ike. She doesn't deserve what they're doing to her. I'm going to get her out on the town, take her mind off it."

"Be careful." I told her to try to reach me again that evening.

As I put down the receiver I snapped my head around as if I'd heard a noise. But the house was quiet.

No, not a noise. It was like when, during the day, you suddenly catch a glimpse of a dream you had the night before. You know the whole thing is there in your mind, but you can't get at it.

6

IT'S LIKE A SMELL, I told myself. The solution to a case is like the way an odor can transport you. You catch a whiff of honeysuckle and you're on your grandmother's porch in the land of Nod, a breath of perfume and you're kissing a girl in '44, you can't even remember her name. That's how the answer arrives, not through reasoning. You can't anticipate. You can't force it any more than you can remember an essence—of glue in first grade, of rented roller skates, of the cinders along the New York Central tracks on a hot day. It always eludes you. You have to breathe the answer.

No, that was bullshit. That was the romantic notion of a guy who couldn't figure what the hell was going on.

From my window, I could just make out the highest buildings of downtown. A haze was settling over the city, the way it does on a hot day. The colonnade on the Powers Building and the art deco bonnet of the Times Square tower were still in the clear, but the rest was lost in a humid, stagnant soup.

Maybe that was a better way to look at it. Fumes and fog were filling my head. Only a few facts stood out. Look at those. Separate the figure from the ground, the meaningful from the trivial. Line up the important details and solve the formula and see what comes after the equal sign.

Nix. Kidding myself again, and mixing metaphors to boot.

But somehow it was within my grasp—if only I had the energy to reach for it. The heat and the exhaustion were weighing me down. I stripped to my shorts, set up a fan, and stretched out on the davenport. The blowing air made my skin crawl. I clicked the switch and watched the blades come to rest. The bristly fabric felt like steel wool against my back. Some idiot down the block was playing a radio just loud enough to reach my ears. I would never be able to sleep.

And I was alert now to a real smell. It wasn't at all subtle. It was the odor of wet charred wood. Of spent smoke. It was the forlorn smell that follows a house fire.

I was inside a roofless building and the timbers were black with cracked coals. The walls were reduced to lace, the windows to fangs. I was looking at the angry blue sky.

Dogs surrounded me. Thick, stinging sunlight streamed in. Through an incinerated door I saw Sandy Mink, naked and nubile. She squatted, took ash on her hands, and began to smear her body black. I had to stop her. She didn't know what she was doing. I had to reach her.

As soon as I took a step, the dogs turned toward me. Their ears perked, growls seeped from their throats. Another step and one tore at me, knocked me to the floor. They all descended, their teeth clacking. I averted my face, closed my eyes, and came awake with a start.

I was sweating. I thought I'd been asleep for two minutes but saw by the clock it was nearly three hours. Someone was pounding on my door. I reached for my pistol without thinking. I stepped into the hallway.

"Yeah?"

"Ike, it's me."

I unlocked the door. Angela didn't wait to be invited in. My foreboding evaporated and suddenly I was breathing pure oxygen. It was painful to smile, but I couldn't help smiling. Her presence was an embrace.

"Look at you," she said. "I called here this morning and a cop answered."

"I had some trouble."

"He started asking me questions. What happened? I thought maybe you wrecked your car on the way home last night and were in traction."

"Disgruntled client."

"Did that? Who was it?"

"The wife in that Gill case. She cut that little girl's throat, then came after me."

"I'm glad you survived. Real glad."

"I had to. I needed to be alive in order to see you."

"I saved you a trip. I'm no sentimental fool, but I've been getting gooseflesh, Ike. Gooseflesh."

"You mean last night?"

She looked around incredulously, as if somebody else might be in the room. "Sure, last night. Like, the things you said, the things you did, the things we did. Like, the lake. Like, back at my place. Jesus, I've never had so much fun since I can't remember when. How about a little glad-to-see-you?"

She put her arms around my neck and I kissed her. The taste of her mouth ignited a rush of memories. The memories washed my fatigue away and made me want to pull that summer dress over her head.

Her hand touched the sore spot on my back and I winced.

"You are a mess," she said. "Tell Mama all about it."

I went over Mrs. Gill's attack, Vicky's escape. It was a strange story that seemed like a feverish delirium. But Angela had the capacity to take it in. She understood, and I imagined she could understand anything. She knew about the wildness that can get out of the human mind and infect the world. Nothing fazed her.

"I dreamed about you," I said when I had finished the story. "It was pure pleasure, except for the end."

"What happened then?"

"You know how taking a drink in a dream never gets you high and leaves you as thirsty as ever? My dream ended with an ache."

"That's my specialty, taking care of aches. It's the nice thing about reality, the way you can drink your fill."

She examined the contents of my liquor cabinet and mixed me a drink that was cold and sweet and bitter and strong. She changed the bloodstained sheets on my bed. She looked through my record collection and made the sweet melodies of Lester Young float onto the hot air. She had me lie down so she could dab my forehead with Aqua Velva. She covered my eyes with a cold washcloth and massaged the muscles of my shoulders and chest, all very motherly.

She did some other things that weren't so motherly, things that took my mind off my troubles and off the sweet earth.

Some time later, I found myself climbing up from the bottom of a well, struggling to reach the light, anxious that the world was leaving me behind.

I pulled myself out of bed and stumbled as I tried to step into a pair of pants. The clock said four-thirty. Cicadas were tearing up the outside air.

Angela was sitting in the kitchen, smoking a cigarette and leafing through a copy of *Argosy*. She had kicked off her shoes and propped her grimy feet on the table.

"Feeling better?"

"Much. Beer?"

"Now you're talking."

I opened a couple bottles of cold pilsner. She saw me tapping pills from my Benzedrine stash and said, "Hey, me too."

I took two and handed her the vial.

"Hear about Palermo?" I said.

"I heard." She put one of the little pills on the tip of her tongue and took a swallow of beer.

"Who did it?"

"God knows. Whoever iced Joe, I'd say. I think Bobo was in on the coup d'etat and they had to get rid of him. I'm not sorry. He was a stupid dink. Now everybody's wondering what next."

"I've got a theory."

"Want to try it out on me?"

I put a match to a Lucky and paced up and down the linoleum. "I keep thinking about those buildings."

"Which are those?"

"The ones somebody's been torching over in the old seventh ward. Somewhere in the deal, there's a lot of money. There has to be."

"Insurance?"

"Maybe, but I think it's something bigger than that. A guy named Paddy Doyle, who owns some of them, hired me to look into it. He was convinced Petrone was behind it, and I think he was on the right track. Last night I had a strong suspicion that Doyle was the one who put the contract on Petrone. He as much as told me he was going to. But I think it goes deeper."

"Deeper how?"

"Something worth killing for, even killing a guy like Petrone. Say Joe was involved. Say he had partners. Say those partners began—"

The telephone interrupted me. Not too many had my home number.

"I got a line on your man Gill," Earl's voice said.

"Eddie Gill?"

"You said you wanted him run down."

"Gill, yes, definitely. Where are you?"

"I tailed him to a farm east of town. I'm calling you from a Cities Service on Empire."

"Okay, wait there, I'll come out."

"Before the plaza, on the left."

"I'll be there in twenty."

I hung up. As I strapped on my .45 and slipped into an old seersucker jacket, I said to Angela, "Want to join the Secret Squadron?"

"I thought I already had."

"How about driving me somewhere?"

"Let's go."

7

HER CONSPICUOUS CADILLAC WAS parked in front of my place with the top down. In daylight, the creamy upholstery and glossy salmon-pink body stood out like a bride in a slaughterhouse.

The flow of air canceled the stifling heat. I let my head drop back. The bennies kicked in and filled my mind with electricity. A glorious throb galloped down my arteries. I watched the branches speed backward above me. A kaleidoscope of leaves winked and shimmered.

"You didn't tell me your theory," she said.

"They're making money, somebody is. But how? How do you make money?"

"I wish I knew the answer to that one. Steal it?"

"You need muscle or capital or both. You need information. You need inside stuff that the other guy doesn't know about. So how does all that fit together?"

"Joe Petrone was always working an angle, I can tell you that, always looking for the edge."

We slipped down the hill into the dugway and passed the Anaconda, where I'd had my intimate meeting with a certain mobster's wife the week before.

"There's Earl's car," I said as we came up the hill on the other side.

She pulled across three lanes of traffic and swung into the service station. Earl stood beside his car watching us. The pink Cadillac didn't raise a ripple on his Buster Keaton features.

"Thanks for the ride," I said to Angela.

"Hey, you can't brush me off. I want to see you in action. Anyway, you might need me, the condition you're in."

"Okay, but you'll have to leave the circus wagon here."

I introduced her to Earl and we both climbed into his car. He asked me about the bandage on my hand.

"Gill's wife," I said. "She tried to take my tonsils out this morning."

"Sweet lady."

"She confessed to killing the girl."

"I thought you told me it was him."

"I read her wrong. She's Old World and I don't understand Old World. I'm strictly New World."

"Then why run down the husband?"

"Funny thing, Earl. He's got links to that arson business. I think Petrone was tied to it, as well."

"Seems like Petrone was tied to everything."

He turned off Empire, away from the shopping strip. After half a mile I realized we were coming down Creek Road from the other end.

Why wasn't I surprised? The jigsaw pieces were beginning to form a picture.

Earl slowed his car near the entrance to the horse farm.

"This is the place," he said. "I can't guarantee he's still inside. It was quarter of when I went to call."

"Pull right in," I told him.

"If you say so."

"Don't worry, I know the party."

We rolled down the long driveway and parked in front of the house.

"He was driving the Edsel," Earl said. "Looks like he's blown."

"Have a look around outside. I'll pay a little visit." I told Angela to wait with Earl.

"You're not going to get shot, are you?" she asked me.

"I've taken enough punishment for one day."

I climbed out and crossed to the front door. In that heat, the effort left me sweating. I rang the bell.

The colored butler who'd served me iced tea answered. "Can I help you?"

"Miss Biltmore."

"I'm sorry, she's not in."

"That's okay, I'll look around."

"I'm afraid that's impossible, sir."

God, wasn't it ever going to cool off? The sun was catching the back of my neck and the man was so polite, it hurt. I reached under my coat and pulled out the Colt with my weak right hand.

"This'll save us a lot of time and bullshit."

"Yes, sir, that it will. It surely will."

"Where is she?"

He pointed upstairs with his eyes.

I slipped the gun back into my holster and strode up the wide staircase feeling light again, cruising on the pep pills. Down the corridor, the door to her room was shut. I twisted the knob and let it swing back.

She turned toward me. She must have just finished taking a cool shower. She was still wet and the imprint of her bikini stood out white on her tan skin. She put an arm across her breasts and flashed her nervous smile on and off six times in rapid succession. Her attempts to laugh came out as a string of peeps. Her eyes darted.

"Where is he?" I said it louder than I had intended.

"Who? Who let you in? What do you want?" She was frantically wrapping herself in a silken robe.

"Gill. Duncan Kerr."

"You can't come in here. Who do you think you are?"

"You know he killed his own sister, don't you?"

"What are you talking about?"

What *was* I talking about? You have to pretend you know something.

"He ran her off the road. She found out Duncan was trimming her husband and he killed her. You helped arrange it. Come clean now, you might just save yourself from the electric chair."

"The electric . . . ?" She tittered as if someone were tickling her feet.

"We're talking about murder and the game is almost over. What's your favorite food?"

"My— What in the world are you talking about?"

"London broil? Banana split? They'll give you anything you want. Just a reminder of what you'll be missing."

"Don't, please."

"They'll shave that blond hair off. They'll strap your arms to the chair. What do you think that feels like? You have to scratch, but you can't reach it."

"I didn't do anything. You've gotta believe that. It wasn't me."

"The electrode has a pad soaked in vinegar. It feels wet and clammy against your temple and down there on your ankle. You breathe that sourness and you wait."

"I didn't do it. I didn't want to do it. I couldn't— He made me."

"You wait and wait. It's only a minute, but it goes by like ten lifetimes. You sit there waiting for the juice and knowing that if you had only played the game right when you had the chance, everything would be different."

"My God, will you stop!"

We were reciting lines from a play. Talk or I'll blow you head off. You killed Miles and you're going over for it.

Her face collapsed on itself, she tented her hands over her nose and mouth, closed her eyes, and let out a high-pitched keen.

"Start talking," I said.

"It was him. It was Duncan."

"He made you."

"Please, you have to help me."

"Sure, I can help you. I want to. But only if you tell me the truth. He hooked you into his plot."

"Yes! I didn't mean to. I didn't know about Avis until later. She was my friend. But I needed him. I had to do what he said."

"He asked you to set her up, right? She came to see you and you sent her out along Maplewood on some pretext."

"Yes. I didn't know, though. You have to believe me."

"You and Kerr cooked up the suicide angle. You had that ready in order to throw off somebody like me, somebody who might get suspicious."

"He told me to." She threw herself face down on the bed and bawled. The silk clung to the dampness on her back and legs.

"You wrote that note yourself."

"Yes," she said through her weeping. "He said. She was threatening him. Telling Joe lies. She was cracked, he said. Psycho. It was dangerous."

"He told you to play house with Slade."

"Oh, God!"

She turned over, quieted her sobs. Her gaze pinned itself to my face. She laid her palms on the mattress and arched her back. I guess it was pure instinct with her. The robe came open. She lifted one leg and pointed her toes. She'd seen a lot of movies, all right.

"Slade was easy pickings for you, wasn't he? Wasn't he?"

Seeing I wasn't going to bite, she pressed her teeth into her upper lip and glared.

"You disgust me," she rasped, pulling the robe closed.

"You could make him jump through hoops."

She sobbed again, really heaving this time. I found a box of Kleenex and offered her one.

"Kerr wanted Petrone dead," I said.

"Duncan made out it was a game." She thought she would try becoming a contrite child. "We had played games, ever since we were kids. And he always made up the rules. I just did what he said. You know? He was—he's a pervert. Did I tell you that? He's the one who's sick. But I got so I needed it. I couldn't escape him. We acted out things until I didn't know what was real and what was just Duncan's imagination."

"You went with Slade?"

"Yes."

"And told people you were Vicky Petrone?"

"It was a game. I didn't know what he was planning. I really and truly didn't. Melvin was nice, dumb but nice. We actually had fun. Duncan told me to give him money. To sleep with him. To suggest things. Melvin would do anything for me."

"Suggest what?"

"If he would kill Joe, it would mean a lot of money. Duncan convinced Melvin he could get away after. They would have it arranged. But they killed him instead. That wasn't right. I told Duncan, that wasn't fair."

"They set the fires in the seventh ward."

"Duncan said he could make so much money on it if he could get hold of that property. It was business."

"Burning people alive in their homes? Burning children to death? That's what you call business?"

The glimpse of what the whole thing was about made her eyes widen. She bit on her fist. "Oh, God. I didn't know, I swear."

"You knew. Why did you think he wanted Petrone dead?"

"For killing Avis, Duncan told me. Only, Joe didn't kill Avis. I knew that. But Duncan said it was the right thing to do."

I was pacing up and down beside the bed when another idea occurred to me. Oh, I was full of ideas.

"What was Gill doing out here just now?"

"What do you mean?"

"Did Kerr have you sleeping with him, too?"

"Eddie Gill? Don't be—that's disgusting."

"He came here to meet Kerr, didn't he?"

She chewed her lip, trying to work out what to say.

I said, "If more people die, you're getting the juice. There won't be any saving you then. Ten thousand volts."

"Please don't. I didn't know."

"What was Gill doing here?"

"You're right. He came to see Duncan."

"For what?"

"I don't know. They talked. They made some phone calls. They went out."

I grabbed her shoulders and pushed her back onto the bed. "Talked about what and went where?"

"You're hurting me, for God's sake. Please!"

I knelt on the bed and put my left hand on her throat. "Tell me!"

She opened and closed her mouth. Her eyes went wild. I let off the pressure.

"Something. About a beach. Beach property. Gill checked on it. Duncan made a phone call. They left. I don't know where they went. I swear."

I let her go and paced to the window. Outside, the sun was descending toward the bright haze in the west. My head was blazing. Time was leaping forward again.

I left Ceecee sobbing on the bed.

Earl had turned his car around and was leaning on the fender talking with Angela when I came out. We piled in and took off.

I said, "Gill rented summer places in Sodus. Penny's out there with the Petrone woman."

"What's the chance he put it together?" he said.

"I don't know. She gave me as a reference. It was her car that shut down the grab this morning. Two plus two. I think I'll head down there, just to be on the safe side."

To Angela I said, "You want to go for a ride?"

"That's all I want."

"Let's go."

"Want me along?" Earl asked.

"No, I want you to get in touch with Tom Cahoon," I said. "Tell him Miss Biltmore would like to make a statement about the Petrone murder. Then head back and watch her place till he gets there. If she bolts, keep on her."

"She could be halfway to Monte Carlo by morning."

"Make sure she's not. When you're done, do what you can to get a line on Kerr and Gill."

We reached the gas station. Angela and I switched to her convertible. Her driving had me gripping the armrest. She picked up Route 104 on the other side of Webster and put her foot on the gas. We flew past the fruit-packing plants that lined the bare strip of concrete, the factories that turned out maraschino cherries, pie fillings, and applesauce.

"How you figure this racket worked, anyway?" she asked me.

"Kerr had contacts galore with the city politicos," I said. "His old man was an architect and in with the winners. Petrone had clout, but they would never let him through the front door of the country club. So Kerr provided the know-how, Petrone handled the muscle. Gill was the cat's-paw."

"Didn't I tell you? Wheels within wheels."

The breeze tore over the top of the windshield, making her hair toss. We turned off and cut along the back roads toward the lake. Along there, it was all orchards. Rows of trees bowed under the weight of green apples.

"Kerr has to have a connection inside the mob," she said. "I can't see him taking the chance of hitting Petrone otherwise."

"I figure that was Palermo. Use him, get rid of him."

"No, somebody else. There's always somebody pulling the strings. I'll lay seven to five Kerr's got a rabbi in the organization. That'll be the guy who'll get credit for taking care of Vicky. It'll earn him points with the boys who give the nod."

In one field a farmer was taking advantage of the stillness to drag a spray rig through his orchard, drenching the ripening fruit with chalky chemicals and tinting the air with a nitrate tang.

"What about the first Mrs. Petrone?" she said. "You think Joe knocked her off?"

"It's just as likely she was reaching for the soap and the radio zapped her. Your warning to Vicky was based on thin air."

"Stupid me."

"Avis was never the little lamb they made her out to be," I said. "She knew what Joe and her brother were up to and she found out that Duncan was cheating her husband. Maybe she tried to cut herself in or maybe she threatened to tell Joe. Duncan set her up, ran her into the gorge, and that was that."

We turned onto Lake Road. You could smell the water now.

"I'm going to be happy to have you around full-time, Ike."

"What are you talking about?"

"I'm putting you on my payroll. You'll be my personal bodyguard."

"What do I have to do?"

"Jump when I say jump."

"And roll over when you say roll over?"

"Natch. I might even make you sit up and beg."

"What if I want to stay independent?"

"Then I'll have to call you in on special assignments." The tires squealed as we leaned around a tight curve. "Like dusting the horses on the merry-go-round." She gave out a wild laugh.

Coming around another corner, she said, "Hey, this is it. Look at all the cars."

8

SODUS POINT WAS A poor man's Riviera, a summer town where girls pranced around the village in too-short shorts and halter tops that showed off their tans, where boys cruised the streets in hot rods and jalopies, brains filled with images of speed and impossible copulation. I had haunted the bars down there myself as a youth.

"This place is hopping," Angela said as we rolled into the village.

"They're celebrating their sesquicentennial."

"What the hell's that?"

"A hundred and fifty years ago Yankee Bill Peters started the first settlement here—a tavern, what else. He served Mohawks and trappers going by on the lake. You can imagine the insanity that went on in that joint."

We stopped at the only traffic light.

"From the looks of it, it hasn't changed much," she said. "How about some more of those uppers?"

I felt spent myself. I tapped four pills from the vial, swallowed two of them dry and put two between her lips with my fingers.

"Now all I need is a cold beer," she said.

The Point had been a mecca for the rabble since just after the war. It was the only resort on the eastern end of Lake Ontario with a boisterous nightlife. It drew merrymakers from as far away as Syracuse and Utica, and from all the hick towns scattered across the dark countryside. Teenagers came to pack the dance halls. Motorcycle hoodlums came to fight. Bumpkins with chaff in their hair and bikini dreams came to soak up draft beer. Young businessmen, canning factory workers, gamblers, sorority girls, wolves, souses, and a diverse collection of lonely souls who were sick and tired of peace and quiet and anxious to let off steam—they all gathered here in summer to chase the mirage of bliss.

The main part of the village sat on a bay, which was sheltered from the lake by a wide sandbar loaded with cottages. A long row of beer joints, dance halls, and restaurants lined the bay shore. They had patios and docks out over the water, very picturesque and easy for vacationers to get to by boat. Whether it was a forty-foot cabin cruiser or a little skiff with a ten-horse Evinrude, everybody down there had a boat.

We skirted the strip and made a turn by the Little League field. To the north, beyond that warren of cottages, a sand beach stretched along the lake itself. It ran from a bluff at one end to a concrete pier at the other. The pier extended a couple hundred yards and guarded the channel that connected the bay and the lake. A light revolved in a tower at the end, sending a beam skimming into the black.

We drove up and down a maze of side streets, most of them dirt lanes, between cabins that had been jerry-rigged out of two-by-fours and driftwood, old clapboards and corrugated tin roofing. Crickets clogged the air with their urging.

"That's it," Angela said. "I see the number."

The windows of the cottage were dark. My car was parked in the dirt patch in front.

"Keep rolling."

"This is the place."

"I know," I said. "Don't look, but there's a guy sitting in that Buick over there. Not a good sign."

"At least it means they haven't found them yet."

"I hope so. The women probably went out on foot. Let's go check the strip."

We parked in a dirt lot close to the village and got out. Above us, a thick swarm of insects danced around the streetlight.

Music and bubbling conversation drifted down from the row of bars. The air was thick with heat.

"Look over there," she said, as we turned onto the sidewalk.

Across the street, Eddie Gill was standing talking to Frankie Delmonico. Two men waited beside them for orders. One had the wide cheekbones and slicked black hair of an Indian. The other was bald and bore a sharp resemblance to a professional wrestler who went by the name Hans Schmidt. While we watched, the group broke up, the minions entering the two closest bars while Gill and Delmonico continued up the street and disappeared among the packs of loiterers who crowded the sidewalk.

"That answers the question," Angela said. "I'm not surprised. Frankie was always a backstabbing skunk."

"He must have offered Kerr and Gill a better deal than they were getting from Petrone."

"The condition being that Kerr knock off the boss," she said, "so Frankie could keep his hands clean. Now Delmonico puts on a show—takes revenge on the wife to convince Mr. Upstairs he's still on the team."

"And maybe ends up running the rackets when the dust settles," I said.

"Do we follow them?"

"Let's see if we can find the women ourselves and get out of here."

"What about calling the cops?"

I shook my head. "All they've got down here is a couple of part-timers. It would take too long to explain it to them, and they'd be out-gunned anyway."

We paid a couple of dollars to enter a dance hall called The Sturgeon. I knew Penny loved to dance.

Stagger Lee! Stagger Lee! Inside, a skinny young man with a guitar slung around his neck was screaming into a microphone. Drums were pounding a raw beat. The throb of an electric bass was making the floor shake.

"I'll circle this way," I told Angela. "You go around there. We'll meet at the back."

I began to work my way to the left, weaving through groups of dancers and past crowded tables. The air was steamy and smelled like seaweed and spilled beer. I lit a smoke. I was flying on the bennies now. The noise and the bustle buoyed me.

The Sturgeon was the largest of half a dozen joints along the strip. The crowd packed the dance floor and stood three-deep along the bar. Half the patrons were wearing bathing suits.

Stagger Lee told Billy . . . The band was playing loud enough to drown all conversation. The patrons were talking anyway, screaming jokes that brought hysterical laughter, shouting secrets that widened eyes.

My gaze, groping in the dimness, skimmed the gyrating bodies. A girl's face, luscious with summer lust, looked back at me across ten feet of smoky air. She broke into a grin so sweet and inviting that it carried me back fifteen years, into my youth. She moved her mouth as if speaking to me, but the remark must have been directed to someone else. She turned away.

. . . *said nobody move and he pulled his—forty-four.* The space in front of the band was mobbed with dancers and jitterbugs. Boys were spinning and twisting their partners. Girls were dancing with girls. One young woman, loaded to the eyeballs, had shed her blouse and was undulating in Bermuda shorts and bra.

"What the hell are you looking at?" a drunken hick roared in my face.

I tried ignoring him, but he grabbed my shoulder. "Lookit the professor," he bawled, fingering my seersucker. I needed the jacket to conceal my shoulder holster. "He's all dressed up like the dog's dinner."

I didn't feel like fighting. "You know," I shouted back, "if your aunt had balls, she'd be your uncle."

"What?" He gave an uncertain laugh, as if he wanted to be in on the joke. I moved on.

Rather than push back through the throng, I made my way out the double doors in the corner and onto a deck overlooking the bay. Streaks of white and blue and green light wavered across the water. I met Angela coming from the other direction.

"No sign of them," she said.

"Let's check the other bars."

As we moved back inside, I glimpsed Duncan Kerr talking to one of the four men working behind the bar. I pointed him out to Angela.

"Stand up by the entrance in case I don't cut him off," I said.

"And what?"

"Keep him from leaving. I'll be right behind."

I cut through the mob toward him. It's funny how you imagine you can read people. Looking at him now, I could see his character printed on his face. The suntan and superficial good looks were a veneer. His mouth was shaped by a lifetime of sneers. His eyes were the selfish eyes of a truculent toddler. He was a man who had never grown up, who still wanted to eat the world, who could carelessly order murder, order families burned from their homes.

Yet I had seen the same face a few days before, sat and talked with him, and been taken by his sincerity and concern. You like to think you can read people, but it's an illusion. Nothing shines through the mask.

I reached him just as he was turning away from the bar. I smiled and held out my hand. He knew he was doing the wrong thing, but habit made him offer his hand in return. I grabbed his wrist and applied a come-along hold they taught us on the police. I goose-walked him along the bar and down a sour corridor past the doors to the rest rooms. We banged through a steel door at the end and were out on one of the docks that extended into the bay.

"Okay, Van Savage, look." He was grinning. "Let's not get rough here."

"Find her?"

"Her? Her, who?"

His left hand was sneaking inside his windbreaker. I swung a compact hook up under his ribs. As he bent forward gasping, I felt the butt of a gun tucked into his waistband and pulled it out, a Luger.

The band, which had meandered through some generic blues riffs, now swung back to "Stagger Lee": . . . *all my money and my brand-new Stetson hat.*

"You're not down here looking for Vicky Petrone?" I said.

He licked his lips as if holding down vomit. His pained eyes looked at me. "Who?"

A dozen boats were tied up on both sides, rocking gently in the placid water. The insistent music poured out the open windows.

"What's this?" I said. We both stared at the gun.

"I'm a wealthy man."

"No kidding."

"I come to a place like this, these people, I need to be able to protect myself. Not much civilization out here in the boondocks."

Gentlemen of the jury, what do you think of that?

"Civilization?" I barked a laugh. "You ran your sister into the gorge."

"You must be crazy." He was starting to get hold of himself.

Stagger Lee killed Billy Lyon for a five-dollar Stetson hat.

"You killed her or you hired it done. The way you hired those houses burned. Orlo Zanek, remember? Those kids who burned to death?"

"I don't know what you're talking about. Burned? You've been misinformed, my friend."

That bad man, oh, cruel Stagger Lee.

"Maybe even Joe Petrone thought you'd gone too far. Arson was one thing, murdering children was something else."

"Joe Petrone? Are you accusing me of killing him, too?" His laughter was sincere.

"I didn't mention it, you did."

"Well, if I had done it, I should get a medal, shouldn't I? I mean, the man was scum. Surely you can see that."

"He was your partner. The miracle mile?"

"Business, Mr. Van Savage." He was growing confident. Maybe

he imagined he could buy me the way he'd bought people all his life. "Like they say, Christmas is over and business is business."

"What business is it that involves lighting a house where children are in their beds?"

"Accidents are unavoidable."

"What business is it that involves killing your own sister?"

"Again, an accident. But you can imagine how I felt, to have a man like that married to my sister. Can't you? I was relieved when she had her mishap. Because then I didn't have to think about that animal putting his greasy, filthy hands on her. I didn't have to think about—"

I hunched my shoulders and spun, pointing the Luger. The sound of the shot from behind me barely rose above the pounding of the drums. Kerr reached for the railing, held to it as he slumped to the deck.

Angela looked at me, her face a blank. She took two quick steps forward and came up beside me. She leaned, lowering her hand as if she were going to take Kerr's pulse. The second shot was duller, the barrel pressed behind his ear.

"He was going for a gun," she said, straightening.

I stared at her. "I have his gun."

"Yep, he was going for a gun." She slipped hers, still smoking, back into her purse. "I saw him. I had to do it."

She lowered her chin and looked at me across her eyebrows. Her face bore no expression whatever. For an instant it shone with a kind of primitive brutality.

She said, "Let's get him in the water, it'll give us time to drift."

Okay. Okay, this was mobtown. This was her world. And Kerr was less than nothing to me.

We eased him headfirst off the end of the dock. The drop to the water was less than a foot. He made no splash. For a few seconds, air caught in his clothes and held him up. Then he slowly disappeared into the black liquid. I dropped the Luger in after him.

She drew some water in her cupped hands to splash on the boards where there was a small spot of blood. She wiped her palms on her skirt. We strolled back through the bar and out.

9

WE WENT TO A place next door called the Driftwood Lounge. A juke was blasting Presley. Hot green light illuminated a pool table. *Don't be cruel.*

I asked the bartender, who was sporting an Abe Lincoln beard, about Penny and Vicky. He said he'd seen them.

To a heart that's true.

That blonde? Are you kidding? What a doll. And another girl, skinny, big eyes. Yes, they had been sitting at the bar earlier, drinking Seven and Sevens.

"She was too much, that blonde. Guys were afraid to talk to her, which in this place is saying something. So you're looking for them, too."

"What do you mean?"

"Fat guy was just in here asking."

"You know where they went?"

He shrugged. "They asked me about the fireworks. The town's shooting a big show over on the beach. Those chicks seemed interested." He looked at his watch. "They're supposed to start about now."

"You told this to the other guy?"

He nodded.

We went back and picked up Angela's car.

"You loved Joe Petrone," I said to her.

She looked at me, evaluating. "You are out of your gourd."

"You wanted him for yourself."

"I could have had ten Petrones."

"You put the Bluebeard idea into Vicky's head hoping to remove her from the picture."

"Don't push it, Ike."

"You resented Petrone, maybe. But you wanted him. After Avis died, you hated Vicky for stepping between you and the prize."

"I'm telling you, you're way off base." She laughed, but with a nervous edge to it.

"Am I? Isn't that the reason you pulled the trigger on Kerr? Because he had Joe murdered?"

"No, I'm just a killer. I forgot to mention that. Just a heartless assassin."

"Heartless? I know that's a lie."

"We swim in lies, all of us. The important thing is to keep your head above water."

We left it at that.

I was growing impatient with the stalled traffic. Revelers over-flowed into the street as they streamed from one bar to another. The lines at the hot dog stands wound past the curbs. Convertibles cruised slowly along the main drag, shirtless young men shouting insults and invitations.

With the cars at a standstill, the crowd flowed around us. I pounded impatiently on the dash, imagining we could have reached the beach quicker on foot. The tide of humanity was heading in that direction.

Angela's car drew hoots of admiration. They whistled at the interior and at the glut of chrome, which picked up the flashing come-on lights of the bars.

It took me a second to realize that the fat man passing right at my elbow, his shirttails hanging loose, was Eddie Gill. Up till then, I had only seen him from a distance. Now I noticed that he had the lips of a man who likes to pet bunnies. His bulbous cheeks jiggled as he walked. Under the streetlights, his sweaty, frog-belly complexion looked like death.

To anyone else, he would have blended in with all those men, descending into middle age, who mix with young people in order to clutch at the dregs of their own youth. To me, he was a reptile. He performed dirty work for rich men. I could imagine his oily line of patter, the words that had convinced Sandy Mink to go with him, the words that had struck a deal with Orlo Zanek. He was a coward and a killer.

By the time I flung open the door, Gill had disappeared into the crowd ahead. The cars in front of the Cadillac were moving on. Horns began to sound behind. I pushed an opening with my left arm, guarding my injured right. I fought my way ahead. Where was he?

"Hey!" Angela came gliding beside me in the car. "Get in."

"I saw him," I said, slipping back into the seat. "Eddie Gill."

"We'll get there before he does." A gap had opened in front of her. She gave the engine some gas, blowing a high hosanna out the glass-pack muffler. People looked and got out of her way.

I kept searching for Gill's squat form, but the crowd was dispersing now, streaming down the lanes that led to the beach.

Everyone was hurrying. Some were carrying aluminum lawn chairs. Families straggled forward, laden with blankets and ice chests. Men were selling cotton candy out of yellow-lit wagons. Children wrapped their mouths around the pink confection.

We turned off and rolled again past Penny's cabin. Still dark. The Buick still parked opposite.

We cut down a street of soft macadam and came out at the edge of the sand beach. Some kids had built a driftwood bonfire. The smoke was tinted with Arabian musk. Beyond, the lake was pure immensity, slick darkness extending forever. Lazy undulations flowed sighing onto the sand.

As we were getting out of the car, an explosion, a flash of light from on high.

The beach was crowded with dark forms. Kids were dancing around the fire. Families sat on blankets eating cold chicken and watermelon from hampers. Furtive couples groped each other under the bayberry bushes.

The first bang must have been a teaser. The onlookers continued to stare into the darkness, waiting for the show to begin. The murmuring silence intensified.

At the other end of the beach, far out on the pier, red railroad flares bounced, outlining the figures of the men preparing pyrotechnics. As I watched, a *whomp* sounded and a trail of sparks skittered into the sky. An immense fiery flower blossomed overhead. Shouts of wonder rose from the crowd.

"I'll go along the water," I told Angela. "You work your way down the beach from here. If you spot them, stick to them and give me a yell. If you don't, meet me at the base of the pier."

"Wait." She grabbed me and kissed me. "You were right, me and Joe," she said quickly. "I thought Joe had Avis killed and I was glad he did. I imagined it gave me a chance. When he went and married Vicky, it was like sticking a knife in my chest. She worked for me, goddamn it. She was nothing, just beautiful."

"Are you with me or not?"

"I'm with you all the way, Ike. None of it matters now. I'm sold on you."

I touched a finger to her chin. She winked and headed off into the dark crowd of watchers.

I moved down to the edge of the lake. The water was black glass. Someone lit a packet of firecrackers near me. They crackled in a dry spasm and tinted the air with sulphur.

Half a dozen distant coughs drifted back from the pier and half a dozen shells burst in the sky and the crowd cheered again. The show had begun. The fire lit up faces. In the wild pink light, I searched for Penny's familiar features, for the spun gold of Vicky's hair.

The explosions came in a regular rhythm now. Each boom rolled along the shore, then returned like distant thunder as it reflected from the bluffs that jutted into the lake.

With every overhead blast, saffron and rouge and cobalt green light washed the crowd. I scanned the faces. Hundreds of pairs of eyes turned upward, hundreds of mouths relaxed into amazed smiles. But I couldn't spot the faces I was looking for.

When I was halfway to the pier, a column of orange sparks heaved upward and branched into a drooping palm tree two hundred feet high. It was followed immediately by a tremendous explosion that drew my eyes toward heaven. Red and blue streaks expanded to fill the sky. The devotees lining the beach roared.

A commotion back along the trees drew my attention. In the glow I spotted Eddie Gill.

He stood by while the Indian and the wrestler grappled with Vicky. They held her by her arms, dragged her. Penny was flailing at them.

Darkness descended on the scene. I could only see shadows. I pulled my pistol and began to run in that direction, dodging the spectators who packed every inch of sand.

Another burst in the sky. Penny was down. Gill and his buddies were half marching, half carrying Vicky away from the lake toward a stand of cottonwood trees beyond. Her brilliant hair stood out like neon.

Angela had already passed beyond them. Now she turned back and was standing in their path. She had her gun in her hand, but she couldn't fire for fear of hitting Vicky. She simply stood there, defiant, waiting.

It was Gill who fired first. I saw the muzzle flash, but the sound was lost in a stunning cannonade from over the lake.

Angela slumped. Gill and his buddies veered, plunging into the obscurity of the trees.

I leapt over a portly man on a folding chaise longue and ran to her. She was kneeling upright on the sand.

"I'm okay," she said. Her hands gripped her belly. A burst of fireworks showed the paleness of her features. "Go on. It's nothing."

Blood was seeping between her fingers.

"I'll take care of her," Penny said at my elbow. "You get to Vicky before they escape. They'll kill her!"

"She needs an ambulance," I said stupidly.

"Of course. Go!"

10

I RAN UP THE beach and into the trees. Every flash from overhead imprinted the shadows of the trunks onto the fine white sand. Then the thicket plunged back into darkness.

I dodged through and came out at the corner of a crowded parking lot. The little group was passing beneath the glow of a street lamp. The two men were dragging Vicky along by the arms. Gill was moving quickly toward a dark blue LTD that sat in the far aisle, its engine running.

I sprinted, shouting. From the sky, a flash and another flash. The echo tumbled along the water, a resonant sound that mingled with the cheers of the crowd.

In the dark, when you're hyped, it's almost impossible to hit a target with a handgun. I decided on a sure shot. I raised my Colt and fired at the car. The window of a back door shattered.

Delmonico, who had been waiting in the passenger seat, piled out on the opposite side. Gill ducked and scrambled around beside him. Delmonico came up with a gun and popped it at me a couple of times.

Chief Sitting Bull let go of Vicky and pointed a big revolver in my direction. He fired. The sky lit up.

Vicky took advantage of the distraction to wrench herself free from the grasp of the wrestler.

She ran.

Gill raised up and fired at her. He didn't take time to aim. Vicky kept running, heading toward the pier, which extended from the corner of the lot. Gill swung around and fired at me.

I set off toward the pier myself, running along the grassy verge that divided the parking lot from the beach. The big Indian angled to cut me off. He fired at me twice as I ran toward him. I waited until I thought I was close enough and pulled the trigger of my own gun.

We both missed.

I met him head-on, lifting a knee to slam it into his chest. We went down. The collision knocked the gun from my hand.

I caught hold of his wrist. He fired his pistol inches from my ear. The shot filled my head with white noise.

I caught hold of the barrel. The heat stung my hand. I held on and twisted. He tried to knee me. The gun came loose and fell to the sand. I brought my fist down hard on his Adam's apple. That took the fight out of him. He clutched both hands around his throat and made a gasping noise.

I broke away and searched briefly for one of the guns. Feeling nothing but sand, I looked around for Vicky. She was about twenty yards out on the pier, running.

Gill was waddling after her. The wrestler had consulted with Delmonico and was now heading in the same direction.

I reached the pier a few seconds after he did. He turned and waved his gun toward me. I dodged. He pulled the trigger. I felt the bullet whisper past my neck on the right side.

The recoil threw his arm toward the sky. I lowered my head and ran at him. He may have shot again before we collided. My skull caught him in the stomach. I drove forward, stumbled. He fell. His hand reached out to break his fall. Reached toward nothing. He tumbled the six feet into the channel.

I would have gone over with him, but I landed facedown on the deck before my momentum could carry me. The concrete skinned my palms.

I clambered back onto my feet. About twenty yards farther along the pier, a young man in a T-shirt was waving his hands at me. He must have worked for the fireworks company. They had roped it off at that point.

"You can't—" I heard him say as I ran past.

Farther out, the men with flares were loading and shooting fireworks shells. The pace of the show was speeding up. They were approaching the finale. I passed them—they were too intent on their business to notice.

They fired a shell from a tube that must have been a foot across. A massive explosion made the water shiver. Grit and ash were raining from the smoke.

I caught a glimpse of Vicky, way out toward the end.

I reached another of the fireworks boys. His flare was dripping flaming phosphorous. He stared at me, shaking his head.

Beyond him a long row of tubes held together in wooden racks stretched all the way to the base of the light. Each tube was fused to its neighbor. The beam from the tower continued to sweep the darkness.

I kept running. Gill had vanished. Had I passed him?

In a tiny pocket of silence, I heard a warning. "Look out!"

I glanced back. The boy with the flare was setting it to the end of the row of tubes. They immediately began to explode, a quick succession of cannon shots. Smoke obscured the shore.

Ahead of me, I caught sight of the fat man. He was standing on the stone pedestal of the light tower, staring into the lake opposite the channel. I followed his gaze and caught sight of Vicky's blond head bobbing above the blackness of the water.

Gill was taking aim with a revolver. He fired. Treading water and trying to get her bearings, Vicky didn't notice when the bullet sent up a little geyser near her head.

Now the shells that had been heaved skyward were going off in a thundering, stuttering barrage of overlapping explosions.

The flame reached the last rack of mortars just as I did. Desperate, I bent down and grabbed one of the crosspieces that kept the tubes upright. I lifted and swung it. The fireworks, like artillery shells, began to angle low over the water. They exploded above the lights of the boats that had anchored to watch the show. The occupants ducked for cover.

I continued to spin the rack. One of the grenades flew past Gill's head. I succeeded in distracting him. He looked back, his face stretched. The next shell crashed into the light tower and exploded right beside him. The blast scorched him and knocked him off his feet. He rolled onto the surface of the pier.

Blinded, screaming, he struggled to his knees. One of the last shells caught him in the chest. With a force that surprised me, it thrust him backward off the pier. He dropped into the water, the bomb in his arms. A second after the ripples closed over him, the shell exploded under water in a glow of eerie orange light and a mass of foam. The bubbles rose to the surface and burst in little puffs of pink smoke. Gill did not rise.

My head was ringing. I yelled to Vicky, who was still paddling aimlessly in the water. She didn't hear me.

The sound of cheering reached me. The finale had pleased the crowd. By tipping the mortars, I had added an element of chaos. Everybody loved it.

Closer to shore, fire raced around a large lath structure. At first, I couldn't make out the pattern. Then I saw it was an American flag. The red, white, and blue flames poured forth a glorious, glowing pennant of smoke.

The crowd on the beach clapped and clapped. The flag hissed. The fire gradually died. The last of the stars and stripes sputtered.

The smoke drifted. Delmonico's car had disappeared from the parking lot. Sure that no one was approaching along the pier, I pulled off my shoes and dove.

TUESDAY

ANGELA WAS DEAD. All the rest was details.

The day afterward, nobody knew exactly how the story would come out. But I could pretty well guess. I spent the morning feeding my version to Tom Cahoon. I knew he would never be able to use all of it.

Cahoon arranged protective custody for Vicky Petrone, and assured me there would be no slipups this time. Once she was cleared of her husband's murder, there would no longer be a need to protect her.

Pretty soon they would fish Duncan Kerr's body from Sodus Bay. The burned corpse of Eddie Gill would wash up somewhere along the lake. Gill's involvement in the arson would come out. Kerr's death would remain a mystery, a subject of whispers in East Avenue parlors.

Ceecee Biltmore would hire an expensive lawyer and make a deal with the district attorney. She would tell the story she had to tell and she would get off. Rich girls usually do.

Frankie Delmonico might get drawn into the case, and he might not. He might take charge of the rackets in Rochester, or he might stay behind the scenes and advise whoever did. What we didn't know at the time was that mobtown had its own justice, that some bird-watchers in the Montezuma swamp would come across a pair of rare sandhill cranes picking at his body one morning about two weeks later.

We didn't know, either, that the miracle mile would never get built—at least not where it had been planned. A year later a Dem-ocrat would take the White House and the shifting political winds would blow the deal away like dust.

I could have predicted the fate of Mrs. Gill. I would have to testify against her. She would be convicted of killing Sandy Mink. She would continue to protest her love for her late husband until they executed her in the electric chair, the last woman to walk into the old death chamber at Sing Sing.

Penny came out of it shaken but unhurt except for a bruise on her jaw. I told her to take a week off with pay and work on her suntan.

Vicky, I was sure, would land on her feet. I hoped she would get out of Rochester, go somewhere new and start over. California, maybe. Everybody was moving to California in those days.

Life would go on, but not for Angela Grecco.

Life would go on and the heat also seemed as if it would go on— maybe until Labor Day finally brought a hint of autumn. That after-noon, when I was done with the police, I had had enough of the heat. I swung around to Eileen's.

Gloria was outside practicing her hula hoop. She was holding her splayed fingers above her head, frowning with concentration.

"Look!" she yelled.

Eileen hadn't connected me with the hullabaloo that was in the papers. She wouldn't have read beyond the headlines, anyway. She had never cared about rackets and conspiracies.

"Let's go out to Durand," I said.

"Yes!" Gloria crowed.

"I was going to take her shopping for school clothes," Eileen said. "But I guess we can do that some other time. She loves the beach."

She gave a weary sigh and I noticed the lines that traced the corners of her mouth. Like the little wrinkles around her eyes, they were permanent now.

"I mean the three of us," I said.

She looked at me curiously.

"Just a day at the lake," I told her. "For old times."

"Can we get hot dogs?" Gloria asked.

Then we were driving through the heat and Gloria was hugging me around the neck from the backseat, delirious at this unexpected family outing.

Then we were on the hot sand and the transparent water was lapping at the shore. Gloria and I swam and splashed and shouted and ducked each other. Boats were forming strings of jewels across the sunlit water.

Then Eileen came down the beach, tucking every strand of hair under her bathing cap. Gloria and I both turned our eyes toward her as she waded in. We gazed at her perfect, meticulous crawl. She sliced through the water with such precision, it almost hurt to watch. She swam way out, then turned back toward shore. Gloria held my hand and hummed a tuneless tune.

Then I went back to lie on the blanket, my heart suddenly too heavy to bear. I stretched out and stared at the limitless blue of the sky.

"Dad, watch!"

Then I raised my head and saw my daughter turn a perfect cartwheel in the sun.